The spell was growing stronger

"I've thought of you every night, Diana." Bryce pulled me closer and kissed me. "I've turned out my light and felt alone, knowing the most important thing in my life was missing. In Greece. Holland. London. Wherever I was, it was wrong because you weren't there."

"It was the same for me. I never want to leave you again." I ran my hands along the wide expanse of his bare back, savoring the feel of him. When we were touching each other everything was different. Stars shone brighter. Peace took the place of turmoil.

"I can't see you very well in the dark," I whispered. "I can only feel you."

"Do I feel good?"

"Wonderful!"

"And you," he said, lightly caressing my breast. "You feel like silk."

Regan Forest has, for a long time, fantasized about creating a character—and then meeting him in real life. That spark generated *Moonspell*, a powerful and poignant love story where that very thing happens to the heroine.

Regan would rather write than eat, she confesses with a laugh. However, she also loves to travel and has never written about a place she hasn't been. (Yes, she's been to Spain, Switzerland and the Kalahari Desert!) Now that her nest is empty she'll be doing a lot more traveling—and a lot more writing.

MOONSPELL

REGAN FOREST

Harlequin Books

TORONTO • NEW YORK • LONDON
AMSTERDAM • PARIS • SYDNEY • HAMBURG
STOCKHOLM • ATHENS • TOKYO • MILAN

*To Margaret Carney,
with gratitude and love . . .*

*With thanks to three special people whose input I
greatly valued in the writing of this book: Jane
Maxey, Wilma Zufelt, and Robert Donaldson of
Glasgow, Scotland.*

Original paperback edition published in Italian by Edizioni Mondadori.

German language edition published in Germany by Cora Verlag GmbH.

ISBN 0-373-79003-1

Cover illustration © Corey Wolfe/The Image Bank

Scottish traditional folk song
Translated from Gaelic

THE BLACK-HAIRED LAD

I'll not climb the brae and I'll not walk the moor,
My voice is gone, and I'll sing no song;
I'll not sleep an hour from Monday to Sunday
While the black-haired lad comes to my mind.

It is a pity I was not with the black-haired lad
On the brow of the hill under the rainstorms,
In a small hollow of the wilds or in some secret place;
And I'll not take a grey-beard while you come to my mind.

Coaxing of mouth you are, the love of the girls you are,
A drinker of wine you are, and a generous man ungrudging;
You are manly and hard-striking, a hunter on the moors;
And I'll not take a grey-beard while you come to my mind.

My handsome black-haired lad, though all think you reckless,
I would marry you without consent of my kindred;
I would fare far with you through dells and wild places,
While the black-haired lad comes to my mind.

My fine black-haired lad, I will not leave you;
If I saw you in company I'd choose you above all the rest.
Though I saw five thousand, sure, I'd think you the best of them,
While the black-haired lad comes to my mind.

Chapter One

NICHOLAS PAUL was the perfect man. Every woman who met him fell in love with him. Thousands of women all over the world thought of Nicholas when they were with other men, lesser men who could never measure up to Nicholas Paul. He was handsome, rich, talented, exciting. He was larger than life. He was everything.

I was in love with Nicholas, too. I'd lived with him for the past five years, the best five years of my life. I knew him better than anyone in the world and loved him more. He was my Nicky. I created him.

He was born within the memories of my heart, born somewhere inside the folds of my brain—an outgrowth of all the emotions I'd ever known and everything I'd ever learned of men. He came to life between the pages of my books—four books now, four adventures.

Ah, he was wonderful, Nicky was. More wonderful than James Bond who came before him, because he was more human somehow, having been created by a woman. Sometimes the sight of a fallen bird would make Nicky turn his head and stand speechless for a moment or two. Women loved him because he was as tender as he was strong. But Nicky wasn't real. He was my creation.

My name is J. D. Nigel. My friends call me Jaye. For a long time people who read Nicholas Paul books believed I was a man. That's what they were supposed to think, because readers don't trust a woman to write about a world-class insurance detective and sometime spy-adventurer such as Nicholas Paul. No one knew the truth, until recently when word got out that the creator of Nicholas Paul was a woman. But now that he's established, men want to be like him and women want to love him. So I'm getting away with it. Nicky's popularity is growing.

When I travel, though, I don't make an issue of who I am. I travel alone to the places where the adventures are to be set, and there I summon Nicky to bring life to the stories that have been steaming and brewing and growing in my imagination.

Because I have traveled so much, I know a lot of people in cities around the world. I had a good life, an exciting life, until something happened one summer night that abruptly turned my world upside down. That night I lost all certainty of what—or who—was real and what—or who—was not.

It HAD BEEN a refreshingly cool spring in Spain that year. When I arrived in Madrid in early summer, the mild weather remained and everyone, grateful for each day of cheating the stifling heat that should be descending upon us, was in high spirits. I had brought Nicky here for our latest adventure, one involving two mysterious murders, the first long unsolved, the second, its duplicate in every detail, half a century later.

One of the scenes that I had in my head—the first of those I wanted to write here—was to take place in a café. The cafés of Madrid were not new to me, but as was my habit, I took myself to my setting to make notes of little things overlooked by the eye of my memory.

It's impossible to carry on a conversation in a café in Madrid because of the noise. People don't sit across from one another and talk. They yell. They scream, they pound on the table. Spanish voices are gay and incredibly loud. I was used to that; it was part of the atmosphere. In a corner with my notebook, I reveled in the fun of writing this adventure story and manipulating the famous detective into and out of trouble.

By Madrid standards it was still early; eleven o'clock and the evening meal was just beginning. I had started to feel hungry myself and was reaching across the table for the menu when something drew my attention to the center of the room. The sight of the man made me draw a quick breath—a breath that almost hurt. It was a stab followed by a pain that began in the back of my throat and traveled down my body to my chest, my heart.

I stared and kept staring, because there, sitting across from me in the café where I had conjured up a scene for him, was Nicholas Paul! The man was exactly Nicholas Paul—the dark hair, the broad shoulders, the body language, the way he leaned forward, listening so intently, cocking his head a certain way to hear what the man across from him was saying. The way he wrinkled his brow and quirked his mouth into a small smile that said he could barely hear, but he was trying. Every gesture, every look, was so familiar. He was no stranger.

It must have been several seconds before I noticed what he was wearing, and when I did, the wild sensations started all over again. My heart raced and stopped, raced and stopped, as if it didn't know what to do—any more than my head knew—because the man sitting there was wearing exactly what Nicky was wearing in the scene that I was forming. Dark slacks, a lightweight, white turtleneck summer shirt, fitted tight across the shoulders. I stared at the shirt. How could he possibly be wearing the same thing Nicky was wearing in this café scene in my head?

One part of me—the part that lived in images and daydreams—wanted to get up out of my chair and walk across the room and say, "Hello, Nicky," almost accepting the fact that what I had imagined was taking place before my eyes. But another part of me was frightened. Coincidences like this just didn't happen.

I tried to rationalize. But the fact remained that his face was as familiar to me as my own. I'd seen it in a thousand daydreams. I was in love with that face and that man, real or not.

If I touched him, would he dissolve like vapor? Was he flesh and blood? Or an apparition?

Unable to move, I simply sat and gaped. He wasn't a Spaniard, I decided; his gestures were not those of a Spaniard. Unfortunately, over the din it was impossible to hear what language they were speaking at his table. Blinking, I looked away as one looks away from the blinding sun, but my eyes quickly found their way back to him.

Perhaps he felt my stare, as people do sometimes. He must have, because his eyes flickered away from the person on whom he'd been so intently gazing. And his gaze didn't wander about the room looking for the source of the energy that was bearing down upon him. Instead he turned his head and looked directly at me, and me alone.

I was dazzled by his silver-blue eyes, eyes that flickered with such surprise. His forehead was knitted in a frown, and every flicker, every movement of muscle in his face showed surprise. My heart was behaving crazily. I tried to draw a breath and couldn't, our eyes locked together in a gaze I'll never forget.

He seemed to know me! Yet he couldn't—this stranger couldn't know me.

Our eyes caught there, above the smoke and noise of the room. I don't know what he was seeing, but I was certain of one thing: he recognized me. He really is Nicky! I thought for one crazy moment.

Then sanity returned. I began to shake. I tried to look away and couldn't. He shifted his attention back to the man who was talking to him. But again his gaze seemed drawn to me.

Stop me from staring! I prayed. Perhaps it was only my staring that was drawing his attention; he was simply reacting to that feeling of being watched.

But no, it was more. His eyes were burning me with silver fire. I don't think I even smiled. Neither did he. He just stared at me as if to say, "I almost... remember."

Shortly afterward I watched them leave. The man stood taller than the others when he rose. In the shadowy interior of the restaurant his face looked incredibly handsome. Just before he reached the exit, he took a pair of sunglasses from his shirt pocket and put them on. How strange I thought, wearing sunglasses to go out into the night. It made me wonder if he was guarding his identity, hiding from someone—or something.

After he had gone, I sat trying to decide if a dream had indeed walked into—and out of—my life.

NICHOLAS PAUL wasn't exclusively my property—not anymore. The whole world knew him. They didn't know me, but they knew and loved Nicky. He belonged to them, and yet he couldn't come out to play unless I brought him, or have new adventures unless I allowed it. I'd brought Nicky to Spain, and there happened to be a man in Madrid who looked and dressed just like him. A coincidence.

Morning light had a sobering effect, especially in that sunny country where the summer sun rises so brightly over the buildings and splashes like diamonds in the fountains. I tried to get back to work, to forget about this coincidence.

There was a scene forming in my mind, to be set in one of my favorite places in the city—near the magnificent statue of Cervantes. It was a site where Nicky, my hero, would make contact with another undercover detective.

Here I was, creating a make-believe plot while living a true story more diabolical than any I could have conjured up in my imagination. . . .

But I'm getting ahead of myself. Early the next afternoon I sat down under the statue of Cervantes with notebook in hand to soak up atmosphere, record impressions, sounds, smells, feelings in the air on this day at the beginning of summer.

Perched on a stone bench, eyes closed, I could envision the scene clearly. Nicky was wearing dark slacks, a white shirt and a loose, very expensive leather vest, with a pocket on each side. He was waiting impatiently. I heard the voices in Spanish—Nicky spoke several languages, of course—and just as the scene was really coming alive in my head, some invisible force grabbed at me and made me open my eyes. I gasped. There, walking in the crowd was Nicholas!

Again. The same man I'd seen last night in the crowded café. The same man whose eyes had met mine.

The same man I'd wanted to rush toward and say "Nicky!"

I scarcely noticed the man with whom he was walking, or anything else... except the clothes. White shirt, brown leather vest, expensively cut, with a pocket on each side.

It was too much for me to comprehend. Terrified, I closed my eyes and had to force myself to open them again. I don't know whether I wanted him to be still there, or whether I wanted him gone. The pavement shimmered in the sun, making waves, making everything unreal. The Spanish sun beat hot upon my head and shoulders; its reflection from the chrome of cars was dazzling. I was being blinded and I couldn't see reality anymore. I couldn't really see this man who was squinting in the summer light. My Nicky wasn't real!

Yet he was right in front of me! He'd jumped out of the pages of my book, leaped out of the fountains of my imagination and was sparkling with life, as if he had been given energy from the air and the sun... and somehow from me.

I sat gaping. He seemed to feel the visual attack, because without missing a step he looked up, not at the enormous statue above, but directly at me. The way he had last night. A strange thought flashed across my mind: he knew this place well or he couldn't have walked by the magnificent statue, so intent on his conversation that he didn't look at it. Of course. Nicholas Paul had been here many times.

My brain was whirling; I was trying to hold on to the past—before today, before last night. His eyes were on me again, with that same expression of surprise and recognition. He wasn't wearing dark glasses, and the sun seemed to be reflected from his eyes; even at that distance I could see it. No sunglasses in the glare of midday, yet he had worn them last night!

He hesitated. His companion was looking around to see what it was that had caught his attention. I saw that other person only as a shadow; my concentration was on the man who must be Nicholas. For one heart-stopping moment I thought, *he's going to come over here!*

With that same I'm-trying-to-remember wrinkle in his forehead, he halted and almost came toward me, but then stopped himself. After all, he didn't know me.

I shivered and sweat under the weight of his stare. He blinked, perhaps sensing my discomfort. There were people walking between us like slashes of darkness, shadows coming and going, filtering sun between their bodies as they moved. It was hypnotizing. Somehow I knew he didn't have the courage to come near me, just as I didn't have the courage to go to him.

Nor would I have had the courage to touch him. He might have been warm; he might have been cold; he might have been nothing but air. He kept walking, and the moment was gone.

Looking away then, talking to his companion, he was leaving me behind, just as he had done last night. I sat staring after him, at his broad shoulders in the vest and the graceful way he walked. Every movement was so familiar to me. The crowd folded in around him, and like water falling into a fountain he became part of the whole and was gone. Again.

A shadow seemed to move across the sun. Fear was gripping me. Two coincidences? How could there be two? Just the man would have been enough. But the clothes? No, something magical was happening, something otherworldly—something my instincts were simultaneously drawn to and warned away from.

It was all I could do to get myself up off that stone bench and walk, but at the same time I was kicked and prodded by a powerful urge not to lose him. I felt my legs moving under me, moving faster along the sidewalk toward the entrance to the subway where I thought they had gone. I started down the steps, searched the thousand faces, but none was his.

Some hidden part of me, I felt, was gone. Nicholas was a part of me, yet he was eluding me, leaving me. I was so confused!

The memory of that look in his eyes burned in my mind. "You?" his eyes had asked. "You?"

I walked in a daze, feeling the heat of the sun heavy upon my shoulders and thinking, did I make this happen? Did I somehow will him here? Could I have touched him? I walked, not knowing or caring where I was going, and thinking crazy thoughts, wild thoughts, thoughts I could hardly believe were really coming from me.

I'd try an experiment, I decided, to see if I could make him materialize. Not in a public place, where the appearance of any stranger might be construed as a coincidence, but somewhere private. Could I, by planning a scene in my head, make it happen again? I had no choice but to try.

MY MADRID ADDRESS was the penthouse of a friend. It was a sprawling apartment in the heart of the city, so rich in atmosphere that I'd already planned to set some scenes there.

The top floor of the ancient building was reached by a painfully slow elevator from a small lobby off the street. Lydia's flat had three entrances, one a front door, the second an opening onto the rooftop, from where one could look out over the city of Madrid, and then cross to a third door at the far end, which led into the flat's long, narrow kitchen.

Lydia was a secretary for an American-based company in Madrid. We'd met years ago through friends, and she always invited me to stay with her when I was in town. She was a musician when she wasn't at the office, and so were many of her friends. There was an old, unpainted piano in one of the three bedrooms and an even older piano in the living room. Guitars sat against the walls and on the blanket-covered couch, and every corner exuded charm. Sagging, creaking wooden floors, rough, solid old furniture. It was too often cold here in winter and hot in summer, but always welcoming to gypsies like me. Lydia's penthouse was one of my favorite places in the world.

In my book in progress, Nicholas Paul would attend a small gathering here, where he would meet some of the characters with whom he'd share his latest adventure.

That afternoon I set the scene vividly in my mind. How would I dress him for tonight? Still in leather. Nicholas often wore leather. The vest. I could add something, a little flair—something no other man would be likely to wear, for this was an experiment.

A narrow scarf around his throat. Nicky could get away with wearing a scarf, a silk scarf in tones of pale blue and brown and tan. A white shirt, sleeves rolled up. Surely no forces that played with coincidence could come up with a costume like that.

I invited a dozen friends, who could have no way of knowing they were part of a scene. Or of a crazy game.

I wouldn't tell any of them that a stranger might be in their midst. The truth was, I didn't really expect him; it would just be too much.

Sherry on the sideboard. Wine, cheese, bread. A gathering to say hello to old friends whom I hadn't yet seen since my return to Madrid two days ago. Arranging the evening, I kept thinking of Nicky as a stranger with the sun—and me—in his eyes, and I walked in a dream.

Lydia was pleased to learn we were having a party. We nibbled the cheese and bread and started drinking wine long before anyone arrived. I said nothing to her about what I was doing. How could I?

It was ridiculous, anyway. A stranger wouldn't show up here uninvited. I *had* invited Nicky in my mind, but how could a living, breathing man walk through that doorway, sprung only from my mind? It couldn't happen. Yet I waited through the longest hours of my life.

The guests didn't begin arriving until nearly ten o'clock, which was typical for Madrid. Trying to calm myself with sherry, I was determined just to enjoy the party, for that was all this was going to be.

It was good to see old friends again and catch up on the gossip. Lydia was at her very best—even a little high, playing her guitar with more skill than she'd exhibited when I'd been here last. It was a hot night. All doors and windows of the apartment were open, letting in the sounds of traffic from the street five stories below, along with muffled shouts and laughter, the barking of dogs.

At midnight some of us were gathered around the piano, singing in English and Spanish; the party was in full sail. I happened to look up and my breath left me, my legs went numb. Nicholas Paul was in the room!

I hadn't seen him enter. I'd forgotten an hour ago to constantly watch the door; the realities of time and the party had served to lessen my belief in miracles. But now he was here, wearing the vest I'd dressed him in and the scarf around his neck.

I'm dreaming this, I thought. The scarf wasn't exactly as I'd envisioned it. The colors were similar, but it was smaller, and he wore it tied at the side of his throat. He wore a smile, too, and that was new. I realized it was the first time I'd seen him smile.

He wasn't smiling at me; he hadn't seen me. But people were greeting him, touching him, shaking his hand, so he couldn't be an apparition. One man, at least, seemed to know who he was. Someone must have invited him!

Reeling, I swept the cobwebs from my mind, sorting through the tangle of old memories. Somewhere there had to be a memory of this man! Claudio was the guest who knew him. When had I met Claudio for the first time? Three years ago when I was here. Nicholas was five years old; damn, it didn't fit.

When then? When could I have seen him? When, before the picture of Nicholas Paul erupted like a volcano in my head? If I'd seen him, it had to have been five years ago at the earliest. When could our paths have crossed?

It wasn't here, I knew, because Lydia didn't know him. And I'd remember. *Surely I'd remember!* My memory was vivid and accurate, a point of pride. The first time I ever saw the face of Nicholas Paul, it appeared against the blackness of night . . . appeared clear and strong on the sill of my imagination. I'd seen his face in a vision . . . not a memory. No, definitely not.

The deeper I plowed through my recollections, the more certain I was that I had never seen this man in the flesh before last night. And even if I had, it still wouldn't make any sense of the distortions of logic that had brought my emotions to a rolling boil. It wouldn't explain how I knew what he would wear or where he would be, even if I'd seen him a thousand times!

My brain-scouring turned up absolutely nothing. I hadn't seen him, hadn't ever known him, and yet we were somehow entangled...frighteningly entangled. Reality had run amok!

Was he really Nicholas Paul—this man who stood across the room...so big, so beautiful and so perfect? No man could be this perfect. I'd known for years that no man could be as perfect as Nicholas. He was created that way. And here I was looking at him, and he was flesh and perfect, and I was speechless and beginning to feel feverish.

He came into the room relaxed, accepting a drink, laughing at someone's joke, while I stood by the piano, taking in his beauty and the miracle of the whole affair, wondering who the hell he was. Wondering at that point who *I* was. I quivered as I anticipated meeting him, I was terrified to meet him...half expecting to be swallowed into my own half-written scene. I'd never been so bedazzled and frustrated and confoundedly confused in my life. Nor ever so awake.

He was lifting his wineglass to take a drink; the glass was in midair, his elbow bent, when his gaze moved up and across the room toward me. His hand stopped moving and hung in midair, as if he'd forgotten what he was going to do; he just stood there, looking at me. And I stared back.

I was strangely aware of myself. What is he seeing? I wondered. My white blouse trimmed in lace, a full, blue cotton skirt, small sandals on my feet, my dark hair pulled back from my face. I might as well have been a mannequin. He was seeing only a mannequin with a stupid and blank expression. I had to move, try to look alive!

He set down his glass without ever taking the intended swallow of the drink. Someone was pulling diligently on his arm, demanding his attention. He turned away reluctantly and was led across the room.

Other people grew fuzzy and time had no measure. Only a few minutes elapsed before he found me. I'd half expected someone to make introductions, but oddly, no one did. I had moved to the kitchen doorway, then turned around and he was there, not smiling, not frowning, just looking at me in that puzzled way.

Approaching, he looked down at me from his great height and said, "Where do I know you from?" Not hello, just, "Where do I know you from?"

Chapter Two

HIS VOICE was Nicky's voice, deep and velvety. His accent was Nicky's too, a hint of Scotland or the far north of England. I looked up at him, trying to find my voice, trying to still my heart.

"I saw you at the café last night, didn't I?" I said.

His smile was questioning and mysterious. "Yes. And today in the city. And now once again. Is it coincidence?"

Trying to smile casually was hard. I answered the only way I knew. "I don't know what it is."

He was struggling with something, as if he couldn't say what he wanted to say any more than I could.

"I'm sure we've met." He held out his hand. "My name is Bryce Macklin."

I swallowed. The name reverberated in my brain like a gong. Bryce Macklin. I said, "I'm Jaye Nigel."

"No, I've not heard your name. I'm sure I'd remember if I had. I'm sure I'd remember you. Funny, I *do* remember you, but I don't know from where. You're American...."

I nodded. His hand felt warm—there was blood in his veins! He breathed air as any other man did. The warmth of his hand left a tingling in my palm where he'd touched it. I wanted to reach out and put my hand on his chest just to make sure he was solid. "Who told you about this gathering tonight?" I asked.

"Claudio did. Lydia's friend Claudio." He looked around the room. "I came in from London two days ago. Claudio and I met at a business meeting this afternoon. He was coming here tonight and suggested I come along." Bryce looked intently at me. "I'm glad I did."

"Do you have business in Madrid?"

"Aye," he answered, then said, "Yes. I work for Charles Haydon."

Everyone knew that Charles Haydon was the most prestigious insurance firm in London. Could this man be a detective, like Nicky?

Before I asked the question he answered it. "I'm an appraiser. Art and weapons, antique weapons. I'm here in Madrid to look at some armor that's privately owned. I work all over Europe and sometimes America. I've been there often. I like America...and Americans." He smiled. "You don't have a drink. Can I get you something?"

"A sherry," I answered softly. He moved toward the sideboard where the bottles were set out. I watched him pour with steady hands, watched the small reflection of light in the liquid that was filling the glass. It was almost hypnotizing in its effect—tiny, velvety rich bubbles. I was feeling light-headed and thought I shouldn't drink, but then I decided it wouldn't make any difference whether I did or not.

I was conscious, I could feel the floor under my feet and the air around me, and I knew that Bryce Macklin was a real man. Why he thought he knew me I couldn't fathom. But there was some strange connection between us. There had to be. I was certain that, regardless of who he was, I had manifested his presence here. Whether he'd met Claudio today or not, it was I who had really brought him.

The apartment was sweltering with the press of people. I turned and made my way through the narrow kitchen and out onto the rooftop, knowing Bryce Macklin would follow me. The night air was cooling, refreshing, sobering. I needed to view the endless expanse of Spanish sky to try to put into perspective my sense of entrapment by forces too mysterious for me to begin to understand.

In less than a minute he came up behind me as I stood at the railing, looking out. Without a word, he handed me the glass and tipped his own glass toward me in a silent, small salute. Curiously, he turned his back on the beautiful view of the city and didn't look out at the night. I didn't drink, only watched him tilt back his head as he swallowed.

"Funny," he said, "I never drink sherry unless I'm in Madrid. It goes with the place somehow. Do you want to go in?"

"It's so hot inside and so beautiful out here on the roof. Just look at that moon."

He didn't look at the moon or even turn around. Somehow he seemed uncomfortable. When his eyes moved back to mine, he was squinting, the way one squints in sunlight. An image came into my mind of Nicky squinting that way on a bright ski slope with the sun reflecting off newly fallen snow. My confused brain began to betray me. I heard myself asking suddenly, "Do you ski?"

A look of surprise crossed his face, for my question was abrupt and had nothing to do with the summer night that wrapped us warmly in a sweet aroma of flowers. Lydia's million flowers, in huge ceramic pots, sat about in profusion on her private rooftop. "I like to ski," he answered. "Do you?"

"A little."

"I never tried skiing until three years ago," he explained. "I always intended to, but you know how it is, we never do the things we say. But three years ago I got a sudden urge and took myself to the Swiss Alps, and in a fortnight I learned to ski." There was almost consternation in his voice.

"Are you good?"

"Yes."

I was making calculations. Three years ago I wrote the book about skiing, in Switzerland, with Nicky flying down the mountain slope like a dark bird. I drank from my glass, hoping he wouldn't notice my shaking fingers. Even though my questions were out of sync with the present moment, there was still much that I had to find out.

Gazing out at the city lights, I pushed for answers. "Do you fly, too?"

While he couldn't have understood why I was asking these out-of-the-blue questions, there was a gentle patience in him. It was odd how his impatience seemed to rise, then shift down, and he'd soften. "Yes, I do fly," he answered.

"Have you flown long? What do you fly? What kind of planes?"

"I started with gliders, in my youth. Until a prop plane my father was flying went down. He was killed and I nearly was. I didn't want to go up again. But about a year ago I took up flying seriously, for my own pleasure."

"A year ago," I repeated.

"Why the strange look?"

My voice quivered. "I'm hitting a lot of lucky guesses, aren't I?"

He wasn't buying it. There was something else, and he knew it, but he couldn't define it. He repeated, "I've known you from somewhere, I'm sure of it."

Thinking about the book I'd written a year ago, in which Nicky had taken up flying, I wanted to ask Bryce more, interrogate him, find out everything about him, but that was awkward. And I couldn't imagine what connection he made with me, why he was feeling this familiarity. It was eerie and growing more so.

His shoulders brushed mine when he turned around. He set his empty glass on the railing, thrust one hand into his pocket and stood looking down at the traffic below us. I glanced up at him, shocked to see that he'd put on dark glasses, just as he had last night before leaving the restaurant. How eccentric!

"Lydia says you're a famous writer of detective novels," he said. "Tell me about your books. I don't read much fiction and I apologize that I've never heard of your work."

I laughed. "I don't expect everyone to know my books. The protagonist in all of them is a man named Nicholas Paul." I watched him closely, but there was no reaction to the sound of Nicky's name. Bryce just stood looking at the view and waiting for me to continue. "They're adventure stories of danger and suspense."

"I'll have to make a point of reading one, now that I've met you."

It was the polite thing to say; he may or may not have meant it. The idea of his reading about Nicholas frightened me. I couldn't help but think he'd see himself, then reason took over and I decided he couldn't possibly see himself in Nicholas Paul. He couldn't see the image inside my head—the mirror image of himself.

"Who is he?" Bryce Macklin asked suddenly.

"Who? Who is who?"

"Your hero. Tell me about the hero of your books. What's his name . . . Nicholas Paul?"

"He's a talented, international-type detective, sometimes playboy, but with a serious side. He's clever and he solves mysteries that come his way. Loves a challenge and always wins. He's multidimensional. He can do anything from teaching kung fu to playing Chopin."

"Hell, I play Chopin." Bryce Macklin grinned.

In the silence that ensued, he turned and looked at me through glasses that were so dark, I could see nothing of his eyes. "That surprises you, I can see. Why would my playing the piano surprise you so much?"

Surprise me? I wanted to blurt out. *Why should it surprise me? I know a great deal about you, Mr. Macklin.* I couldn't share my thoughts, of course; I had to play the game. "You don't look like a man who plays Chopin. But then, neither does Nicholas Paul."

He looked down at his hands and flexed his fingers. "Does it take a certain kind of man to play music?"

"I guess not. Nor to love music." My awkwardness must have been obvious to him. To overcome the awkwardness I asked, "And kung fu?"

He laughed. "Doesn't every guy know martial arts these days?"

His accent sounded almost American then, as if he'd shifted and become somebody else. "I'm not all that good at kung fu," he added. "Been doing it for years, but it's the sort of thing you have to do every day until it becomes second nature. None of the moves are natural for humans. They're moves copied from certain animals, you know. It's necessary to practice the techniques until you can do them without thinking, and that takes a lot of time."

"So does playing Chopin."

He nodded. "There's never enough time to do all the things one wants to do, is there?"

"How long have you played?"

"The piano? All my life."

Yes, I thought. So had Nicky. I wanted to ask more about the martial arts, but it was getting too uncomfortable and he wanted to talk about me. I was evading questions about my personal life, but only because I feared there was so little time to learn about him. As in the story of Cinderella, the clock would strike midnight, he'd disappear, and I might never see him again.

But I couldn't divert him. He bombarded me with questions and I hurried through polite answers. The Arizona desert was home, I explained, but my summers were for Europe. Second to my career was a love of literature and music. And adventure. I recited the usual brief essay: I was single and thirty-two, divorced once, seven years ago, no children. No, I answered, I hadn't been in New York last December. He was obviously looking for some clue as to where we might have met, but I was convinced there were no clues.

Looking back, now I know that I was wrong. There were clues—bizarre, incomprehensible clues. Such as the dark glasses that he wore.

"How did you get started writing books?" he asked.

"I've written since I was a child."

"But these Nicholas Paul books? How did you spawn those?"

"The idea just came to me. I always liked James Bond stories, but I thought Bond was too much a male fantasy. A man's idea of a man. To James Bond women are objects. I wanted a hero women as well as men could fantasize about—an individual who was deeper and more human than 007."

It was hard to tell whether Bryce Macklin understood or not. I had the feeling he'd lost his concentration and was far away, thinking of something else. But in a moment he was back and questioning again.

"When did you write the first one?"

His questions revealed the same intense curiosity that had provoked mine. He, too, wanted answers. I owed him honesty. "Five years ago. It was unusual how the idea of Nicholas Paul came to me. I was in London researching a book on druids. This particular night I was alone..."

I paused, looking out at the starry sky, remembering. There had been stars that night, too. The sky had been so dark and full of stars, an eerie night with no wind at all. I continued. "I was standing outside my tiny leased bungalow looking at the sky. There was to be an eclipse that night and I'd come out to see it. The moon disappeared and left the earth so dark. I watched in fascination. The air was so strange, as if time were standing still. And that was when it came to me, this idea of Nicholas Paul. During an eclipse of the moon."

Bryce Macklin jerked both hands out of his pockets and turned away from the view of the street, turned completely around to face me. "An eclipse?"

"Yes. I think that's rather symbolic, don't you?"

He frowned. "I remember."

I felt a shiver crawl up my spine, felt my knees grow so weak that I thought I might lose my balance and fall. To protect myself I backed away from the railing. We, he and I, were standing too close to the edge of another reality that neither of us understood. "You remember?"

His voice was incredibly deep. "I remember the eclipse five years ago, though I'd rather not. It was a night I'd prefer to forget."

"Tell me."

He shuddered almost imperceptibly, a shudder telling me that whatever he remembered was something quite terrible.

"I was in London, too. I'd flown down from my home in Edinburgh to visit the woman who had been my childhood nanny. She took a job in London after I left home for boarding school. Grizel was a second mother to me and she hadn't been well. We had dinner together at her flat and, in retrospect, she asked me an uncommon lot of questions about myself that night. I think she was worried about me, didn't approve of the way I was living. We talked about the eclipse and waited for it. Grizel knew a great deal about the night sky. She used to tell me I was a moon child, and that my moods were affected by the phases of the moon. But I didn't notice it myself. At least, I don't think I did."

He shuffled his feet. It was plain he didn't want to talk about that night, although he was willing to tell me. Or was he? A long silence made me unsure.

Gently I reached out to touch his arm, and his warmth shot through me like a current. He didn't feel exactly the same as other men, and I couldn't explain in what way; I only knew there was something like electricity shooting through my fingers and up my arm. "Please go on," I begged. "What happened the night of the eclipse?"

His face changed. He took a deep breath. "I wish I knew for certain. Lord, I wish I knew for certain. I didn't see the entire eclipse, only the darkest part of it, but Grizel watched it all. I remember thinking how frightened ancient men must have been to see the moon disappearing from the sky. The shadow got larger and the moon got smaller, and I began to feel light-headed. I thought at first it was the wine, then I knew it wasn't. I thought, good Lord, I'm coming down with a bug. I never fall ill. But that night I knew I was in trouble when I heard Grizel say, 'Bryce, dear, you look pale as goat cheese. Are you all right?' I wasn't all right, and I knew it. It kept getting worse, as if a heavy weight was pressing on me and I was suffocating.

"I didn't wish to alarm her. She always tended to baby me too much, and with her ill herself, I hated to burden her with worry about me. But when I started to get up, I couldn't walk. The pressure was increasing, yet my head kept getting lighter, as if I were being split in two—the damnedest sensation I ever had. I kept looking at the shadow on that bloody moon, trying to decide what the moon had to do with me. I was blaming the moon, so obviously I was delirious."

Bryce stopped talking and forced a smile. "You don't want to hear all this."

"But I do."

"Why?" His voice conveyed regret that he had broached the subject in the first place. "This is a dull story. Nothing entertaining in it. Don't know why I told you."

"But I want to know."

He repeated, "Why?"

"Because it was that night. The night of the eclipse," I said, as if that were any kind of answer.

He searched my eyes, appearing almost to find what he sought, but not quite. And then a shadow came over his face, just as shadow had covered the moon that night.

"Och, it's not a pleasant story." He looked away and I knew he wasn't going to tell me more.

But I wasn't satisfied with that. I prodded. "You were sick?"

"Yes, I was ill. Very ill."

There was something more to it than that, I knew, but I was a stranger and whatever he balked at telling me was personal. I couldn't question him further without invading his privacy, yet I ached to know why he seemed to think his illness had something to do with the eclipse. I felt the chill again.

Shivering beside him, remembering the first instant I saw him last night, I knew for certain it was true: his illness did have something to do with the eclipse. And with Nicholas Paul!

Clouds danced before an almost full moon. The party behind us was getting louder as the hour grew later, and more guests were moving out to the rooftop to enjoy the coolness. For a little while the night had belonged to us—just us—but we weren't alone any longer. I felt the man's restlessness again. Or was it my own?

"I must leave," he said. "I have a very early appointment in the morning."

"No one has early-morning appointments in Madrid."

He laughed. "The appointment is with an American who's buying some armor I'm to appraise."

"An American? Oh, that explains it."

When we started back inside, he removed the dark glasses. Unbearably curious, I asked, "Bryce, why the . . . uh—" I gestured to the glasses in his hand. "Do you have a double life as a fugitive?"

"I apologize for the dark glasses. My eyes are...bothering me."

"Something serious?"

"No...but painful."

Back inside, he hurriedly said good-night to one or two people he'd met, to Claudio and Lydia and finally to me. "I enjoyed meeting you, talking to you," he said, his unblinking, light blue eyes hinting that the goodbye was not final.

I BECAME more spirit than flesh after Bryce Macklin left Lydia's *ático* that night. Conversations with late guests were a blur. I remember returning to the rooftop and looking at the moon and wanting very much to be alone, to try to think. In the small hours, when I had the opportunity to talk to Lydia alone, I found I could say nothing about what had happened. She wouldn't believe me; who would? But it wasn't just that. Something else held me back. I was a victim of my own fear. Indeed I was almost choking on it.

I lay in bed and thought of two men who were identical twins—except that one was real and one was not. Through the open window, moonlight was streaming in onto the pink-and-yellow-flowered sheets. It cast an eerie glow over everything, making the ancient building seem still older and the mystery deeper. I remembered every word, every gesture of Bryce Macklin's. And the more I thought about him, the more I was helplessly propelled to pursue this thing, no matter what. My curiosity was frantic; the pull to Bryce Macklin was too powerful to fight.

On the one hand, I was certain I'd manifested his presence tonight. On the other, he'd had a logical reason for being there; he'd met Claudio in the city. Maybe it was coincidence. No, it wasn't. Fear and curiosity swirled through me, but the curiosity was stronger than the fear. I decided to try to manifest Bryce Macklin's presence once again, and this time I wouldn't leave anything to chance. The next experiment would tell me for sure.

THREE SUMMERS AGO I had visited a medieval castle ruin in the environs of Madrid. Austere, dark, solitary and abandoned to the ravages of time, the castle lay in the quiet countryside. Its dark, deep moat, once full of water, was now overgrown with grasses. Wind echoed through its towers. If Bryce Macklin showed up in a place this isolated, it couldn't possibly be coincidence.

I went out there alone in a borrowed car, Nicky's scene taking shape in my head as I drove. The breeze was hot that afternoon, burning my face; it was a relief to get out of the car. The air had a strange feel to it, as though promising rain, but there wasn't a single cloud in the sky. A hawk sailed high on the wind.

With notepad and pencil, I plopped into the soft grass as the shadow of the castle loomed over me like a monster. There couldn't have been a more appropriate place for Nicholas than a medieval castle, I thought, and got to work.

He had been summoned there, I wrote, because of a baffling homicide, the second such incident to occur at this unlikely site. The body was found in the same location in the tower and lying in the same position as it was in the previous murder, but the first killing had occurred in the 1930s—half a century earlier! There was not a mark on either body. The 1935 homicide had never been solved; poison was suspected but never proved. This time, though, an expert—Nicholas Paul—had been summoned.

Nicky came alone to the empty castle, dressed in blue jeans and a T-shirt advertising a Jamaican scuba diving club. I was engrossed in the scene, lost in the intrigue, when something caused me to look up. Like a phantom rising out of the castle shadow, Bryce Macklin appeared!

He was wandering over the grass like a gypsy, in jeans and a T-shirt, hands in his pockets, watching the hawk circle over the highest tower. And he was almost upon me before he saw me.

Startled, he stopped dead still. "Jaye? What the hell? I don't believe this!" Confusion etched his voice.

I was too stunned to answer right away. Although I'd told myself he might turn up out here, I knew now that I hadn't really expected it. "Hi," I said stupidly.

"What are you ... doing here?" His voice dropped away.

I sucked in my breath before I asked him the same question, although I wasn't sure I had courage enough to hear his answer. "What are *you* doing here?"

With a shrug, he sat down beside me. "The city's hot, and I wanted a break from the heat and the noise and the smells of cooking and exhaust fumes. I've been to this castle before."

Leaning back on his elbows, he took a deep breath of air filled with the fragrance of wildflowers and sunshine, looked at the sky and then at me. That was when I noticed he wasn't wearing sunglasses.

"I don't understand it, Jaye. There's something funny going on. When did you decide to come out here?"

"This morning, lying in my bed, thinking about a scene in my book." I could hardly admit I'd been thinking of him and little else since I first saw him the night before last, and I couldn't look at him. I gazed at the ancient fortress instead. "Nothing stimulates the imagination more than a castle ruin. Did you know there are ravens in this castle?"

"You mean flying inside?"

"They fly the stairwells. It's frightening."

"This is one of the eeriest castles I've ever been in," he said. "Bad vibrations inside. Evil things have happened in this castle."

"You feel it, too?"

"Aye. The first time I walked the ramparts, I tripped for no reason, as if something pushed me. Nearly fell. I'd have broken my neck if I had. It's a long way down from up there."

"As if something pushed you?"

"It seemed so at the time."

I looked up at the ruin. "The tower stairs echo and whine and the dungeons are hideously quiet. You're right, the evil lingers even with the erosion of time."

Bryce smiled. "Want to go in?"

"Do you?"

"Sure. Evil fascinates me."

The way he said it made me shiver. "What's fascinating about evil?"

"Evil has power. It penetrates. I'm fascinated by the pull of opposites and how they affect each other—evil and good, dark and light, moon and sun . . ." He rose and offered a hand to help me up.

As he pulled me up, I got a strong mental image of Satan poking his fiery fork at a silver cloud, and I found myself searching Bryce Macklin's eyes for a glimpse, some glimpse, into his soul. What I saw in his eyes wasn't evil, but it was dark and uncomfortable.

"Moon and sun, dark and light?" I asked as we walked. "Does that mean you equate the moon with evil?"

"Doesn't everyone?"

"I don't. No, certainly not everyone does. Why do you?"

"I never thought about why. I told you about Grizel last night, my nanny. She was a practitioner of what she called 'the old religion,' meaning Celtic rituals. When I was a tot, she convinced me I had a connection to the moon, because I was born within thirteen hours of a lunar eclipse."

"You *were*? Just like Nicky! In a sense, he was born during a lunar eclipse."

"Your hero character? Aye, so you said."

This further coincidence began to eat at me. Coming on the heels of his remarks about evil, it was very disturbing. Bryce took my hand when he reached the moat, for the slope was steep and the grass slippery. The drawbridge had long since disappeared.

"Did your nanny tell you the moon represented evil?"

"Not represented. She believed the moon itself was evil, especially to me because of the timing of my birth. She always warned me never to look directly into the center of the moon."

"Why?"

"I don't remember. Maybe I never knew."

We entered an archway where the old gate had been. A grass-grown bailey opened before us. The silence seemed to scream at us intruders. I hung back. On the opposite wall were the great iron gates that led into the keep; they were closed.

"A gatekeeper should be here," Bryce said.

"No one's here. The doors are padlocked."

"Hell, we can't get in then."

Bryce looked up at a dark-winged bird that flew out of one of the high slits in the walls of the keep. His eyes might have been bothering him last night, but they didn't flinch in today's bright sunlight.

I sat down on the stone bench reserved for the gate-keeper. Leery as I was of walking the haunted halls of that evil castle, I wouldn't have admitted it. "The shade feels good. I was getting pretty hot in the sun, even with the breeze."

"So was I." He sank onto the soft grass opposite the bench and leaned against the gate. "I must be inter-rupting your work. You came out here to be alone."

"Oh, no! No, I'm glad for your company. But didn't you come to be alone, too?"

"I don't know why I came here. Just a whim."

"Do you often do things . . . on whims?"

"Often enough."

I tried to keep my voice steady while I steered back to dangerous waters—the subject of the moon. "Bryce, you said your nanny warned you not to look directly into the center of the moon. Did you take the warning seriously?"

"Aye, when I was a lad."

"And now that you're a man? Do you ever look into the center of the moon?"

"I can't. But not because of my nanny's supersti-tions. The moon hurts my eyes."

When he said this, the jagged shadow of the battle-ments above us darkened, as if a cloud had blocked the sun, but there were no clouds. "What? The moon hurts your eyes?"

"Moonlight burns and tends to blind me, and I get headaches from it. Some times are worse than others. It's especially bad when the moon is full."

"That's why you wear dark glasses at night, but not in the bright sunlight. I've never heard of anyone being so sensitive to the moon. It's very...unusual, isn't it?"

"I don't know. Is it?" He smiled. "Grizel didn't seem to think so."

"She watched the eclipse with you."

"She could look directly at the moon. I couldn't."

"How strange, Bryce. How very...strange."

He shrugged, seeming to have no enthusiasm for the subject of his headaches and the moon, a subject too far removed from this sunlit hour to be important. But my instincts were on full alert, telling me—no, warning me—that it was important.

"Is Grizel still in London?" I asked.

"She died a few months after the eclipse. That night was the last time I saw her."

I longed to tell Bryce the truth about why I came to be here at the castle today, but how could I? Was I supposed to tell him he was here because I'd willed him to be present, although I didn't know why? This sophisticated, educated man would never accept so bizarre an explanation. I drew the secret inside me and held it there, wrapped tightly in my fear. I could see no purpose being served if Bryce believed I was insane.

As we talked, it was hard to separate Bryce from Nicky, yet I was goaded by a feeling that the two were rivals. A human being and a fictional character rivals? Maybe I *was* insane.

"I wish I'd brought my camera. Landscape photos are a hobby of mine." Pausing, he studied me. "Actually, you make a lovelier picture, Jaye—a twentieth-century woman against a medieval backdrop. From where I sit there's a silver halo frizzing your dark hair with light, and the shadows of the folds in your skirt would photograph dramatically."

"You sound like a professional."

"No, photography is a creative outlet."

"Like piano?"

"Better. For me it requires more imagination."

This was exactly the answer Nicky would have given. I had to remind myself for the hundredth time that this man was not Nicky. Who he was, though, I still didn't know.

The stone bench was uncomfortable, and the rough wall of the castle keep was hard against my back. "Where is your home now?"

"Edinburgh. But I spend more time in London, so I have a flat there. Rather, I share a flat with another chap, who travels as much as I do."

"And your family?"

"No family, since my mother died when I was twenty-five." He shifted his legs. "That bench can't be very comfortable. Why not sit here beside me on the grass and tell me about Arizona? It's one of the places I've never been."

During the next half hour I became better acquainted with Bryce, and he with me. I almost called him Nicky a time or two, but gradually Nicky was fading from my mind and Bryce was coming clearer. I half expected Bryce to disappear as magically as he had come, like a puff of smoke or the dream he was, but instead he sat idly picking at the grass, looking at me oddly from time to time, as though trying to remember why I was so familiar to him.

Although usually ready for any adventure, I was glad we hadn't been able to get into the bleak medieval ruin, because Bryce in sunshine was enough to deal with. There was something about this castle that was spooking me.

With the shadow of the enormous structure hovering over us, I asked, "How could the castle's shadow be as cool as this?"

"The shadow holds the chill of the keep's interior."

"How could it?"

"It's the chill of this castle's past," Bryce said. "Can't you feel it?"

My knee touched his as I leaned forward. "I don't...know. What do you feel?"

He looked up at the brooding walls. "I get bad vibrations from this place, Jaye. I'm going back to town to do some work. Shall we have dinner together tonight?"

"I'd...like to," I answered, wondering if he actually had some psychic sense of this castle's stormy history, or if his bad vibrations had more to do with whatever unknown force had brought him out here today—to me.

"I'll call for you at Lydia's flat about eight o'clock, if that's all right with you."

Tonight it will be Bryce, not Nicky, I thought. *I won't manifest him this time. Tonight he'll come because he wants to.*

Won't he?

Chapter Three

THAT EARLY-SUMMER NIGHT in Madrid a warm breeze moved along the dark streets, giving life to shadows. We walked hand in hand, looking into shop windows and popping into music-livened bars where people stood drinking, laughing and eating calamari, the popular snacks of dried squid. It was a gay night in the season when much of the city's population had left for the southern beaches. Those who stayed had abandoned their stuffy apartments for companionship and fresh air.

The moon was almost full. Bryce wore his dark glasses without further apology whenever we stepped out into the night. My dress of cloud-blue organza flowed in the breeze as I walked and my heels clicked on the sidewalk.

"You always wear blue," Bryce said.

"Usually."

"The blue matches your eyes. I like it, but it's a cool color, like the sea or the sky—your cool exterior. Why do you try to conceal your warmth, Jaye?"

"Do I?"

"I think so. There's much more warmth in you than you'd have the world believe. I caught many glimpses of it this afternoon. Maybe the facade of coolness has to do with whatever else you're concealing."

Fear pricked at me. "Do you have a reason to think I'm concealing something?"

"Many reasons, but it's hard to define them. It might be just intuition."

I thanked heaven for lucky timing; we had reached the restaurant Bryce had selected for dinner, and I pretended to be distracted from the subject. I wasn't fooling him, of course, but under the circumstances, I dared neither confirm nor deny his suspicions.

We entered the centuries-old building through a door off a narrow street and climbed a steep stairway to a quaint candle-lit restaurant on the second floor. Bryce addressed the maître d' by name and spoke to him in Spanish. Just as Nicky would have done.

No, I couldn't think of Nicky! He was securely tucked away for the night between the covers of my notebook, where he belonged. Bryce was a part of the living, breathing city—a city he knew better than I—and I would let him lead me as far away from Nicky as possible.

My obsession that evening centered on discovering who Bryce was. He looked so handsome sitting across from me with the flickering light of a candle softly illuminating his face. It was hard for me to convince myself that this man was not the one I loved. Loving Bryce was as tempting as a pool of blue water on a scorching day. My only defense against slipping in was to make a fierce effort to keep separating him from Nicholas Paul—especially in moments when I seriously wondered if he *was* Nicky.

Bryce ordered for both of us. My hunger was less for food than for information. Because he already suspected something, I forced calm into my voice. "Are you married?"

He looked surprised. "I'd have told you if I was."

"Have you ever been?"

"Several years ago."

"Divorced?"

"My wife died."

"I'm sorry. Would you rather not talk about her?"

"She was Australian and very beautiful, and she loved me." The sentence had a gentle finality that discouraged further questions about the woman he had married.

I pushed sideways. "Do you work out of Edinburgh or London?"

"Both," he answered as the waiter brought our wine. He tasted it, gave his approval and waited until both glasses were filled. He didn't bother with a toast, only a small salute as he raised his glass, then continued. "My company has offices in both cities, with the main office in London. I enjoy Edinburgh in summer, and somewhere farther south in winter."

"As a Scot, you must be well accustomed to cold."

"Cold doesn't bother me. It's the darkness. In Scotland winter days have very few hours of light."

What a relief it was to me to discover something about Bryce that was the opposite of Nicky! Nicky thrived on darkness, with much of his adventurous life unfolding in the night hours; he preferred to sleep mornings. And Nicky squinted in sunlight, not moonlight.

"Do you think your nanny instilled in you superstitions about darkness?" I asked.

"Perhaps. I've sometimes wondered. When I was a lad I used to go out onto the moors alone. We lived in a large house in the country, and sometimes I'd ride or hike over the hills. I'd go to my favorite places along the river with my dogs. They were fine, carefree days, but I didn't like nights out on the moors. I'd head home quickly at twilight. I think Grizel did put stories in my head.'' He took a sip of wine and smiled. ''I'll wager you too were afraid of the dark when you were a wee'un.''

''Horribly. My brothers told me the big bad wolf was under my bed. I didn't dare hang an arm or leg over the edge, or the wolf would get me.''

''It was never one of your brothers under the bed?''

''No, but eventually I got even with those two. The father of one of my friends had a clothing store. The friend and I took a mannequin from the storeroom, put a gorilla mask on it and hid it in my brothers' closet. The boys ran half a block before they stopped to breathe.''

Bryce laughed. ''Sounds like the start of a war.''

''A war that never ended. I had glue in my rubber boots and bugs in the bottom of my ice-cream cones.''

''Sounds like life at my boarding school. Revenge can keep a kid busy.''

I chuckled. ''One of the worst things I ever did was put Alka-Seltzer in my brothers' fish tank. What was the worst thing *you* ever did in boarding school?''

When Bryce broke a hard roll, crumbs flew all over the tablecloth. He buttered a bite and popped it into his mouth, all the time with a thoughtful expression on his face, plainly trying to remember long-ago days. ''There was a boy named Jamison James, who stole from the other boys and planted the goods under my mattress, to get me in trouble. No one believed my innocence, and I was whipped in front of the whole school. I swore revenge. My opportunity came when the old plumbing at school had to be replaced. We were without showers for three days, forced to use a bathtub that we had to fill ourselves from a water supply next door. Jamison played around in the tub and made everybody else late for dinner. The second day I stole three bottles of meat tenderizer from the kitchen and emptied them into his bathwater.''

''Good heavens!''

''He was mildly cooked. And we had bliss without Jamison for days.''

I grinned across the table. ''The kid who thought up a revenge like that was as mean as he was clever.''

''He had a mean streak, I'll admit. Someday I'll tell you what I did to the headmaster, who wouldn't listen to my pleas of innocence and whipped me.''

''Oh Bryce, tell me!''

He hesitated, then smiled. ''It was bloody bad. When he threw out a pile of periodicals, an accomplice and I removed all the address labels and carefully pasted them on pornography magazines. We piled the magazines with some things the school had collected for charity, and they were collected by a local women's group.''

''I'm shocked! Was there a scandal?''

''A bloody good scandal.'' Bryce chuckled. ''He was dismissed. Then somebody discovered that the dates on the labels didn't correspond to the dates on the periodicals, and the hoax was uncovered. But I was never caught. Every boy he ever whipped was suspect, and there were plenty of us.''

''I hope you never get mad at *me*!''

''Och, Jaye. Why would I ever get angry with you?'' His voice was teasing. ''Sweet as you are. You'd not do anything mean to me, would you?''

What *could* I do to him? I wondered. If I could make him dress a certain way and show up at a certain place, what *could* I do to him? And what would he do when he discovered this . . . this power I had over him?

He had moved on to another subject. "You don't fit the role of a writer of high-adventure mysteries. Soft and feminine as you are, and wearing antique pearls. Can I buy one of your books in Madrid?"

"If you can read Spanish."

"I can if I have to, but I'd rather read it in English, the way you wrote it."

"Lydia has a couple of them."

"I'll borrow one, then."

The idea of Bryce reading one of my books was uncomfortable, and I knew even then that my discomfort was another warning that something was terribly wrong—hideously strange—about our friendship, Bryce's and mine. How could I have heeded those warnings, even if I'd tried? I still don't know. But I do know that the beauty of him distracted me completely. His deep voice was like music carried on the night air. His hand over mine on the table held me spellbound by its warmth and strength. And I chose to ignore all the warnings.

SEVERAL OF LYDIA'S FRIENDS were gathered in her flat when we got back from dinner at midnight. Emerging from the slow elevator, we heard voices and laughter coming from inside. I was disappointed, having hoped for the chance to say good-night to Bryce in private.

He didn't linger. As soon as he'd met Lydia's guests and obtained one of my books from her, he left with a quick kiss on my forehead and a promise to call.

Maybe it was better he didn't kiss me good-night, I decided after he was gone, because I wasn't sure how I would have reacted. My attraction to him was frightening in its intensity. I don't know whether I was more afraid of myself or of him. And then there was this mystery we were caught up in that neither Bryce nor anyone else would believe...

I could tell him, I reasoned, and then wondered if Bryce would walk out of my life if he thought I was insane. *Could* he walk out of my life, if he wanted to? Or did I have the power, through Nicky, to bring him back?

Bryce had asked me why I'd shivered on a hot summer night. I could hardly tell him it had happened because I was forgetting what it felt like to be warm.

TWO DAYS WENT BY and he didn't call. I was a mess, and so was my life; I didn't dare work on my manuscript. I sat by fountains watching the birds. I walked hot, narrow streets, unproductive and wildly frustrated. Here I was with a contract deadline to meet, and I couldn't write.

It was a terrible temptation to try to bring him back into my life again by just picking up the damned pad and pencil and writing about Nicky. But if I did that, I'd never know if Bryce really wanted to see me. I wanted to know the answer to that question more than I wanted anything else. My creative energy joined with the forces of fear to invade my sleep with harrowing nightmares.

On the third day he called and invited me to go with him to the Prado. I'd been there several times, and so, I was sure, had he. Though one never tired of the works of the masters, I wondered why he'd chosen to look at art when that was the business of his daily life. It didn't matter; I'd have gone anywhere with him.

We walked through the echoing halls for hours, gazing upon the compositions of Raphael and El Greco and Velázquez, and Goya. Bryce was very quiet in the museum. But all he had to do to set my senses afire was to touch me with his shoulder or take my hand.

I remember there were footsteps other than our own, and I would look back over my shoulder, unable to shake the feeling that we weren't alone...that someone or something was following us. Yet the great halls held only tourists and wandering students. I wondered then and I wonder now if it was Nicky's presence, haunting us.

To my relief, Lydia's passion for concerts kept her and her friends away from the flat that evening. Bryce and I returned to a dimly lit, empty house. We fixed sandwiches and poured drinks, kicked off our shoes and made ourselves comfortable in the living room—he sprawled on one couch and I on the other. Through the open window came the sounds of music from another apartment and the growl of cars from the street below.

Suddenly he said, "I couldn't put your book down until I finished it."

"Does that mean you liked it?"

"It pleases me to say I liked it very much. I waited until now to tell you so I could toast you." He held his glass in the air. "To *Times of the Tides*. Where do you get your story ideas, Jaye? If I didn't know better, I'd swear you'd been shadowing me, taking notes on my life. For example, the part about Nicholas Paul getting speared in the leg while scuba diving. The same thing happened to me."

I nearly choked. My body turned to ice. I had allowed myself to believe that nothing more could shock me after everything I'd lived through during the past two days. But this! How far, in the name of heaven, did the identification of Bryce and Nicky go?

I wasn't sure I had the strength to hear what he was about to tell me. Bryce didn't seem to notice my stunned stare as he reclined comfortably in the soft lamplight. "One summer I took up diving in the Mediterranean. Several of us were on the deck of the boat, just after we surfaced from a dive. One bloke's shark gun discharged and hit me in the right thigh. A freak accident. Of course, your man Nicholas was shot by an adversary during a fight, but the spear wound in the thigh was the same. Very curious."

Taking a sip of sherry, he smiled. "I can tell you, Jaye, you did an incredible job of describing what a spear wound feels like. It was one of the worst things I ever experienced. Painful as hell. The way you wrote about it, one would think you'd been through it yourself."

I ingested a dose of a raw fear like a swallow of poison. Bryce had been seriously injured!

From across the narrow room he studied me. "Is something wrong? You've gone chalk white."

If I opened my mouth, I'd stutter. My hands were sweating and my knees had gone weak. Was it possible that some boundary of physical reality as we knew it had burst? Was it possible *I* was the cause of his injury? No! It couldn't be! And yet, holding on to some thin thread of coincidence was no longer rational. This wasn't coincidence, and I knew it.

"What summer did this accident happen?" I asked weakly.

"Three years ago, the first summer I got into scuba diving."

He needn't have answered; I already knew.

Bryce patted his thigh. "Hell of a scar. Nicholas Paul must have one just like it."

"Yes . . . I guess he must have."

In jeans and T-shirt, the man in front of me looked more American than British as he sat back grinning. "You know, there's something about Nicholas Paul that bothers me."

My fists tightened. "Something about Nicholas?"

"I can't pinpoint it exactly. But see . . . I can predict everything he's going to do. One thing he's not is impulsive."

Bryce had already left the subject of the spear-gun incident, but I could think of nothing else. I had to force myself to respond to what he was saying. "You think Nicky ought to be more impulsive?"

"Well . . . I'm impulsive. Maybe I was identifying with him. You must be a damn good writer, because I felt as if I knew your character, right from the start of the book. It was a little like the feeling I got when I met you. That feeling of knowing you still bothers me. Where might we have met? You mentioned Switzerland once. Could it have been Switzerland?"

We hadn't met in Switzerland, yet pursuing the subject of where our paths had crossed would be a vehicle for probing details of Bryce's life, so I would play along. "I was researching a book in Nendaz, in the mountains above Sion."

"That could be it. I was once on a ski holiday in Haute Nendaz. Were you skiing up there?"

"Yes, but I'm sure I'd remember you if I'd ever seen you."

This remark clearly pleased him. "I'd remember you, too." He sighed deeply. "I had to leave Nendaz in a hurry. Another of my disastrous holidays."

Terror just kept slamming at me. Nicholas Paul had nearly been killed in Haute Nendaz! I closed my eyes because I couldn't look at Bryce. I felt as if I had a fever—there was heat behind my eyes, my body had gone weak and my stomach was getting queasy. I made myself ask, "Why was your ski holiday disastrous?"

"I'm accident-prone. The cable broke on the lift car, the big lift that carries skiers from the village to the summit, and I was damn near killed."

"Oh . . . your shoulder . . ." I muttered, before I realized I had actually said it aloud.

Bryce straightened. "How the devil could you know I hurt my shoulder?"

"Did you?"

"I shattered the bone in my shoulder and broke my wrist in the fall. It should have been worse. The authorities who investigated said it was a miracle I escaped with my life. So I suppose I can't howl too loud. But I haven't skied since. How did you know it was my shoulder?"

"A . . . a guess . . . I don't . . . Bryce, was anyone else hurt?"

"No, I was alone on the lift."

His blue eyes conveyed suspicion. I shrank into the role of a criminal desperately concealing a violent crime. What would happen, when Bryce got hold of my Switzerland book and read about Nicky fracturing his shoulder, when the cable of a ski lift was cut and the car fell?

I couldn't take any more. Bryce had been hurt worse than Nicky. What had prevented his death? Had I? Had Nicky?

Fear and helplessness were whacking at my sanity like a bayonet. It was becoming hideously clear to me that I couldn't keep this secret from Bryce. I had to say something! But what?

Instead of facing it, I rationalized that I needed more evidence before I told him what had happened to Nicholas Paul in Switzerland. But this stall was only an excuse for cowardice, I was simply terrified of what he would say.

Picking up his empty glass from the table, I went to the sideboard to refill it. How my knees held me up was a mystery. I filled my own glass again before I sat down with a false show of nonchalance, rearranged the pillows at my back, and tried to think how to bring up the subject of Africa.

I raised my glass. "Here's to Switzerland, where we might have met. And to Africa, where we might have met. Here's to the great gray-green greasy Limpopo...where we might have met."

His gaze was riveted on my eyes, searching. "Why would you mention the Limpopo River out of the blue?"

"I researched a book at Kruger National Park once, near the Limpopo. I thought maybe you'd been there, too."

"What the hell, Jaye! What are you, psychic?"

"So you have been there!"

"The Limpopo doesn't flow through Kruger," he said suspiciously.

"Not quite, no. I was up at the river border, though. What were you doing in Africa?"

"I went to Durban on business two years ago and took the opportunity to see the wildlife at Kruger. It was mid-October, the week the north section of the reserve was opened up for the summer season."

"Two years ago. Malaria was bad that year in the north regions."

The suspicion in Bryce's eyes was deepening by the minute. He knew I was deliberately throwing out hints about . . . something. It seemed that the best way to approach the truth was gradually, like this. There was no question in my mind now that Bryce did have to be told the truth, for his own safety, whether he believed it or not. I felt as if I were holding a stick of dynamite with a lighted fuse.

Swallowing hard, I pressed on. "How long were you at Kruger?"

"About a week."

"Did you stay in the little rondovals?"

"I stayed at several of the camps. Did you?"

"Yes. And walked about the camps at night. It's very dark when they turn off the electricity at night."

Alerted that I was leading up to something, Bryce hung on my every word, but he said nothing, only stared.

I said, "Puff adders abound in that part of Africa."

His stare became threatening. It frightened me. He repeated the words *puff adder* as if the serpent's venom were carried in his voice.

"Did you have an encounter with a venomous snake?" I asked.

"How the hell do you know that?" He rose from the sofa. "Damn it, Jaye! This is bloody weird!"

My hands were so cold by now that they were numb. "The snake wasn't in your rondoval, was it?"

"No, on a footpath. I was told later that puff adders have a habit of sleeping on paths at night."

"And you were bitten?"

"You obviously already know that I was!"

"How bad was it?"

"My leg turned blue and swelled up like a melon, and the pain was excruciating. Luckily there was a supply of antivenom at the camp, and they shot me full of it. For a week I couldn't walk because of the snakebite, and I couldn't sit down because of the needles."

I closed my eyes in agony. *It was my fault!* a voice inside me screamed.

"Jaye," he demanded. "How did you manage to find out so much about me, and why would you be digging into my past, anyhow?"

"I haven't been digging into your past. I was merely guessing... about the snake."

"You don't expect me to believe that, I hope."

"One of my books, *Bulawayo Sunrise,* took place in that area. In the novel the ivory hunters tried to kill Nicholas by putting a puff adder in his hut while he slept. Nicholas was bitten when he stepped on the snake in the morning."

Bryce's eyes narrowed. "You knew about the snake. You knew I'd broken my shoulder in Switzerland. You used the incident of the spear gun in your book. How long have you had me followed? And why would you keep insisting we've never met? I think you knew about the cable breaking, too. But *how* did you know?"

"I didn't know, damn it! I swear I didn't know!" My guess is that my eyes portrayed my agony, because Bryce didn't leap on me, even though he was plainly convinced I had been lying to him all along.

"Something foul is in the wind," he said viciously. "I think you'd better tell me what it is."

"I can tell you, but I can't explain it," I began, shaking. "In my book *Alpine Conundrum*, Nicholas Paul broke his shoulder when someone cut the cable of a ski lift car on a slope in Switzerland, and the car fell.

The idea came out of my head. So did the spear-gun incident. And so did the snake. They all happened in my books. There seems to be a series of events that happened to Nicholas Paul and also to you.''

"*Seems* to be?"

"Bryce...I..."

"I don't get it!" he raged. "Why would you be following me around the world? Why me? How could you follow me without my knowing and...and *why*?"

"Please. I never saw you or heard of you before you showed up in the café a couple of nights ago. I don't know why the same things happened to you that happened to Nicholas in the books. I don't know why!'' My voice had risen to a near scream.

Even as I said this, a new thought exploded in the center of my brain. Maybe I had the sequence reversed! Maybe I wasn't causing these things to happen to Bryce; perhaps what happened to him was somehow being conveyed to me, and I was picking it up and using it in my writing. I began to pray that it was so.

Bryce sat down on the edge of the couch across from me and leaned forward, elbows on his knees. His eyes were so blue that they mesmerized me, and his lips were tight and stiff. "Let me digest this. What happens to me happens to your fictional man, Nicky.''

"Yes, or the other way around. And it's even more complicated than that, Bryce. It isn't just the...your accidents. It's your being in these settings. Your diving and flying and skiing when Nicky does those things. It's your being at a windy castle when I was writing a scene there.''

"What? Two days ago?"

"Yes."

He straightened. "That doesn't make any sense!"

"No, it doesn't, and I can't explain it."

"And I don't believe it!"

At that moment I was almost afraid of Bryce Macklin. If he had a temper anything like Nicky's, I didn't want to be at the receiving end of it. I said, "Absurd as this is, I had to tell you. Bryce, I couldn't *not* tell you!"

"You're leaving something out."

"Yes." I stared at my hands in my lap. Helpless hands. "Your resemblance to Nicholas Paul is what I left out. The two of you are so identical in looks that I couldn't believe my eyes when I first saw you in the café."

"I resemble a man who doesn't exist?"

"He does exist. Millions of people could describe Nicky in vivid detail. You read the book, think about it. He came from my imagination, that's true, but the image of him in my mind—from my first concept of him— is a carbon copy of you."

Head down, looking at the floor, Bryce raked his fingers through his thick, dark hair. His voice was husky with frustration when he spoke. "We saw each other four times in four days in this city. That's stretching coincidence bloody far. I knew it, but I didn't let myself think about it much. You're saying it definitely wasn't coincidence."

"It was me writing about Nicky."

"Bloody hell. How do I know you weren't following me?"

"How do *I* know you weren't following *me*?"

"What?"

My shoulders sagged. "I know you weren't following me. And I was there first—at the fountain, at the party, at the castle..."

I wrote the scenes before you showed up looking just like Nicky.''

Thinking back, I'm sure I didn't expect Bryce to believe me. He wasn't a gullible man, and if anything ever sounded absurd, this freakish story did. Yet his body bore the same scars as Nicky's.

To my surprise, Bryce laughed deeply, unrestrained. "I missed the point of the joke. Or is it forthcoming?''

"I wish it were a joke,'' I said miserably.

He rose and went to pour himself another drink. The tears brimming my eyes might be convincing him I wasn't joking, but he had yet to be persuaded that I was sane. "If there was something bizarre about our meeting, why haven't you said anything?'' he inquired.

"Said what? That I wasn't sure if you were imaginary or real? That I can write a scene about Nicky and you end up in it?''

"What you're saying isn't possible.''

"Of course it isn't. I think . . . I think you *are* Nicky. I found you on the night of a lunar eclipse, but I don't know how I found you! There must be . . .'' My voice faded; I didn't want to say the words.

He walked to the window with his drink. "There must be what?''

"Forces at work . . . forces beyond our understanding.'' I sat in agonized stillness, studying the back of Bryce's head, his broad shoulders and the curves of his body that I knew so well before I ever met him.

In only seconds he turned from the window, wincing, with one hand shielding his eyes.

"Moonlight?'' I asked, but it wasn't really a question. A round summer moon hung over the ancient city of Madrid, casting a silver-white glow around the shadows. It was so bright that one full look at it had sent him reeling. He leaned against the side of Lydia's upright piano, his back to the window. When he uncovered his eyes, I hated the expression with which he looked at me. The part of Bryce Macklin I didn't know had surfaced; I felt it and feared it.

For a full minute he stood there in silence. Then suddenly he challenged me. "If what you say is true, then prove it."

I stared dumbly.

"Go on, Jaye, prove it! Find your notebook and write something about Nicholas Paul.'

My heart constricted with fear. "I've never done this with you actually present. I have no *control* over any of this, Bryce! I can't—"

His voice was hard. "You have total control over your fictional character, haven't you?"

"Of course, but—"

"Then take control of him. Get the damned book and write something about him now. Or are you afraid to?"

Chapter Four

BRYCE'S CHALLENGE scared me to death. I wanted to prove to him that what I said was true, but because I didn't know why it happened and whether or not it always did, to try this in his presence was to dive into the mysterious unknown. I wasn't ready for it!

But what choice did I have? My knees quivered when I rose to get my notebook. I sat down at Lydia's dining table at the far end of the long, narrow living room and read over pages of the scene I'd last written—at the castle.

It was difficult to focus on the story, when my own situation was so perilous. If this "test" didn't work, Bryce would be convinced I was crazy. If it did, it would prove he was in danger from me. No matter what happened, I was in trouble. And so was he.

Bryce stationed himself like a military guard near the piano, arms across his chest in a defiant stance. The moonlight was at his back.

I closed my eyes. "I must concentrate to form vivid images of my scenes before I write them, like running a movie in my head. I need to think about what I'm going to write."

"Take your time."

The pressure was unbearable. Whether Bryce's presence would neutralize the effects of my writing or make them stronger, I had no way of knowing. While my extreme fear interfered with concentration, I decided it would be easiest to duplicate our present setting—this timeworn room with its silence, its shadows and its wood-framed window, forming a membrane of glass between us, the night sky and the moon.

I fought to let go of reality and bring Nicky's face before me, to release my senses to the fantasy of Nicky's world. As if through a camera lens, I zoomed in on the room, focusing hard to try to cancel out the skepticism that Bryce was exuding. The pressure was giving me a terrible stomachache.

I had to conjure up a situation that was both powerful and simple. My mind whirled until awareness of what Bryce was doing across the room vanished, and I was there instead with Nicky, walking him through a fictional scene.

Nineteen minutes later by the big clock on the wall, I looked up from the paper, weak from tension. Bryce was sitting stiffly on the piano bench. The room was cloaked in a foreboding silence.

"Well?" he asked finally.

"It's only a portion of a scene," I said. "I can't get much written in twenty minutes."

He cocked his head skeptically, the expression in his eyes changing like revolving lights from anger to confusion to challenge. I tensed and could barely move.

He rose and stretched impatiently. It was obvious that he had already decided the experiment had failed. The tension in his shoulders relaxed.

"So much for that," he said. "Nothing is a bit different from how it was when you sat down there to write." He stretched again, more luxuriously this time. "It's not easy to sit still so long, waiting for some kind of voodoo to get me. Where the hell is my sherry glass?"

"Have you been right there at the piano all the time I've been writing?"

"Like a well-behaved statue."

I remained at the wooden table while he poured himself the drink. He paced the room, glass in hand, sipping slowly, but not going near the window, until he settled on the couch where I'd been sitting earlier and pushed a cushion behind his back. On the table next to the couch were Lydia's sewing basket and a skirt she had been hemming. When Bryce reached over to move the sewing basket, so as to make a place to set his glass, he jerked back, cursing, and accidentally knocked the basket and a pincushion to the floor.

"Damn! That material is full of pins!"

A small trickle of blood fell onto his white shirt. He sucked at the tiny wound. I sat stock-still at the table, watching him.

When he was satisfied that his finger was no longer bleeding, and had cursed again at the pain, Bryce sat back and looked at me. "Well. What now?"

"What do you mean?' I asked softly.

"I mean about your wild theory. Are you going to tell me it didn't work because I was here in the room while you were writing? Come on, Jaye, you're the one with the runaway imagination. What did you write?" His tone wasn't friendly.

My chair scraped loudly on the bare wooden floor when I scooted it back to rise. I picked up the writing tablet and handed it to him without saying a word.

"Go ahead," he insisted. "Read it to me."

Before I sat down on the bench, I turned on the lamp above the piano. Bryce was still sucking at his pricked finger. The notebook quivered in my hands as I began to read.

"The curtains were blowing in a warm breeze, a breeze that blew off the rising moon. Moonlight filtered in softly, like white mist. Nicholas entered the room with trepidation, for the shadows moved with a life of their own. Too much had happened here. The ghost of Gillian's past lurked so darkly in the shadows, Nicholas sensed he was not alone. By this time, in this room, he could not trust his senses."

I looked up from the page. Bryce was watching me closely, and I could tell he was impatient with me, as someone is impatient with an incorrigible child. I was being silently accused of raising a storm from the settled dust of a prevailing calm. I read on.

"Everything within the four aging walls seemed dead, and yet everything appeared to be alive. Nicholas had been set up, he knew. It was a trap. He walked the length of the room, checked the front door and the landing of the outside fire escape. The fire escape looked too rickety to hold the weight of a man.

"Something moved behind him in the shadows. Nicholas turned swiftly, and as he did, his hand brushed the top of the paint-chipped table that stood at the end of the sofa. He jerked in alarm when a sharp stab of pain rose in his finger. Spots of dark red blood dripped from the punctured finger onto his shirt. Fully expecting to see a serpent or a spider slither off the table, Nicholas uncovered instead a blue silk pincushion and a kerchief pinned for hemming.

"The breathy curse he emitted in the shock of a sudden jab of pain would alert anyone else who was hidden in the apartment, and Nicholas knew it. When he turned, there was a figure in the doorway."

I looked up for the second time. There is no word in my vocabulary to describe the look on Bryce's face. He was sitting forward, his body frozen as if he had fallen into a trance.

What could I say to him—to my victim? I set down the notebook on the piano bench beside me and rubbed my aching neck, moving my head from side to side to try to free myself of the pain that had settled in my neck and shoulders.

An eternity elapsed in the brittle silence. Gradually his senses came back from numbness; his left hand moved along his chin. The hostility in the light blue eyes was replaced by vacant disbelief. He gazed at the pricked finger, rubbing his thumb over the tiny puncture as if he were trying to nullify the wound by wiping it away.

Finally, as if sensing himself foredoomed, he spoke huskily. "Then it's true."

Tears had formed in my eyes. "Yes."

He was humbled, mystified. "What is it, Jaye? What does it mean?"

"If only I knew. I'm bewildered. This might have been going on ever since . . . since Nicky. I can't understand why we've never met in these five years, unless you were always behind Nicky in your travels. Until now—until Madrid."

"It's bloody voodoo," he said in a voice so soft I could barely hear it.

I swallowed. "What are we going to do?"

"We have to find out what this is about." He looked at his finger again and then at me, disbelievingly. "You knew I'd hurt myself on a pin!"

"I didn't know you would. I knew Nicky would."

His eyes closed.

"The experiment proved one thing, though. This... power, or whatever it is, is being transmitted from me to you, not the other way around."

"What?"

"I mean I'm not picking up things you do and writing about them. I think them up before they happen to you."

"It's like a curse—a spell."

"I'm not a witch!"

"Aren't you? How the hell else can this be explained?"

"I don't believe in such things!"

"Neither do I," he said. "Although I... used to..."

"Are you serious? Evil spells? Oh, Bryce, you're too practical a sort of man to be discussing witches without smiling."

The expression in his eyes hit me with such a wallop that I reeled. Squinting slightly to block out some inflow of light, he fixed his unwavering gaze on me, but his eyes didn't seem to see me. He was seeing something, though, and whatever it was existed in a realm beyond my own vision. It was eerie.

"You've put some kind of a spell on me," he said.

"Don't be ridiculous!" He *was* discussing witchcraft, but was not smiling.

"You explain it, then."

"I... I can't," I stammered, intimidated by his accusing tone. He had put me on the defensive, which didn't surprise me. It was only too obvious which of us was the victim. Steadying my voice with effort, I attempted to pry at the window of his thoughts. "Bryce, why would you say such a thing, right after you admitted you didn't believe in witchcraft?"

"Witchcraft seems to be what you Americans call a buzzword," he answered. "I no longer believe in...the kind of witchcraft you mean, but the borders of it are rather vague to me. That is to say, the borders between the explainable and the unexplainable are impossible to draw. This phenomenon has every earmark of a spell."

I was aghast. "You're assuming I'm a witch?"

"Yes."

"Even though neither of us believes in witches!"

"I don't believe what just happened in this room, either. Look, Jaye. There are thousands of people who believe in outside forces. Millions, probably. Beliefs are only that—beliefs. Mine have no more or less value or truth than anybody else's. Nothing in our own belief systems can explain this, so we're forced to look elsewhere. What other choice have we got?"

Even though intellectually I knew he was right, I was stunned that any man's beliefs should be so flexible. Or was it only the words he spoke that were flexible? The disbelief in his eyes was certainly evident enough—disbelief, resentment—and utter confusion.

"A belief in outside forces?" I repeated. "What outside forces are you talking about?"

"I'm grasping at bloody straws," Bryce answered, rubbing his chin nervously. "I don't know what the hell I mean."

Perhaps he really didn't, then, but I began to wonder. Bryce's remarks at the Spanish castle came rushing back to me—remarks about a nanny who was a "practitioner" of the old religion. And the hint just now that he might have once believed in...in witchcraft. Why? Because of her? Because he had been taught from infancy to fear the moon?

We stared at each other. Gradually his eyes began to soften. He was beginning to see himself less as my victim and more as a victim along with me, connected with me in some bigger thing—beyond our understanding.

The softening of his eyes sent a rush of relief through me. I desperately needed a sign from him that he didn't see me as his enemy.

"It would seem," he said philosophically, "as if we're in some kind of trouble."

"Damn. I thought I was just going about the business of my life, writing books...and then one day...there's you..."

"Let's try to think. You told me the idea of Nicholas Paul was born during a lunar eclipse."

"The same night you fell so ill."

"I was with Grizel. The last time I ever saw her. She told me she had seen a dove fly round her head, which meant she thought she was going to die. I passed it off as old superstition." Bryce scratched his head, frowning, trying to remember that long-ago night. "Grizel was in a strange mood," he said. "Singing a folk song, and telling me she wished I could find love again and marry some wonderful girl. She was scolding me because she didn't like most of my women friends. She thought they all were frivolous."

"Were they?"

"Yes."

My gaze darted away, then back.

"I wasn't inclined to want to marry again," he offered in his own defense. He was looking at the floor.

"You and I are both wondering the same thing, aren't we, Jaye? We're wondering if the eclipse of the moon has anything to do with the unexplainable connection between you and me."

"The thought is on my mind, but it's so farfetched."

"It is farfetched. But think. Think about the eclipse, about everything before and after. Anything strange at all. Think back."

"I was looking at the sky that night with my mind on the project I had just begun—a historical novel set in London, which I'd come to London to research. My head was full of that other book, when for no reason that I could fathom, the concept of Nicholas suddenly came to me."

Bryce sat forward. "Just like that? Out of the blue?"

"Out of the black, more accurately. He just...was there, shoving out the characters who were already walking around in my imagination, and he wasn't part of the London book, not Nicky. He wanted...hell, he practically demanded, a book of his own."

"And got it."

"Absolutely. He was wonderful! I'd never done a character as surreal as Nicky before, nor had I particularly liked his sort of books, but I was overcome with the desire to write them, and I knew I could. I had a strong feeling about it, and the character was forming vividly in my head. He was very alive from the moment I first saw his eyes...blue eyes...out of the black night."

"And the character looked like me? Even then?"

"Yes. Exactly you. Features, coloring, build, everything."

"It's weird."

"More than weird." I picked up my notebook nervously and set it back down.

"Grizel," he said.

"What?"

"Grizel and her Celtic magic." Bryce swore a terrible oath, then continued. "The ancient magic. I grew up with it and as a bairn I believed it, although my mother never took Grizel seriously and told me the things she said were nonsense. She accused Grizel of being fairy-struck, which only made it all more dark and real to me—wee lad that I was."

"Fairy-struck?" I got up from the piano bench, went to Bryce and touched his arm. "What kinds of things...were dark and real to you?"

"The fairies were real," he said without blinking. "Spirits that haunted woods and streams."

"Tiny, sparkly nymphs darting from flower to flower? Those kinds of fairies?"

Bryce laughed with a frown. "I'm not talking about children's stories, Jaye. I'm talking about the spirits of those who lived before, dwelling in dark woods and dark water, fairies who kidnapped children, spirits who were in communion with darkness. Grizel cautioned me all the time about getting into trouble with the fairy spirits, the brownies. She warned me about the dangers of the night, and sewed iron nails into the seams of my clothes to ward off—" He stopped.

"To ward off—what?" I knew what he was going to say, and I dreaded hearing him say it.

"Spells," he answered, wincing as if the word soured in his mouth. "To ward off spells."

My vision clouded. "Oh, Bryce."

He fidgeted in the chair.

"Surely she didn't actually believe in...the fairies?"

"As I look back, I'm not absolutely sure. I know Grizel had a strong bond to nature, which she instilled in me. She was so moved by the beauty and the magic of nature, and she would never harm a flower or a tree. Thinking about it as an adult, I don't know whether she believed in the fairies and goblins, or whether it was just her way of teaching her wee charge to respect nature as she did. There are those who still believe, though, Jaye. The religion of the ancient Celts is not dead and never will be."

"Superstitions."

"Aye, so we tend to call it now."

"There was much beauty and romance in it . . ."

"Och! And horror. Savage cruelty. You'd not want to know."

The way he said it somehow brought the horror closer. I thought of robed druids and wizards, sacred fires and mysterious forces of earth and sky, and I thought again of the eclipse. I was growing so uncomfortable that I could barely sit still. I, for one, was not superstitious. But I was beginning to wonder about Bryce. He had been brought up on this . . . this dead religion that was not dead, and it was a part of him, whether he consciously believed it all or not.

With dread, I said again, "But . . . surely your nanny didn't really—?"

"She was a gentle woman," Bryce interrupted. "But she did have an uncanny understanding of nature and its forces, and knowledge of the occult passed down in her family for generations. She talked about my birth connection to the moon and to the eclipse. That's got to be it, Jaye—the explanation of the unexplainable. Grizel was dabbling in spells."

"You think she put some kind of spell on you? But it's . . . impossible!"

"Your being able to make me prick myself with a pin is also impossible." He rubbed his forehead. "Because of the coincidence of the eclipse, there's just no other way to figure this out. Nothing happens without a cause. If you don't have witch's powers, then it must have been Grizel."

"But . . . but Bryce, could she?"

He closed his eyes. "Probably."

I couldn't believe this. I asked, "Have you ever seen a . . . uh . . . spell before?"

"No, not that I'm aware of. My nanny didn't go around chanting, if that's what you're picturing. She took me for walks on the moors and told me about the trees and flowers and the sun and the hills, and how there used to be wonderful oak groves growing in the homelands, and she taught me not to fear death, because she believed the soul never dies."

"Then why? Why would she . . . dabble in spells, as you say . . . something like this?"

"I have no idea why."

"Oh, if only she were alive, so we could ask her! Bryce, it was the druids who practiced the magic, wasn't it? The priests?"

"Apparently there were plenty of witches and bards around to help them, not to mention the gods and goblins and the thousand spirits. It was a world of magic, Jaye, in those days."

I gazed at him, trying to read him, reminding myself that this wasn't new to him. Whether or not he believed it, at least it wasn't new. For me it was a fairy story, for him it was . . . the past.

As if he read my mind, he said, "I'm a Scot, you know. A Celt myself. The mysticism of the druids is part of my heritage."

"Mine, too. My own ancestors left your islands only two generations ago. Bryce, there must be someone who's a student of the old magic! If we could find somebody who knows about such things."

"Grizel had two sisters who, as far as I know, are still living in Scotland. One of them never married, and I believe the other is a widow. I'll try to find them. At least it's some kind of a start."

I leaned weakly into him. "I'm terrified. The Nicholas Paul books are my livelihood. I can't just stop writing! But if I don't stop writing, what happens to you?"

To my surprise, he threw both arms around me and held me in his comforting warmth. "This is a mess. I have no idea how you could have got mixed up in it—if it was Grizel's magic. Hell, I can't fathom any of this! I'm hearing us talk about it, still not believing it."

"I've been getting the impression that you do believe it."

"On the contrary. I don't. School made a complete skeptic of me long ago."

"Perhaps not as complete as you would like to think."

"A shock like this jolts one out of comfortable obtuseness. We have to start looking in cracks we'd rather weren't there."

"And I? How was I pulled in, then? I most certainly was in the wrong place at the wrong time—when Grizel was . . . uh . . . dabbling in spells."

"No, it doesn't work that way. You were definitely selected, that much I know. It wasn't chance."

"She couldn't have known me."

Bryce gave me a squeeze. "Maybe somehow she did. But one way or another we're on the right track. The more I think about it, the more I'm sure."

I sighed shakily. "I just don't...see how you can say that so calmly."

"Calmly? That's what the spirits of my warrior ancestors would like to believe of me. The truth is, my knees are shaking like hell. I don't like this one wee bit." He paused. "I have to leave Madrid tomorrow because my business is finished here. I wasn't planning to go to Edinburgh, but I'd better take some time to look into this. I also need some time to try to absorb it. Perhaps back by the rivers of my childhood, I can get more insight."

"You said your childhood home was a very large country estate."

"My ancestral home is a museum now, but the grounds and the surrounding countryside are as they always were. All my secret places are still secret and still mine. I'll take a few days to walk the old moors again and to find Grizel's sisters, if they're still alive, please God."

I could feel the roughness of his beard against my face. And then, with little warning, the softness of his lips. He kissed my forehead and my cheek, and finally my mouth. His lips lingered on mine, and his kiss defined itself. It was not a kiss of passion, but of caring. *You're not alone,* his kiss said. I'm with you. We'll work through this thing together. He was conveying his strength in the gentleness of his kiss. With the fearlessness of those warrior ancestors, he meant to take charge of uncovering this grisly mystery we were caught in. Fears be damned.

I swam in the sensations of his kiss. No other man had ever kissed me this way; certainly no other man had ever awakened the response in me that Bryce did. I lost what small hold I still had on reality under the spell of his lips, and my strength left me. My stomach went whirly. I savored the feel of his skin as I touched his face, his neck and his shoulders through the thin shirt. The feel of him sent my senses soaring. Should my reactions to his kiss and to the touch of his body have been a surprise to me? Hardly. I still could not successfully differentiate between Bryce and Nicky, and I was in love with Nicky.

And therefore with Bryce.

His fingertips caressed my face. "Jaye, the first moment I saw you, I felt an incredible attraction to you. Out on Lydia's rooftop it was all I could do to stop myself kissing you. I resented the dictates of society that wouldn't allow it. Very out of character for me to be tempted to behave like a barbarian."

"You knew there was something strange about our meeting. You kept saying it in various ways."

"I thought you were the most beautiful woman I'd ever seen." He settled back with his arm around my shoulders, and said, "I'm remembering back to the eclipse. Grizel was complaining that I'd turned into what she called a 'jet-setter,' a term she probably picked up from television. She challenged my ability to choose the right woman, and said if I couldn't make the proper choice, she would make it for me." His eyes closed. "Aye, by the saints, Grizel has done just that. I'd swear it!"

"Chosen? What are you talking about?"

Bryce closed his eyes and began to hum a haunting tune. Then he softly sang the disturbing refrain.

"I'll not climb the brae and I'll not walk the moor,
My voice is gone, and I'll sing no song;
I'll not sleep an hour from Monday to Sunday
While the black-haired lad comes to my mind."

I caught my breath. "What is it?"

"The old Scottish folk tune Grizel was singing on the night of the eclipse. It's coming back to me."

I waited.

"My handsome black-haired lad, though all think you reckless
I would marry you without consent of my kindred;
I would fare far with you through dells and wild places,
While the black-haired lad comes to my mind.

My fine black-haired lad, I will not leave you;
If I saw you in company I'd choose you above all the rest.
Though I saw five thousand, sure, I'd think you the best
Of them, while the black-haired lad comes to my mind."

I touched Bryce's black hair and said nothing. There seemed nothing to say. It was only a folk song, after all. Wasn't it?

No, it was a spell.

I finally asked, "Is there more?"

"The song? Aye, but I can't seem to remember."

"She was mischievous."

He said nothing. Evidently he was still thinking about the song.

"I hate her name," I said softly.

"Grizel?"

"It sounds so...mean."

"She wasn't mean. She loved me. And I loved her. I'll admit she was overprotective. Tell me, why does your Nicholas have a phobia about cats? Why won't he go near a cat? It was a surprise when I read it, but now it fits."

"You? You're afraid of cats?"

"I guess fear is the right word. It's a phobia from my formative years. Grizel always kept cats, all kinds of cats, and this one white cat in particular hated me and I hated it. If I picked it up, I'd get scratched and bitten. It would sneak into my room at night and walk around on my bed, and I blamed all my nightmares on that cat. Cats are evil. I still can't stand them. Like Nicholas. But it seemed so out of character for so suave a detective to fear cats."

"I decided on his cat phobia for two reasons—one because it *was* out of character, to give this otherwise perfect man a human failing, so he'd seem more real. The other reason was simply a suspense tactic. His fear gets Nicky into trouble once in a while. If there's a cat around, the reader sort of perks up, waiting for something. At least I *thought* those were my reasons."

"People in Scotland once believed witches could transform themselves into cats," Bryce said. "It was an old Celtic belief that fairies could look out through the eyes of cats into the human world, so nobody would look into a cat's eyes."

"Grizel taught you these things?"

"I assume so, because I seem to have always known them. Since I had this phobia about cats from childhood, it would appear that some ideas are transmitted from me to you, after all. We both know it wasn't co-incidence—whatever rational reasons you thought you had for giving Nicky the same phobia.''

I shivered. He felt it and moved still closer to me, sheltering me from the world. I needed his strength, and whether he knew it or not, he needed mine.

"Tomorrow night you'll be in Scotland," I said sadly.

"I'll miss you. How long do you plan to stay in Spain?"

''A few more weeks. But these . . . developments are going to affect my writing schedule. I'm afraid to write now.''

A dark shadow crossed Bryce's eyes. I knew he was only beginning to comprehend the extent of my power over him. He was controlled by me, at my whim. And realizing it, he was anything but pleased.

The elevator doors clanged in the outside hall. We heard voices. Bryce glanced at me and then at his watch. With a quick kiss on my cheek he rose, ready to leave.

"You're not staying for a drink with Lydia and her friends?"

"I couldn't handle small talk right now. I couldn't put on a act and pretend the world is still right side up."

As the sound of footsteps invaded the kitchen, Bryce touched my hair. "I'll telephone. In the meantime, please keep Nicky out of any plane crashes, will you?"

Bryce slipped out of the main entrance while Lydia's friends came in from the rooftop and through the back door. I was bothered by his remark about airplanes. Did he believe I was able to kill him? *Was* I able to kill him— with a few words on my writing tablet? I shuddered and had to feign a headache with Lydia's friends, because I couldn't face them any easier than Bryce could.

DAYS WITHOUT BRYCE were overwhelmingly restless. Missing him. Wondering what he was doing in Scotland and if he was learning anything about ancient spells. Wanting him to hold me. Wondering why he didn't contact me. Wondering in the early waking hours if he'd ever happened at all—if I had only dreamed him. My notebook lay on the dining table on top of a pile of papers that comprised the outline of *España Farewell*, the novel I had begun in Spain and should be getting well into by now.

Confiding in Lydia might have helped a little, but something stopped me. If I knew her, she would spend a day shrieking disbelief, question me endlessly, and accidentally leak my wild story to half a dozen people. Never had I felt more alone, because something had linked Bryce to me—some bond—and then he had left. In spite of his silence the bond was still there.

He phoned on the evening of the tenth day. His voice sounded different; I blamed the bad connection.

"Jaye, I'm in Edinburgh. I was here only a couple of days before I got called back to London on business, and I've only now been able to get back. Can you come up here?"

My heart had lurched at the first sound of his voice. His accent sounded stronger than before and exuded urgency. "What's going on?" I asked.

"I've stumbled on something interesting."

The phone line crackled and hissed. "I can barely hear you, Bryce. What have you found?"

"I can't explain on the phone, especially with a bad connection like this. Will you come?"

"I'll take the first flight out in the morning."

"There's an eight-thirty flight on British Airways that connects easily with the London-Edinburgh shuttle. Unless I hear otherwise, I'll see you then."

The phone crackled again, and I think we were cut off. I was staring at the receiver in my hand when Lydia came out of her bedroom in her underwear, brushing her long, blond hair. "Who was it?"

"Bryce Macklin, calling from Scotland. He wants me to meet him in Edinburgh tomorrow."

"Aha! At his expense? Airfares to Britain are atrocious."

"Bryce is . . . helping me with some research."

Lydia grinned. "Bryce is captivated by you. This call doesn't surprise me in the least. The fascination is mutual I know that, too."

I smiled. "I can't very well deny it."

"He's too handsome for his own good, and much too conceited."

I went to the kitchen to pour each of us a glass of ice tea. "I don't find him conceited," I called back through the archway.

"At best he's not particularly friendly. That night when he walked in here with Claudio, every woman wanted to be introduced to him. He saw you and was almost rude about ignoring everybody else. Of course, you wouldn't have noticed. All you noticed was him."

I handed her the tea. "I doubt that he meant to be rude."

"Of course he did. Bryce runs all over the bloody world, mixing with his aristocratic clients. His manners are impeccable. When he wants, he can charm the wings off an angel. This isn't that big a town, you know. Things get around. Claudio says Bryce has a reputation for being unpredictable and moody."

I shrugged and sat down. "How would Claudio know?"

"Bryce comes to Madrid often, but people here know little or nothing about him. Surely you caught that mysterious air? Does he ever talk about himself?"

"Yes. He never talks about his wife, but he'll talk openly about other things." I realized as I said it that Bryce *wasn't* fond of talking about himself. People doubtless spent considerable time with him without knowing him at all, because he wanted it that way.

Lydia scowled at me. "He's married?"

"His wife died several years ago."

She sat down across from me at the dining table. "Why does he want you to go to Scotland? You didn't mention Scotland when you were telling me about this latest book."

"Well, Nicky is trotting the globe, as usual."

"Like our handsome friend, Macklin."

"Rather, yes," I said and smiled, mimicking her very British accent, the way she liked to mimic mine. The sound of Bryce's voice was still echoing in my brain. He had sounded rushed and frustrated. What could he have found?

"Is he a fabulous lover?" Lydia asked suddenly.

"What? I'm shocked you'd ask!"

"You are not."

"I've only known him three days."

"So?" She raised her arms in mock helplessness. "Oh, blast, I keep forgetting you're an American prude, Jaye D."

"And Bryce is a gentleman."

"Bryce is an Englishman."

"He's not. He's a Scot."

"He's just a smart predator, that one. Frankly, I don't see how you could resist him. You won't for long."

I watched the dew form on my glass of tea and thought of the mist on Scottish moors. Bryce had found something he didn't want to talk about on the phone. It was something frightening—I knew that from the sound of his voice. The hours until tomorrow were going to be agonizingly long.

Chapter Five

FOR A SPLIT SECOND I was sure I had gone mad. When my flight landed and I saw Bryce standing at the Edinburgh terminal waiting for me, I thought he was Nicky and I had crossed the invisible line into Nicky's make-believe world. The sensation quickly subsided; Nicky disappeared, and Bryce stood before me with a single red rose in his hand.

He embraced me. His heart beat against mine. I hadn't realized how much I'd missed him until the shuttle flight left London and I was flying toward the skies of Scotland—silver-blue skies, the color of Bryce's eyes.

Wearing dark slacks and a woolen sweater in hues of blue, Bryce took my small nylon bag and headed in the direction of the baggage claim area. "I didn't check any luggage," I said.

"Just this? Are you in a hurry to return to Madrid?"

"I never travel with more than I can easily carry."

He grinned. "I'm impressed. I didn't know there was a woman on the entire earth who likes to travel light."

He led me toward a red sports car in the airport parking lot, opened the door for me, and set my bag in the tiny boot. Once in the driver's seat, he leaned over and kissed me. The kiss lingered and became deeper and stronger. My knees grew weak, my heartbeat quickened and I could barely breathe for the sensations overpowering me. His kiss was positively debilitating.

"Welcome to Scotland, love." Bryce looked at his watch. "Did you have lunch?"

"I ate in London," I answered, allowing the sounds and smells of the parking lot to bring me back to the present. "Bryce, I can barely stand the suspense! I have to know what you found."

He started the engine. "I found Grizel's sisters. It's not going to be easy explaining to you everything I learned from them. I wanted you to meet them yourself. They're both quite elderly and live in a wee house in Dunfermline. They're expecting us."

"Dunfermline. Is it far?"

"It's as close to the airport as Edinburgh, but in the opposite direction—just over the Firth of Forth bridge. We're almost there."

Bryce's apparent need for urgency was making me very apprehensive. Concentrating on the perfect beauty and rich color of the rose he'd given me, I tried to calm myself. "Tell me about the sisters. Did you explain to them what was happening?"

"Not at first, but then it became necessary in order to get any information from them."

"How on earth did they react?"

"Not like other people would have. They weren't the least taken aback. I hate to scare you, Jaye, but you'll know soon enough—Grizel's sisters are witches."

I stared across at him as the engine droned softly and the roadway opened up before us.

He glanced at me. "They prefer to be called sorcerers rather than witches."

"They admit they're . . . sorcerers?"

"It's an old, long-practiced art, passed down for generations. Grizel was a witch, too. I probably always knew that. I thought of her when I thought of spells, when you and I were talking."

I didn't like the sound of this at all. "Bryce, are we dealing with black magic?"

"Forces of evil? I don't...I don't think so. My mother must have known Grizel was a witch, but she didn't seem worried by it, because Grizel was so devoted to me. I think I was the son she never had. For all I know, Grizel and my mother might have had some kind of...understanding, because one never interfered much with the other."

"Then it isn't...it isn't black?"

"What do you mean?"

How could he not know what I meant? I wondered. "The sorcery...is it black witchcraft? *Is* it evil, Bryce? Do you know for sure this isn't black? How could it not be?"

His eyes were on the traffic. "Grizel had a dark side, to be sure, and these women do, too. It's easy to sense. But the darkness probably comes from the past. They seem gentle enough, if a wee bit strange."

"Darkness from the past? I don't understand."

"The old religion casts a long, low shadow, Jaye, rather like a crouching thing, never quite hidden. The ancients were no strangers to evil. They recognized the power of it, and certainly practiced it, but they worshiped the powers of light."

"Witches don't."

He glanced at me. "Do you know about witches?"

"Not a damn thing. Except that they like cats and do spells."

"Grizel's sisters say they want to help us. That's what's important."

I reached to touch his arm. "*Can* they help us?"

"They're busy gathering more information. I hope they'll have something to tell us."

"Does this mean we're definitely dealing with a . . . a spell?"

"Aye. There's no doubt of it."

"You sound convinced. I can't accept it that easily. Maybe it's a . . . bad dream."

He touched my hand. "If so, it's not all bad—you're in it."

The sky became darker as we drove. A few drops of rain spattered the windshield. Bryce's mood was changing, too. His joy at greeting me was giving way to a mood as bleak as the Scottish skies. I was sure he was thinking of the witches.

"Bryce? Why would your nanny put a spell on you if she loved you?"

"The sisters are looking through some of her journals. She left a trunk they never opened until I turned up here yesterday. It's to be hoped they've found some clues in there." He looked at me again. "The sisters are anxious to meet you. I told them you're a famous author."

We crossed the great Forth Bridge on a highway that Bryce said would lead us north into the Highlands if we kept going, and I couldn't help but wish we *could* keep going, and forget about the witches. My usual lust for adventure and my natural writer's curiosity were sealed off somewhere behind a wall of fear. All this was going beyond adventure—to the borders of terror.

A tall, ancient tower rose into view as we approached Dunfermline. "The old abbey ruins," Bryce said. "Robert the Bruce is buried there, all but his heart. When we get closer, you'll see his name lettered on the tower parapet."

"All but his heart?"

"His heart is elsewhere, in Melrose Abbey. Dunfermline was the site of a royal palace, where a Scottish king was married in the year 1070. You may want to visit the ruins."

"After we've seen the witches, I may be a ruin myself."

"I could give you the minitour—Andrew Carnegie's birthplace—a wee house where his parents rented the attic."

"Bryce, you're trying to distract me! What is it? What are you trying to distract me from?"

"From my own fears, I suppose. We're getting into something here that could be evil."

"You said the witches seemed harmless."

"I didn't say harmless. I said they seemed gentle. Their manners are gentle. They're old women. No, I think it's memories of Grizel that bother me. I recall the first time I saw the sea tides. Grizel told me the moon caused the tides and caused the same tides in my blood. She said the force of the moon pulled on me like it pulled the tides. It was my most impressive lesson about the moon's power. She also told me moonlight was light reflected from the eyes of cats with yellow eyes."

"It does sound evil," I whispered, more to myself than to him.

He bypassed the main roads of the town and turned onto a quiet, treeless street lined with little gray and tan houses that stood side by side. Lace curtains at every window softened the bleakness. Seagulls were crying overhead when we got out of the car. A dog barked somewhere around a corner. On this summer afternoon of misty drizzle there was no one on the narrow sidewalk and no sound of traffic.

Bryce knocked only once before the door opened. Childhood stories of Hansel and Gretel did nothing to prepare me for my first sight of a real witch. Morag Campbell wore a rose silk dress with a floral design and a collar of antique lace. Her white hair softly framed her face. Her cheeks were pink, her skin was almost free of wrinkles and her smile welcoming. She reminded me of summer.

"Come in," she offered after the introductions, and turning to me, asked, "Did you have a pleasant flight from Madrid?"

"Thank you, yes. It's a relief to be out of the Spanish heat."

"And into our infernal rain. Always rain. Tea is ready by now, and I've just lit a wee fire to take off the damp chill."

We were led from the entry into a dimly lighted sitting room. As soon as we entered, a large gray cat appeared as if from nowhere, and jumped up onto one of the chairs. Bryce recoiled so fast that he backed into the side of the door.

The woman turned, glanced at Bryce and the cat, and then back to Bryce.

"I'm sorry," he apologized, but he didn't seem to mean it.

"The cat?"

"I don't...like cats."

"I see."

"I'm sure it's a fine, friendly cat, Mrs. Campbell, but I've got this bloody phobia about cats."

Morag Campbell scooped up the cat in her arms and disappeared for a moment or two. A door at the end of the hallway opened and closed.

"Fergus was supposed to be in the kitchen," the witch said when she returned, while she motioned us into the sitting room. It had been obvious to her that Bryce wouldn't have entered the room as long as the cat Fergus was there.

I'd expected the other sister to be here; she was not. A peat fire burned in the fireplace, throwing an orange glow into the room. The furniture must have been in its place for half a century, at least. Faded floral curtains hung at the windows. A muted floral carpet covered the floor. The musty odor of candles hung in the air. Two seascapes and a faded photo of a bride and groom hung on gray-pink walls. It might have been a typical sitting room, except for the plaster cast on the mantel of an upright, open hand. Something about the hand bothered me, but my intuition warned me against asking about it.

A low serving table was set for tea, with pastries and cookies and tiny sandwiches. Morag motioned us to sit and began to pour.

"Elspeth will join us in a few minutes," she said in her strong Scottish accent. "She's upstairs, searching for something, and insisted we go ahead without her."

I was handed a gold-trimmed cup and saucer, and helped myself to the milk and sugar. The small serviettes were lace-trimmed, obviously handmade and very old. Bryce sat beside me on the sofa, outwardly at ease now; the ritual of tea served well as a tension breaker, and was second nature to a man who had grown up with it.

The old woman sought to put me at ease. "I cannot tell you my surprise when I opened my door to see this young man standing before me. That instant I knew who he was, I did, though I had not set eyes on Bryce since he was the weest lad. His smile, aye the smile, I remembered, and the blue of the eyes, and sure, the black of his hair." She grinned at Bryce. "So bonny a lad he is still."

"Hardly a lad anymore," he said.

She lifted a plate of scones from the table and offered one to me. "He's told me all about you, lass. About your books. Elspeth found *Bulawayo Sunrise* in a bookshop and we're reading it now. I like it, I do. A right good mystery. The bookshop owner swore I was wrong about the author being a woman, and later on I shall take much pleasure in telling him I met you personally."

Morag sipped her tea and laughed softly, but behind the laugh was something else, some kind of secret. *She has found out something,* I thought. Bryce was probably thinking the same thing.

She continued. "Bryce has told us the strange circumstances of how the two of you met."

"Frightening circumstances," I said.

"Aye, so." Cocking her head, she studied us. "Don't you both look fine together, but sure you would. It was my sister chose the pair of you."

Bryce sat forward. "You're sure, then?"

"Aye, we were sure yesterday, but we wanted proof. Since then we've found some of Grizel's notes. Elspeth is still going through old books and papers, looking for any reference to this specific spell."

"Is it possible for a spell to get stronger as time goes on?" I asked.

"Aye, and this one has. It's why you two finally had to meet—such was the spell's first purpose."

"There's a second purpose?" Bryce asked.

"That you marry each other, of course!"

I flushed. Bryce fell silent. The moment was awkward. Morag Campbell's face was white above her lace collar. Her face once had been very pretty.

She looked steadily at Bryce. "Everything you told us we found in her journal—her disapproval over how you were living, concern for your loneliness after losing your young wife. Her belief that she could find the right wife for you."

"And she chose Jaye?"

"She did. She chose the virtues and characteristics, and Jaye fitted perfectly."

I could feel Bryce's eyes on me as I spoke. "But it's far more complicated than that. This character of mine..."

"Aye, the book character. Nicholas Paul. Dynamic man he is, too. His description is Bryce's, anyone could see that."

Bryce was becoming impatient. "What does Nicholas Paul have to do with anything, Mrs. Campbell?"

The old woman's eyes darkened as she set down her cup. Her mouth was tight. I sat stiffly, afraid to breathe.

"Nicholas Paul is you, lad. This lovely lassie found you at once in her head, but she could not find you in person for a long time to come. So you became Nicholas."

"I don't know what the devil Grizel was dabbling in, but obviously something went wrong," Bryce muttered.

"This is what we believe. Some unforeseen force came into play. The power of the spell is very strong, because it draws its power from the moon."

Elspeth MacCreath appeared suddenly in the doorway—a tall, thin woman wearing a black woolen skirt and rust-colored silk blouse covered by a black cardigan. Her hair, unlike Morag's, was done up in a tight bun at the back of her neck. I thought of winter when I saw her; she was older, colder than her sister. She, like Grizel, had never married. A stack of papers was folded in Elspeth's thin arms.

Bryce rose as she entered and introduced us. I noticed how big he looked in this room with three women, all of small stature. Elspeth MacCreath grasped her papers with one hand and shook my hand with the other, then sat down in the overstuffed chair reserved for her and balanced the pages on her lap.

When Morag poured Elspeth's tea, the two exchanged glances. Elspeth had found something upstairs, and whatever it was didn't greatly please her, if one were to judge by the dark expression in her eyes. I felt Bryce tense beside me.

"It's a pleasure to meet you," Elspeth said to me. "Sure, I did enjoy your book. One would not picture the author to look like you."

"I'm glad you enjoyed it," I responded politely.

"Have you found the pages?" Morag asked her sister impatiently.

"Aye, I have." Elspeth took a sip of tea and looked at us. "Did Morag explain what I was looking for?"

"I did not," Morag said, rising from her chair. "I thought it best to see if we could find it." From a table she picked up an old, worn book and opened it. The printing was in Gaelic. "We've been through our entire library. Most of our books have been passed down in our family for generations. We possess two books on ancient magic.''

"The druids did not write of any of these mystical or magical things. Rather, the bards passed on traditions by word of mouth. The books were written later and therefore leave many questions unanswered, yet they are helpful. We found this book yesterday, the one we were looking for, but the pertinent pages have been torn from it. We knew Grizel must have torn them out, because they have to do with the spell she used on you.''

"That meant a search through two trunks of Grizel's belongings, in the hope that the pages would be there,'' Elspeth added. She patted the papers on her lap. "And at last, just now, I found them. We missed them the first time.''

"Thanks be,'' Morag muttered softly.

Her sister scowled. "A priceless book ruined. A priceless book! For centuries to own it was to risk death. Grizel was always such a scamp.'' She looked at each of us in turn. "I've had no time to study these papers. I must take a few minutes to look at them.''

Bryce's piercing gaze moved from one witch to another, and I didn't like the look in his eyes. He leaned forward. "Something is changed since yesterday, Miss MacCreath. I sense it. You're holding something back.''

She met the challenge of his gaze. "I have not analyzed all the facts. I must finish reading these.''

Morag reached for the papers, shuffled through a few handwritten sheets on top, and pulled out some yellowed pages torn from a book. Looking at them, she stiffened and touched her right hand to her lace collar, then retreated into silence. It was obvious she didn't like what she saw. Bryce and I exchanged concerned glances, while Elspeth took a sip of her tea.

Handing the papers back to Elspeth, Morag looked at me. "What do you know of sorcery, lass?"

"Virtually nothing. Except it was once widely practiced in Scotland."

"Our family—the MacCreaths of Ochil—came from the Ochil Hills, northeast of Glen Devon, between the river Devon and Castle Gloume."

"Good Lord," Bryce said and scowled. "The area known as the gathering place of witches. I've read of the witches of Dollar who held meetings in that glen below Campbell Castle."

"Aye. Campbell it's called now."

"About forty witches went to trial in that area back in the mid-1600s," Bryce explained to me.

"And most were executed at the Crook of Devon," Morag said. "In the seventeenth century over a thousand people in Scotland were put to death for practicing witchcraft." She lifted a small biscuit from the tea tray and smiled. "Believe me when I say the books were kept well hidden until 1736, when witchcraft was declared no longer punishable by death."

"Do you practice it openly?" I asked her.

"Do we? Oh my, no. Not the way you mean. We are aware of the forces of nature and we sometimes call upon them. To be sure, many folks talk, but we have never admitted to the practice of sorcery. Yesterday, aye, we did, when Grizel's favorite lad brought this problem to us. But of course, he already suspected our...secret."

"Everyone knows there will always be witches in the hills of Ochil," Elspeth said. Grimly she handed the papers to her sister. "Grizel knew far more of the ancient art of sorcery then either of us has ever known. As a child her second sight was very strong—"

"That is to say, she was more psychic than either of us," Morag interrupted.

Bryce muttered a Gaelic word. *"Taibhs."*

Morag turned to me. "Today we recognize that psychic experiences of some kind happen to nearly everybody, but once they were attributed to the fairy spirits. As for the *taibhs*, the second sight, aye, Grizel as a child had dreams about what was to come, glimpses into the future. Perhaps she gave credit to the fairies for it. I do not know."

Elspeth shuffled papers impatiently. "Now then, Bryce, let us review this very carefully. On the night of the eclipse, did Grizel give you any sort of potion to drink?"

He looked shocked. "Of course not. We were drinking wine."

"It probably contained a potion," Elspeth told him.

" 'Potion' is perhaps not the best choice of words," Morag said. "It conjures up bats' wings and doves' hearts. If Grizel used anything, it was a drug to act with the wine to relax you, so you would be less alert to what was going on around you and more receptive to suggestion. Do you recall being sleepy?"

"I recall being sick." No longer able to sit still, Bryce rose and began to pace, hands in his pockets. "How did she do it? Just tell me how the hell she did it!"

"We don't know. I wish we did. Please try to be patient. And try to remember all you can. Were there candles on the table?"

"Aye. Grizel always used candles."

"Do you recall what color they were?"

"Red, I think. I'm not sure. What difference could that possibly make?"

"We're trying to determine how much she relied on the old magic and how much on the new. Red candles symbolize love. For a love spell. Was there incense in the room?"

"I should say so! The smell was nauseating after a while. But I was used to Grizel using incense. I thought nothing of it."

I twisted nervously in my chair. Incense and candles. I used them myself, for fun and atmosphere. They meant nothing, surely. This was all superstition! And yet...something very strange had come from that night.

"Think back," Elspeth urged Bryce. "Relax and think back and tell us everything you remember."

He sighed wearily, which must have meant he'd been going over and over this, himself, in the past few days. "Grizel didn't seem well," he began. "She was excited about the eclipse—she always was about anything happening in the sky—but for long moments she seemed completely distracted, as though she were somewhere else. We talked—mostly about me. She was concerned about my future."

"Aye, so you said. And she held your hand."

"She held my hand for a long time, but that was the sort of thing she always did. She still thought of me as a bairn, and for me as well the years would fold away. She was unusually sentimental and somewhat sad that night." He paused. "She extracted from me a promise to stop smoking, a promise I've kept."

Elspeth gazed into Bryce's blue eyes. "These spells traditionally require chants. I'm surprised she didn't feel compelled to offer up a chant, just—"

"The song?" I asked.

"What song?" both women asked in unison.

"Bryce sang part of it for me the other night. A song called 'The Black-haired Lad.'"

The way the sisters looked at each other, it was obvious they knew the song. "Was it part of the spell?" I asked.

"Aye," Elspeth said. "And you are right, Jaye, the song took the place of a chant. It is a love song, and the spell is a love spell."

"We're going in circles!" Bryce complained, pacing again.

"No, we're not," Elspeth assured him. "We've learned a great deal. Why not sit down and have a bit more tea and we'll try to explain as well as we can what happened."

Morag carefully smoothed her skirt and cleared her throat. She sat with her feet crossed at the ankle, her shoulders straight, her silver hair catching the misty light from the window. She seemed to be talking to me more than to Bryce, perhaps because I hadn't grown up with this and needed more help in understanding it.

"We—my sisters and I—are students of the old ways," she began slowly. "Insofar as we study what little is known of the ancients. But we are the inhabitants of this century, and as such, we must try to build a bridge across the ages. One does not live in the past, one merely tries to understand its legacy. The magic of the druidic Celts was powerful magic, but only because they understood their own power. It is the same power we recognize today and call by other names. The incredible power, for example, brought about by creative imaging."

Now we were moving into something familiar. I'd read about athletes who used "visualization" techniques to help them excel. I'd talked to people who visualized to aid their power of concentration, and by so doing shape their goals. It seemed basic logic to me. But I'd heard and read about creative imaging as if the idea was new. Maybe it wasn't so new...

"In ancient times," Morag offered, "people didn't have the capacity to visualize—of bringing vivid images deliberately to mind—that we have today. We are inundated with photography in every form from infancy. We're schooled in the visual arts, if you will. We have wide-screen and 3-D films, films in our sitting rooms day and night. We've seen the bottom of the sea, and the tops of mountains we'll never climb. We've seen bacteria and we've viewed the earth from space. We can visualize things we desire vividly with great skill. Early witches, like the primitive witches of today, depended upon props to help focus concentration. We no longer need the candles, potions, dolls, herbs and the like. We need only to understand how to focus thoughts..."

Bryce finally sat down. "You're saying Grizel used the power of her mind to cast that damned spell?"

"Aye. She used both methods, Bryce. She utilized the old knowledge, not of *how* magic works, but *why*. She used the candles, the chant, the incense, even some kind of potion that made you open to suggestion. There may have been other props that you weren't aware of."

"But," Elspeth said, "Grizel might not have put great faith in the props, because she seems to have used so few. Love spells are powerful, and they traditionally depend on secret potions. How she was able to draw that much power in, no one but Grizel will ever know. People do it, but the desire must be tremendous, inspired by great love or great hate. My guess is that Grizel had been concentrating on that spell for a long time, and the eclipse somehow enabled her to incorporate the moon's power."

"But how is it humanly possible to draw power from a heavenly body?" I asked.

"All nature is one," Morag explained. "All in the universe is connected. The moon's pull on earth is part of the natural scheme of things. The force that pulls the tides affects the tides of our blood. Grizel channeled the power. I don't know how. I couldn't do it. But somehow she did."

"For a love spell?" Bryce wailed. "A *love* spell cast on two people who'd never met? It's balmy, and it didn't work right. Something went wrong."

"Something to do with the moon," Elspeth answered. "Our theory is that the moon moving out of the shadow during the eclipse caused a tremendous surge of power."

"Then why didn't I fall in love?"

"You did," Morag said. "And she fell in love with you. But for some reason you were unable to find her, and she was unable to find you."

Bryce and I stared at each other.

"Grizel chose Jaye for you," Elspeth said. "That is to say, she chose a woman with all of Jaye's qualities and left it to the higher spirits to identify her. Jaye picked up the image of you and created Nicholas Paul, who is not Nicholas at all. He is Bryce Macklin."

This subject of his being in love had Bryce as rattled and embarrassed as I was. "Why didn't I get a strong visual image of Jaye?"

"For two reasons. One, Grizel didn't know her as she knew you. She herself didn't know exactly what Jaye looked like. And secondly, you may well have received an image of her, but you are not a writer who would stop to analyze your visions, hold on to them and use them. You wouldn't have been able to recognize Jaye until you saw her in the flesh."

Bryce took a cookie from the tea table and stuffed it into his mouth. "Are you hearing this, Jaye?"

"Yes." I was unable to hide my discomfort.

"It's true, isn't it? Damn, it's true."

I was afraid there was no way of ever discovering how Grizel actually pulled this off, or what her original intention might have been. "Did I make the spell stronger by creating Nicky?" I asked.

"Aye, unquestionably. But you had little choice. The two of you were destined to meet, whatever you did."

"Destined or not, we can't live with this," Bryce said suddenly. "Jaye can control me—control my life—with her notebook and her whims. I can't cope with that. And she can't write as long as everything she creates for Nicky also happens to me. We have to find a way to reverse this. That's why we need the two of you. There has to be some bloody way out of this."

The witches looked at each other in a way that made my heart sink. Finally Elspeth spoke. "The spell cannot be broken."

Bryce jerked his hands out of his pockets. "What?"

I felt the blood drain from my face. The course of my career passed before my eyes.

"We have checked and cross-checked," she said. "The pages Grizel tore from the book confirm that this is a very ancient philter, a sacrament, if you will. The spell was cast in conjunction with the planets. Your astral scheme is here in Grizel's notes, Bryce. You are Cancer, a child of the moon. The moon is the planet of brooding. She is not friendly to Venus in your scheme."

"None of that makes sense to me! You'll have to translate. What are you trying to tell us? If the damn thing got on, it can get off!"

The old woman's voice was gentle, patient and filled with pity, and the pity scared me.

"I'm trying to explain, my dear, that the spell is more than a philter. The planets are involved. The concentration of the mind is potent, but not potent enough to change this. We want to help, but there is nothing we can do."

Bryce and I were both on the edge of panic. He because he was no longer in control of his own life, and I because I had already signed a four-book contract, and there were deals being cut for me to adapt my books to screenplays. I couldn't just drop Nicholas Paul! Yet if I didn't...if I didn't, it was too frightening to think what might happen.

"If I were to stop writing about Nicholas Paul, would that put an end to the...the connection Bryce and I have?" I asked weakly.

"Not at all," Morag answered. "The spell is there whether you write or not, because Bryce will still be here and he is Nicholas."

"But my control over him is through Nicholas. That part would cease."

"Aye, that's so. But the moon spell—the love spell—would continue."

"And Jaye loses her livelihood!" Bryce was almost yelling now. He rubbed the back of his neck. "Miss MacCreath, there has to be a way to reverse this spell! Surely if a spell can be put on, it can be taken off!"

"Nothing short of death can reverse this one," Elspeth said softly. "Grizel was determined you find a lifelong love. Only when one of you dies will it be broken."

I sat forward on my chair, feeling my face drain of blood. "It can't be," I muttered.

"I'm afraid it is," the old woman answered. "There is truly nothing we can do."

Chapter Six

THE PAST surrounded us in the form of ancient tomb-stones—high stones, flat, wide stones, crude and polished stones, stones broken and leaning like unevenly planted trees in a grassy field. Bryce and I walked the abbey graveyard in silence. Not feeling the drizzle, reading the names without registering them in my mind, I thought only of finality. How could it be that death alone could break this cursed spell?

Bryce had suggested we come to the abbey grounds, not because he wanted to show me historical Scotland, but because he wasn't ready to return to Edinburgh, accepting what we had learned here in Dunfermline. We needed time to absorb it.

Of the abbey I remember little more than the gigantic buttresses, and the pillars and arches of the nave of the abbey church. And Bryce beside me.

He was brooding and silent, and so was I. I sensed that his frustration wanted to come out in anger, but he didn't know against whom to direct his anger. I was feeling a terrible sense of loss, even while I recognized the other thing between us—the love. I loved this mysterious Scotsman and he loved me, and not by choice. We couldn't understand the love that came from somewhere outside us, but we could feel it more every hour we were together. So, confused, with the looming walls of the abbey at our backs, we aimlessly walked the grounds our ancestors had walked so long ago.

At length he took my hand, the first time he had touched me since we left the house of the witches.

I was still teetering on the edge of denial. Softly I asked, "Bryce, is this...it is true? Do you truly believe it?"

He walked several steps, head down, before he answered. "Aye, it's true. There's another realm of reality, right enough, and we've somehow slipped over into it."

"Or been pushed." I paused. "I do know there's another plane of reality. Too many psychic phenomena can't be explained by our oversimplified, materialistic approach. I know there's a great deal we don't understand...and yet, *this*..."

"This," he said gently, "is some kind of misuse of energy—of power, if you will. When I think back on the atmosphere of my childhood, I remember how these powers were taken for granted. I've seen magic before, Jaye."

I pictured his childhood, the long, dark days of winter, the icy winds of the moors, the mist...the sound of tumbling rivers on moonless nights.... "What magic have you seen?"

"Small things, compared to this. Wishes come true. Precognition. Animals appearing suddenly where they shouldn't be...I'd have to press my memory for the odd happenings that a child called magic, but which the adults shoved off as coincidence. Part of me is still that child and knows what the adult never will." He looked at me. "Aye, I have seen magic. And so have you, and this...we're pawns in it, and probably will never truly understand it."

"But how can we *cope* with it?"

"We can't. But we're stuck. There's no point in denying what I feel for you, Jaye. No point in pretending. I'm in love with you, and it's because of a witch's spell.'' His voice became bitter, and I knew the bitterness rose out of the awful helplessness.

He continued. ''Maybe I'd be in love with you anyway, but there's no way of knowing, is there? Do you feel...love for me?''

''From the moment I saw you.''

''Praise God! And I...we...don't know if it's real!''

''Five years,'' I said. ''It took over five years for the spell to bring us together. We were often in the same places because of it, yet we never saw each other. Five years of all my relationships going wrong. Yours, too, I presume.''

''Och aye. Five years of feeling this thing deep in my gut and not being able to define it. Like an itch I couldn't scratch.''

''Years,'' I said helplessly, ''of impulses you couldn't explain. Of living the adventures of a character in a damn book.''

''I thought Grizel's sisters would have an answer.'' He dropped my hand. ''I can't live with this! I can't ask you to give up your career, but I can't go on being that...that character, either. What am I supposed to do, stand by and wait for your editor to decide Nicholas will be taken prisoner by mad terrorists and tortured? Or wonder when in an unexpected moment I'll be knocked unconscious or shot in the belly or find myself wracked with the fevers of malaria?''

''Bryce, please! I'd never do those things to you!''

''What will you do, then? Send Nicky to tea parties and charity balls and keep him out of trouble? Have you written since I left Madrid?''

"No. And I won't again. I can't...again." I couldn't conceal from Bryce that my saying it brought me to the edge of tears.

I felt the strong grip of his hand, clutching my arm protectively. I couldn't look at him, because I didn't want him to see my tears. "Bryce, what are we going to do?"

"Right now, we're going home. It's raining again and we're starting to walk in circles.

IT WAS RAINING HARD by the time we reached Bryce's apartment in Edinburgh. He took for granted that I'd stay with him. The Bryce Macklin I'd met in Madrid wouldn't have done that, but circumstances were different now. We had just been told that we were destined to love each other for as long as we both lived, whether we wanted to or not. So we could now admit that every time we made eye contact or touched, it was all we could do to pull away. The physical desires were strong and growing stronger, and now we knew there wasn't any use in fighting them.

His apartment was boldly furnished with Scandinavian furniture, in stark contrast to the frowning little house in which we'd spent the afternoon. Bryce carried my bag to the bedroom and set about mixing us drinks on the counter of his small kitchen.

"Do you want Scotch?"

"Have you a little wine?"

"Some chilled cabernet, I think."

"That's fine."

Bryce took a healthy swallow from his glass, unbuttoned his wet shirt and threw it over a chair.

I remained standing in my damp skirt and sweater, shivering, until he said, "If you want to get out of your

wet clothes, you're welcome to one of my dressing
gowns. There's one on a hook in the bathroom. Help
yourself.''

Neither of us was very wet, but the evening was turning cold, and the dampness was clammy and uncomfortable. When I came out of the bathroom wearing his
blue cotton robe, wrapped nearly twice around and the
short sleeves hitting well below my elbow, Bryce had
lighted a fire in the bedroom fireplace. He was bare-
foot and bare-chested, and the firelight glowed softly on
his skin. It was a large, sparsely furnished room, with a
queen-size bed, a long, low, mirrored dresser across one
end, a chair with a reading lamp above it, and some
bookshelves. Books and magazines lay haphazardly on
the table and the floor around the chair, but otherwise
the room was almost too neat to look lived in.

I sipped the wine and watched him bend over the
fireplace to push back a sizzling log. The blaze rushed
and filled the entire room with an orange glow.

"I have steam heat," he said. "But the fireplace is
sufficient for summer evenings."

A moment later he was beside me, gently lifting my
glass from my hand and setting it on the table. For a
long time he merely looked at me, holding both my
hands in his, between us, between our hearts. Slowly he
drew me to him and held me in a poignant silence, a silence that meant there were no words to say. We had
said them all, walking among the tombstones and driving back to Edinburgh. We had wailed and cursed the
forces of sorcery. We had made futile attempts at discussing the future, which seemed flat, like a flat earth
over whose edge we had fallen, plunging into uncer-
tainty.

Now there were only the two of us, and I grasped the illusion that Bryce's arms were the only place on earth in which to escape the inescapable.

Bryce's arms...the only place where I belonged.

Bryce's kiss...to make me forgot every other kiss I'd ever known. Bryce's kiss...open-mouthed and lingering, fired by the passion of his breath. Bryce's hands...warm against my breasts.

Floating in the netherworld of my million dreams of love, I whispered, "I wish we didn't know...."

"We don't know," he whispered back, kissing my throat softly. "I'd have loved you anyway... I've searched too long for you."

"And I for you."

He lifted the robe from my shoulders and let it slide to the floor, loosened his belt and stepped out of his slacks. Kissing me, he pulled me onto the bed. I tumbled on top of him, clinging to him.

"We're already bonded," he said. "I'll never leave you."

Had we not been so mesmerized by the spell and by each other, we might have resented the helplessness of our passion. But we were deeply in love, and all thoughts of the rain and witches and the chant of an ancient song were gone. Even thoughts of Nicky had faded like mist blown off by a wind from the sea. All else blew away, and only Bryce and I remained. Alone.

And aching.

He lowered my bra straps and kissed my shoulders, then my breasts. Soft sounds of music came from the living room. He must have turned on a stereo, but I hadn't really heard the music until now, when it filled a pause of silence with its beauty. The firelight filled the bedroom with a beauty of its own, and the room became a place of magic. Whether these moments were real or a dream no longer mattered. I was with the man I loved.

"There's something I want to know about you," he said, kissing my breasts, caressing with his tongue.

"Mmm?"

"How ticklish are you?" With his fingers teasing my ribs, I writhed and giggled. We began to roll about on the bed like children, needing the play, the lightness, the release.

"I don't believe in any of it," he said.

"I don't believe in it, either," I answered, because we needed to pretend.

I discovered he was ticklish, too. When I poked at his ribs, he doubled over, and came back for revenge by holding my hands above my head and blowing softly on my face. I wriggled for a moment before our eyes caught and held, and we became quite still, looking at each other as if we were seeing something new, something we'd never seen before.

As in fact we were. We were seeing a moment from which there was no turning back. I lay still, held by the strong grip of his hands. Pale blue eyes fixed on mine— making love to me, seizing my fever, my spirit and my soul.

In those eyes I saw the reflection of myself. As surely as if he had already made love to me with his body, he gave a precious part of himself to me—such was the power of love in Bryce's eyes. I accepted, unblinking.

From here there was no turning back.

He drew a heavy breath as he loosened his grasp on my hands. The play was already over, the loving had begun. I reached up to cup his face in my hands. His whiskers grazed my fingers like coarse sand as he smiled softly down at me. He looked so handsome that I needed the warmth of his skin and his breath to prove to myself that he was real.

"Who'd have thought of lace as a barrier?" he muttered, removing the lace I wore next to my skin and replacing it with his hands. Sweet shivers slid through my body when I felt the sensations of his lips on my breasts and stomach.

My hands moved the length of his muscular back to the elastic of his briefs. He rolled onto his back and raised himself to allow me to slide them off. I stared unashamedly at the perfection of his body—the virile male body I had seen so often and so vividly in my imagination. Everything about my lover was so familiar and so new at the same time, as if I had known him forever, as if we had only just met. He had not come from my dreams—my dreams had come from him! Nicky was no more than a photo of him—a black and white picture that faded with too much light. Bryce was the light—as alive as sunshine.

Alive and aroused, he welcomed my admiring gaze. I touched the deep surgical scar on his shoulder and the ragged one on his right thigh—the scar left by an underwater spear gun. Tears formed in my eyes and spilled down my cheeks.

He ran his fingers through my hair as I pressed my lips to the scars. "What's the matter, Jaye?"

"Your injuries were worse than I'd imagined. I don't know how to deal with this."

"You don't have to deal with it. It's part of the past."

"You've suffered so much pain because of me."

"Because of Grizel, my sweet, not because of you."

I found the scar on his leg, the one left by the fangs of a venomous snake, and kissed it, too. Bryce lay almost motionless, allowing me to explore his body.

"Your kisses feel good," he said. "Your lips are so soft. And your tears are making the kisses very wet." He stroked my hair. "But I don't want you to cry."

"It's only . . . it's emotion," I whispered.

"I know . . ." He eased my hand gently along his thigh. "Touch all of me. Lay your claim to me and to no other man but me."

I reached out to him with my dreams and with my aching. To touch him was to touch reality and fantasy simultaneously, like touching earth and sky together.

Bryce moaned at the sensation of my fingers, caressing, circling, teasing. "Sorcery be damned," he grunted. "*This* is sorcery."

Cupping my breasts, he urged me closer and kissed me. Kissed me deep and deeper until my head was swimming. Held me tightly against him, and finally, lips still on mine, he eased me over while his strong hands caressed me, claimed my body, rendered me helpless to the sensations of his explicit adoration. My limbs quivered and trembled and I thought again of the tumbling brook—warm silver water moving erotically over me, flowing against every part of me. Weak and floating, I surrendered.

"You are so beautiful," he whispered. Passion deepened his voice.

Inside my head my own voice screamed, *I want you! Desperately. Now!* I'm sure I never uttered the words, but Bryce seemed to hear them; he responded at once. I pressed my palms against the hard muscles of his hips as he moved up and over me. My heart was pounding violently; my insides coiled and churned like water caught in an undertow of rapids. I held my breath...

Bryce was looking at my eyes, asking something. I blinked and then remembered. "It's...all right," I said, even as I wondered, if it hadn't been all right, could we have stopped? If it hadn't been all right, I'd have had to let him know before now. Bryce trusted me. I trusted him.

His gaze locked on mine as he eased his body into mine, gently, slowly, allowing me the intense joy of the first sensations of him. The essence of Bryce was power. With all my being, I accepted his lusty, full-blooded power. His strength flowed to me, filled me, bolstered and became a part of me.

I absorbed his astounding strength, not just for these moments or this hour, but forever.

When he moved, the planet turned and I with it. I held tightly to him, vaguely aware that my nails were digging into his flesh, but afraid to let go for fear of falling. Or was it fear of flying? My grasp didn't seem to hurt him, if he felt it at all.

Then I no longer cared where I was hurled, as long as Bryce was with me. He found the rhythm of my pounding pulse—or his own; our rhythms were the same. Our bodies moved as one tidal ebb and flow, one tidal rise...rising...rising...

His eyes...oh, his eyes! They were flames searing mine, burning me, daring me, reaching where his voice could not reach.

I grasped him in wild desperation as the fire shot through my limbs and my trembling body surged toward the swift, unbearable drench of passion's flood.

"My love!" he moaned from somewhere far away. "My love..."

I cried his name in helpless surrender. The flood caught me. Raging and raging, it dashed and whirled me against the center of ecstasy. Bryce hastened to lose all restraints of his own, to stay with me.

A groan rolled from his throat, then another. He closed his eyes. I felt his shudder as if it were my own.

I BECAME AWARE of the room again, now darkened by shadows of twilight that would have been deep night, had we not been in such a northerly sector of the globe. The fire burned brightly; shadows of flames flickered against the walls and over the pale blue sheets of Bryce's bed. The curtains moved softly in a breeze from a window he had left cracked open. The night was growing colder, but near the fire and in the steamy embrace of Bryce's body it was warm. When his breathing was close to normal and his heartbeat stilled its thundering, he reached down to pull a cotton quilt over us.

I raised myself on one elbow and kissed his closed eyes. "You said you'd love me...anyway," I whispered. "I'd love you anyway, I know it."

He smiled. "Tell me you want no man but me."

"I want no man but you."

"Because of a bloody spell."

"The spell has nothing to do with it," I insisted.

"We have no way of knowing for sure." Slowly he opened his eyes and looked up at me. "You have the loveliest eyes I've ever seen. They're the deepest blue. And your skin is the color of white heather...here, where the sun hasn't touched you. Have I told you how beautiful you are?"

"You're bewitched."

"Perhaps. But I'm not blind."

"Nor am I, my fine, black-haired lad, when I see such beauty in you."

"My Highland ancestors would flash swords to hear a man called beautiful."

"What do they know? Ask my million readers what makes a man beautiful."

"You mean Nicky. Nicky is the black-haired lad, not me. I'm not Nicky."

"The witches believe you are."

"Witches have never been particularly famous for their wisdom. I'm grateful to my nanny for giving me you, in spite of the problems. A bloody computer couldn't have matched us better. You're everything I ever wanted in a woman." He fell into a thoughtful silence, during which he reached up and touched my face. "Making love with you is fantastic. I've never known it could be so fantastic."

I laid my head against his chest. Our love had made me forget how upset I'd been about the mess we were in. I fought back thoughts of it now. The night had more love in it and more joy than any night of my life till now, and I wanted to savor it and forget the horrendous price we had to pay for it.

Bryce stroked my hair and the back of my neck. "Jaye," he asked softly. "What's your real name?"

The question startled me. "How do you know it isn't Jaye?"

"Because it doesn't fit you. In fact, the fit is so bad I hesitate every time I say it. What is your name?"

"I'd rather not tell you. It's a silly name."

"It probably begins with the letter *J*."

"Good deduction, but I can't tell you. You'll laugh."

"I won't laugh. I want to know your name."

I scowled and sighed. "It's Jasmine. Like the flower. Jasmine doesn't fit me any better, and you know it."

Bryce wrinkled his nose. I could tell he was killing himself to keep from laughing. "You're right; it doesn't. What's the *D* for?"

"My middle name. Diana."

"Ah!" he breathed. "Ah, yes! Diana. Goddess of the moon."

I felt a little shiver go through me. "That's an interesting coincidence."

"I don't believe in coincidences. A beautiful name— Diana. It's you. It's the you that belongs to me."

I'd always felt the name Jaye was too tailored for me to wear comfortably, yet I couldn't help but wonder if his desire to call me something other than my writing name was an attempt to distance himself from the reality of my power over him.

"When we left Dunfermline you were determined to beat this damn spell," I said.

"I didn't want to accept the prognosis that we're enslaved by a concoction of herbs and some hocus-pocus for the rest of our natural lives."

"I wonder if it would help for me to distance myself from you."

"Distance yourself?" Bryce's chest heaved in a sigh. "Remember when Nicky woke in a remote Portuguese village and there was a chicken on his bed?"

I began to feel a little weak. "Of course I remember."

"Where were you when you wrote that scene?"

"I was in Portugal. Why?"

"I haven't been in the south of Portugal for eight years. But once in England when I was staying at the home of a friend, I woke one morning to find a big crow sitting on my bed, looking at me."

"You woke with a crow on your bed?"

"He was sitting there with a stupid how-should-I-know-what-I'm-doing-here look on his face. Just like Nicky's chicken."

"Oh, no."

"A wild crow. Flew right in through the window. I'm glad it wasn't a cat, the way I hate bloody cats. My point is that distancing yourself from me won't help."

"Bryce... what about...?"

He waited. "What about what?"

"Nicky...is quite the playboy. He's slept with his fair share of gorgeous women."

"Aye, he has."

I didn't like the way he agreed with me. It told me more than I wanted to know.

His voice darkened. "I guess I don't know what of my life is real and what isn't. That's a hell of a feeling, Diana."

"Yes, it must be."

"Even our being here. You could have manufactured this as easily as anything else."

I raised my head in horror. "How can you say that?"

"It's within your power to do it."

"Do you think I'm that sort of person?"

"No. But the point is, I can't determine which of my actions are my own and which are whims of yours. It's a bloody nightmare."

I lapsed into uncomfortable silence. Moments ago it had felt so good. Now, that I had given in to the unbearable desires, doubts were surfacing again.

He recognized the pain in my silence, and began to stroke my arm. "I'm sorry for the outburst. It's just . . . you can't know how it feels to be controlled by another person. Like a puppet. A puppet made of straw and wood. You can make the puppet sing and you can make him dance.'' He ground his teeth in anger.

"I wouldn't . . .'' I said weakly, knowing full well I wasn't in complete control of my own thoughts—thoughts that could cause problems for Bryce.

"What will you do, then? Never think or write about Nicholas Paul again? Break your contracts? Refuse to do the screenplays? Find a monastery in the Himalayas and train yourself to keep from thinking?''

"I have to try.''

"No. Trying to put the bloody spell on hold isn't going to work. It's a powerful force we're under. We'll live in constant fear of it, and it will find ways to manifest itself. It'll seep back like moonlight through cracks in a wall. You can't give up your work any more than I could give up mine. I suppose we'll have to live with you in control of my destiny.''

I felt sick. Bryce was in agony over this. Understandably so. And it wasn't going to get any better. This was the worst thing we had to face. *It wasn't going to get any better.*

He lay staring at the flickering shadows on the ceiling. "You suggested earlier that we should get away from each other, and I said it wouldn't help. But now that I think more about it, I realize it's the only solution we have. Maybe it won't help much, but we'll just have to get as far away from each other as we can.''

My heart sank at the thought. "But the spell keeps getting stronger.''

"I know. But I don't know any other way to try to fight it, do you?''

"No,'' I answered miserably.

"You have to keep on writing."

"And what about you?"

"I'll survive. Nicky is indestructible, isn't he?"

"Oh, sure. And what sort of life will you have?"

"The same life I have now. Heaven knows, it isn't dull."

"You've had one horrible injury after another. Anything that ever happens to you, you'll think it's because of me."

"It probably will be. I'll just have to learn to live with it."

"You've been constantly saying you *couldn't* live with it!"

"Words come cheap. There isn't any choice. The only way we can keep this thing from ruining both our lives is to carry on as though we don't know about it. You write your books, and I won't know what you write."

"No."

"Damn it, Diana. I'm going to exert what little power I have and bloody order you to leave me and write your books and pretend I don't exist."

"Oh, terrific! You're ordering me to ruin your life!"

"I'm trying to keep you from being destroyed."

"I hate martyrs!"

"Well, I'm sure as hell not going to have the woman I love martyr herself for me! That would be the ultimate humiliation."

Silence fell around us. The fire crackled. I fought to keep from crying. Fighting wasn't going to bring a solution. Nothing would. I felt his tension.

And I felt his love. Bryce gently began to stroke my bare shoulder. "My sweet Diana. I never wanted a woman the way I want you. Yours is the most giving love I've ever known. I want you so much my body aches. I want you now, again.''

"I want you again," I said. "I want your love more than I've ever wanted anything."

He kicked away the quilt that covered us and drew me to himself, kissing me deeply.

"I love you," I whispered to him.

"I love you," he whispered back.

"How can we stand this, Bryce? One minute vowing to stay together forever, the next minute vowing to part? It's so...so crazy...so impossible...."

"Let's not...talk about it now," he said, brushing my neck with kisses. "Later...we'll...decide..."

Later won't be any better, I thought, but the thought faded as quickly as the shadows of the fire, because his kisses were upon me, moving over my body, and I could think of nothing but how much I loved him.

Chapter Seven

WEAK RAYS of sunlight were showing through the cracks in the curtains when I woke. Bryce slept on his side, facing me, his hand resting on my arm. Still tingling from the sensations of love, I lay for a time and watched him sleep. It was a troubled sleep; he couldn't lie still.

Lying next to him in bed, I felt a sense of belonging unlike any I'd ever known. I'd suffered a deep restlessness for several years, always feeling misplaced wherever I was, always wondering if there was a place over the next hill where I'd feel at home and want to stay—a place where I belonged. Thinking back, I supposed the worst of the restlessness began when Nicky was conceived—the night of the eclipse. Now I understood. It was here I belonged.

And yet I didn't. Bryce had said last night he thought we ought to part, and I couldn't argue with his logic. But I didn't want to leave him. I almost hoped our love for each other would be so strong that we wouldn't be able to part, but trying to imagine a life together was impossible at this point. I'd have to drop Nicky, but others would write the screenplays. Because Nicky was far better known than I, my publisher could even get someone else to write the books, and then what would happen? Since Nicky and Bryce were one, what would happen to Bryce if someone else took over the care and feeding and adventures of Nicholas Paul?

The unanswered questions had no end.

Bryce stirred, opened his eyes, gazed at me and smiled sleepily. "You're still here. I thought maybe you were only a dream."

"It was a very vivid dream," I answered.

"I'll relive it a thousand times." He stretched his arms. "You must be starving. We should have eaten dinner last night."

"Who was thinking of dinner? Can I make you some breakfast?"

"It's too early for me to eat, but if—"

"No, I'm not hungry, either. I don't want to get up."

"Neither do I."

He kissed me good-morning, and I would have been happy to stay there in his bed with him forever.

But it was not to be. Bryce said softly, "I'm driving down to London today and back to work. You're welcome to stay here as long as you like, or drive down with me. I thought about us spending another day here together, but that would only make things harder for us. The longer we put off our parting, the more difficult it will be."

I stared at him.

He reached for my hand. "Leaving you is the hardest thing I've ever done in my life. Diana, if there was any other choice open to us, I'd take it. But you must understand. As much as I love you, I love my honor more. A man can have no honor or identity as a man if he is controlled by a woman—or by anyone. You wouldn't have a man, my love. If I can't be in your life as a man, I won't be in your life at all."

The cold shadows of early morning surrounding us were so heavy that they seemed to have weight. I could feel them upon my shoulders. My eyes moved to the crumpled sheets that covered us. Everything, including Bryce's handsome face, blurred in my tears. My words nearly choked me. "This parting then—it's forever?"

He flinched. His voice was husky. "It has to be, Diana. I'll be destroyed by this thing if you're around me. And you with me. There's a chance you can pull away, find something else. Some life, at least."

"You're convinced you'd be destroyed?"

"I'd rather be dead than be a puppet, a shell of a man outside, with someone else in my body that isn't me. If you're far away, I'll not be so aware of it."

It was impossible to protest what I knew was true. I said, "I'm giving up Nicky."

"I'd feel better if you didn't."

"I have to, whether we're together or not. Do you never want to see me again?"

"What I want has nothing to do with this decision. I'll probably never love anyone but you for as long as I live. But we can't see each other again, for both our sakes."

The pain is going to kill me, I thought. But I wouldn't plead. I knew he was right.

Bryce reached over and brushed at my tears with his fingertips. His eyes were clearly saying, *I don't want to send you away.* "I don't want to hurt you."

"I don't want to hurt you either, Bryce. Ever."

My hand trembled in his. Even then I was aware of the problems that faced me. The instant Bryce released my hand, a premonition came slamming down upon me—a premonition so strong that I nearly reeled. This was not the end of us! Not the end of it. By far the greatest of the pain was still to come.

I ARRIVED BACK at Lydia's Madrid apartment late that afternoon, aching from the emotional overload of the past twenty-four hours. Bryce and I didn't make love again, because it would have been too painful. We showered and dressed and ate breakfast in the coffee shop of an Edinburgh hotel before starting back to London. He drove me straight to Heathrow, where I caught the flight to Madrid. Bryce timed it well; he had most of the flight schedules out of London memorized.

We didn't talk about the witches anymore. There was nothing that hadn't been said. Nor did we talk about the future, because from where we stood on that bleak, drizzly day in Britain, there wasn't any future to discuss.

Bryce's eyes filled with tears when he kissed me goodbye at the airport. His hands were trembling. I felt him watching me as I walked down the concourse to my plane, but I didn't turn around. He'd already seen too many of my tears.

A stranger who was not a stranger had walked into my life and out again, and left me an emotional and physical wreck.

In the late afternoon I spent at least an hour on the rooftop, looking out upon the skyline of Madrid and thinking of Bryce. Lydia would be surprised to find me back already when she got home from work, and I was going to have a hell of a time trying to explain it.

At dusk I went inside and read over the notes I had written on my current book, trying to figure out what I was going to do. I couldn't think at all, except about Bryce's warmth in bed, and his voice and his eyes. I had never felt so lonely, so desperate or so confused.

Bryce expected me to keep on writing the Nicholas Paul series? With Nicky's death threats and close calls? Nicky's sliding in and out of bed with princesses or high-wire artists? Could Nicky move in and out of his daring adventures without ever getting hurt? No. I couldn't do it anymore! My Nicholas Paul books were doomed. And if I broke the contracts with all the money involved in that series, I'd probably never sell another book of any kind to anybody. I would be blackballed. The career I'd worked so hard for was over. The man I loved was off limits to me because he was afraid of me. I didn't know where to go or what to do.

Wrapped in gloom, I reclined on the couch in Lydia's living room, fell into a fitful, exhausted sleep and dreamed of cackling witches stirring potions in a cauldron. I saw Bryce's face in moonlight and his tears turning hard as diamonds in the light of a white, full moon.

THE NIGHTMARE didn't disappear when I woke. It continued for weeks. I decided I couldn't say anything to my editors about not making my deadline until I had something to submit in its place. Another book idea. Some new chapters. *Something.* I lay awake nights, trying to figure out how to explain what was not explainable. I couldn't tell the truth, and no lie was sufficient. I must have thrown a ream of paper into the trash. Paragraphs abandoned in midsentence with oaths of frustration. It was no damned use.

It was impossible to exorcise Nicky from my thoughts or to stop daydreaming about the book I'd been in the middle of. Every time I thought of Nicky I was afraid Bryce would somehow be affected by the thought. I even wondered if the momentum of the power built, like the venom of a black widow spider builds when it hasn't bitten in a long time, so that when the bite does come, the effects of the venom are intensified.

When the city closed in on me, I traveled some in Spain, driving the roads of La Mancha, thinking of Don Quixote and his impossible dream. I drove down to the coast, where the sea breeze cooled the summer air, and the festive nights were filled with music.

I took notes. I wrote quiet scenes of Nicky contemplating the silver olive groves at the edge of the sea. I gave him solitude, but I shouldn't have been doing it. I shouldn't have been writing of Nicky at all.

I gave up trying to force myself to write a book in Spain, and bought a ticket home.

My last night in Madrid, Lydia threw a party for me. Of all things—a party. I couldn't talk her out of it. Afterward, when the guests had left and I had helped clean up and Lydia had gone to bed, I stood at the window of the bedroom, sleepless and miserable. My career was as good as over. I missed Bryce so deeply that it hurt. My chances of ever finding love again were squelched by the lingering curse of a witch's spell. I was bound eternally to a man I couldn't have.

"Until death do you part," I repeated bitterly into the darkness. Bryce and I were both trapped, until one of us died.

And Nicholas? I had lost him, too. Nicky might as well have been dead.

Suddenly I straightened and began to rub my eyes. *Nicky!* With a racing heart, I paced the shadow-filled room. My thoughts spun wildly. "Wait!" I said aloud to the moonlight. "Wait! Maybe there's a way!"

It was very late, I had drunk wine at the party, and my mind was working crazily, but I was on the safe side of hysterics. Perhaps it didn't make complete sense, yet somewhere through the darkness and the near hysteria glimmered a ray of hope.

A plan began to form. I had thought of a way to break the spell!

The plan had a serious drawback: it was extremely dangerous. Horribly risky. Bryce would have to cooperate, and it would be asking a great deal of him. Thinking about it made me break out in perspiration. But we *had* to try!

I spent the rest of that hot Spanish night pacing the sagging wooden floor of Lydia's penthouse and plotting murder.

IN THE MORNING, exhausted, yet exhilarated by the newfound hope of getting our lives back, I canceled my flight to the States and set about trying to locate Bryce. I hadn't come up with a workable murder, but it didn't dampen my enthusiasm. I was a creative person; I'd think of something. What did dampen my enthusiasm, though, was the thought of the danger.

It had been six weeks since we said goodbye, the longest six weeks of my life. Bryce's London office informed me that he had been in Greece, but was presently in Amsterdam and was expected back in London late tomorrow. I got the impression from the secretary I talked with that he wasn't scheduled to be in London very long. So there wasn't much time. I had to be in London when he got there.

I wasn't too keen on the idea of surprising Bryce, but it was the best thing to do. Better that he didn't have a chance to form any preconceived notions about why I was walking back into his life, when I had agreed that I would not. Of course, any ideas, however far-out, on how to break the spell would be welcome to him. Except perhaps this one.

I arrived at Heathrow in midafternoon, and because I'd been too tired to eat all day, I was feeling weak when I needed all the strength I could muster to face Bryce. I made myself eat some lunch at the airport before I took a taxi to his London apartment, gambling that he had already returned from Amsterdam. If he hadn't, I would find a nearby pub with a telephone and wait for him, and hope I was still sober by the time he got in. The closer the actual encounter came, the more I was succumbing to all the fluttery feelings of nervous frustration.

The doorman at the apartment building wore a uniform and a pleasant smile. I rang Bryce's third-floor apartment from the tiny but elegant lobby and looked at my watch. A quarter to five.

After a long wait, a buzz came back, meaning "Come up." As I was being lifted back to his world, I was so jittery that I wanted to abolish all slow elevators from the face of the earth.

The man who opened the door was not Bryce. Only then did I remember he had told me he shared the apartment with another man, who also traveled a great deal and for whom the apartment served more as a London base than a home. He was a young man, younger than Bryce, blond, attractive, wearing dark slacks and a shirt hanging out, which he was still buttoning.

He smiled. "Hello!"

I forced a smile. "Oh, hello. Am I lucky enough to catch Bryce at home?"

"I don't think Bryce is in town, actually. I can probably find out for you. Come in."

I felt foolish carrying the suitcase; this would make a great impression. Whatever thoughts he had about it, though, he kept politely to himself. Maybe women showing up at Bryce's door with luggage weren't all that unusual. He probably thought I was an airline hostess just in from New York.

I set down the bag just inside the door. "I spoke with his office yesterday from Madrid, and was told he should be back from Amsterdam this afternoon."

"Why don't I phone his office and check?" He motioned for me to sit down.

"I'd appreciate it, but if he's at the office, please don't tell him anyone is here. I want to...uh...surprise him."

"I got it." He smiled and finished buttoning his shirt. "I'm Colin King, by the way."

"Jaye Nigel." I wanted to say Diana. Only at that moment did I realize how desperately I wanted to be Diana.

He ducked through an archway to the phone. I looked around the apartment. Very small, very elegant, furnished with much glass and chrome. Under globe lights the furniture was sleek, some lacquered black, some white. The carpet was deep brown and soft and the sofa was brown leather, giving comfortable warmth to an otherwise cold atmosphere. The place was neat, as though a housekeeper had just been there. On the walls were strange, impressionistic paintings in bright shades of blue and lavender and pink and silver.

I heard Colin thank someone on the telephone. He returned, tucking in his shirt. "He left Amsterdam today and is due back in the office tomorrow morning. That means he should be here soon."

"Do you mind if I wait?"

"Not at all. I'll make some tea."

"Are you getting ready to leave?"

"I'm not rushed. And the water is already hot." He was in the kitchen before I could reply.

In two or three minutes he was back, carrying a round oriental tray that I assumed one of them had picked up in Japan. It was lacquered black with a floral design in mother-of-pearl, and it held a tea set and two white cups. Typically English, Colin King had slipped on a jacket and tie before ceremoniously pouring the tea, sitting across from me, making a final adjustment to his white and blue paisley necktie.

"Are you hungry?"

"No, I've just eaten, actually," I answered, accepting the tea. I was trembling enough to cause the cup to shake on the saucer. He glanced at me curiously, but was too polite to mention it. I took note that his manner was far more formal than Bryce's. A highborn Englishman, I thought. "Are you and Bryce with the same firm?" I asked.

"No. I'm in the import business. Textiles. I spend a great deal of my time in the Far East. Like Bryce, I'm in and out of London. I haven't seen him for three or four weeks, maybe five. You say you've just flown over from Madrid? I hear Spain is having a stifling summer."

"I escaped to the coast for a week or two."

He stirred a third spoonful of sugar into his tea. "You're American. Are you on holiday?"

"I've been doing research on a book. I'm a writer."

"Now I know why your name is familiar! I assumed I'd heard Bryce mention it, but it's the books. I read on planes, and I've read two of your books. By damn, I enjoyed them, too. Never figured the author to be a woman, though."

"I'm glad you enjoyed them. I met Bryce in Madrid in early summer."

"Lucky for him."

How wrong that was, I thought, but I merely smiled and sipped my tea and tried to keep from looking at my watch every few minutes. "I don't want to keep you," I said. "I know you were getting ready to go out."

He glanced at his watch. "I'm honored and intrigued at meeting you, Jaye Nigel, and I'd prefer staying here to talk about your books, but I do have an appointment I ought not be late for. Please make yourself comfortable. Bryce probably won't be much longer if his flight wasn't delayed."

Twenty excruciating minutes passed before I heard a key in the lock. I braced myself, standing against the window with my back to the light. Bryce was startled to see me. He set down his suitcase, which hit the carpeted floor with a dull thud. And the room turned deathly silent.

"Diana?"

"I'm sorry to surprise you this way, Bryce. Colin let me in and made tea and then he had to leave. It's imperative that I talk to you."

If he felt joy in seeing me, he concealed it well. No hug to welcome me. No smile of reassurance. I had broken a solemn agreement, and the sight of me was trouble.

As for me—I was thoroughly shaken by how handsome he looked in his expensive business suit. Immaculate, uncrumpled. But he was frowning.

"What's wrong?" he asked.

"Everything has been wrong since I last saw you, but I didn't come to dwell on that. I have to talk to you about an idea I've come up with. I think I've figured out how to break the spell."

He stared. "I don't think that's possible."

"I think it *is*. My idea is terribly dangerous, but you must listen to it, Bryce. There might be a chance."

His eyes changed, softened. He looked at me as if he were trying to decide whether I was real or an illusion. At last he blinked, came toward me and opened his arms.

"Diana. I've missed you. I've stared at the phone in the dead of night wanting to pick it up and dial you, not daring to, forcing myself not to do it."

"Would you ever have done it?"

"No."

It felt so good in his arms that for a moment I forgot how scared I was. We dared not kiss each other for fear of losing ourselves in the kiss, as we had done too often in the past. The effects of the spell were strong. Tingling sensations. The ache of longing. I fought it hard and drew away.

"The tea is still hot. Colin's tea."

Bryce looked dazed. "I need something stronger than tea. You?"

"Now that you mention it, yes."

Loosening his tie, Bryce went to a sideboard on which a few liquor bottles were stored. "Sherry, gin or whisky?"

"Sherry, if it's more or less dry."

He made drinks and motioned me to sit down, then sat across from me. "You're nervous as hell, Diana."

"I hate my idea. I hate it. But I thought at least…we might discuss it. There's so much at stake."

He sat back with the drink in his hand. "All right. I'm listening."

I cleared my throat. "Well. The sisters were definite on one thing—that the only way the spell can be broken is through death. I got to thinking about that, Bryce. There aren't two of us involved in this. There are three of us—you and Nicky and myself. Suppose it was Nicky who died? Suppose there were a way of killing Nicky without killing you? He would be gone, buried, laid to rest forever, you would be alive and the connection would be broken."

He thought about this. "You're right! If the connection to Nicky were broken, the spell should be broken. But if you kill Nicky, you'll probably kill me."

"That's the problem. But did you hear what you just said, Bryce? You said *probably*. Maybe there's a way."

He set down his glass. "Have you thought of one?"

"Not so far. But I'm working on it. I'm thinking till my brain aches. I thought perhaps if we put our ideas together we might come up with something. Do you realize what it would mean if we could do it?"

"It would mean having our lives back again. It would mean you and I could be together. For that I'd risk anything. I'd risk dying."

I winced. "I wouldn't dare kill Nicky quickly. But I thought if he were to die slowly, that I'd have the power to...to save him at the last minute if I had to. Oh, Bryce, I don't want to play around with your life. We'd have to be terribly careful! But we can't know what would happen unless we try."

"It's a bloody big *if*." He rubbed his chin thoughtfully. "But if Nicky were dead, it would free me. It would mean the end of your Nicholas Paul books, though."

"They've ended, anyway. I can't do them anymore. But as the situation with Nicky stands now, if I just drop him, someone else could take him up and write the books. If he's dead, they can't have him, and I can replace him with another character. I've been thinking about it for hours. No one ever imagines the hero of a series like mine can die. The reader expects him to get out of every predicament. But if he *didn't* survive one of his plights, imagine the impact! I'd introduce a new hero. My readers would never know if the new hero was going to survive or not, and the suspense would be doubled. But of course my books are not the concern here. Breaking the spell is what matters." I looked away from him. "I haven't been able to write. You surely didn't really think I could."

"I hoped you could. But I'll admit to being nervous about it."

I could barely taste the sherry. "Well. Do we try?"

"We have to try! It's a good idea, Diana. Maybe we *can* do it."

"I don't want you to get hurt."

"We can't avoid my getting hurt. I just hope we can avoid killing me."

Tears began to sting behind my eyes. I fought them back. "I'm terrified of this, Bryce. I'm confident that if I have to, I can save Nicky at the last minute. All I've been able to come up with is his falling ill with a life-threatening disease. People can rally from illness."

Bryce pulled off his tie, tossed it onto a chair and took off his jacket, though the room seemed cold to me; I was glad to be wearing a heavy suit.

"Let's try to think this through," he said. "On the basis of what we already know, and a little of what I've been researching."

"You've been researching?"

"I've tried. It's difficult, because so little is known of the druidic religion. What's been passed down is very impure, as you might imagine, all bound up in superstition. That they practiced magic of all kinds is undisputed, everything from changing into other forms of animals or nature to making themselves invisible."

"You told me their beliefs about death—that the soul can't die."

Bryce nodded. "And they would sacrifice one life for another." He scratched his head. "I wonder if that might apply, Diana? The druids didn't look on death as a natural phenomenon, but rather as the work of the spirits. So if a Druid was dying, he believed his life would be spared if he offered another as a sacrifice, to satisfy the demands of the spirit. Not unlike your idea of sacrificing Nicky's life for mine."

"The spirit being the moon, in this case?"

"Spirit, force, I don't know. It sounds pagan as hell. The spell is pagan. But it's still based on some knowledge of how the forces of nature work."

"That's the secret of breaking the spell, isn't it? To try to work with the force that's influenced by the power of the mind."

"Right!" Bryce said. He disappeared into his bedroom and came out a minute later, wearing jeans and pulling a sweatshirt over his head. He settled onto the sofa, sprawling comfortably. "Mind energy! It's the strongest natural force of all. The Druids knew it, and so do we. That much we've got working for us, love. We know about mind energy."

"You speak with such conviction," I said. "How can you be so sure mind energy is stronger than the forces of the moon?"

"I can't be sure. I'm guessing. If I'm wrong, I'll die with Nicky."

I swallowed. "I didn't think of . . . my idea in exactly that context."

"Nevertheless, I think it's what your idea boils down to. And defining it that way, it's a chance worth trying."

"Human sacrifice?" I asked. "I hope it wasn't practiced as a common thing . . ."

"I'm afraid it was."

I contemplated this. "People must have felt helpless against the powers of their gods—against all things they couldn't understand, like death. If they wholly believed they might live through an illness by offering someone to die in their place, the power of the subconscious might help keep them alive, mightn't it?"

"Certainly. Or the reverse. It's common knowledge that people can be killed by spells, if they believe they will be."

"All in the power of mind. But what about us? We were suffering the effects of this spell without knowing anything about it."

"I can't explain that, and we'll probably never know what outside powers Grizel was able to tap. Hell, I've been trying to understand some of this, and I still don't, but I'm learning more about the Celtic consciousness. If you hadn't come back, I'd eventually have begged you to. I was just holding off until I had some ideas on how to fight this, but you came up with something first."

"To follow through on your earlier suggestion," I said, "let's analyze what little we do know. In Madrid you pricked your finger not longer than ten minutes after I wrote the scene. That was a very short time delay. During the five years I've been moving Nicky and you around like players on a chessboard, I wonder how close to being simultaneous your accidents were."

"There's no way to check. But it's possible the delay has grown shorter as the spell got stronger. From what happened in Madrid, at Lydia's apartment, we have to assume the effects will be almost immediate. When Nicky draws his last breath, mine won't be far behind. You won't have much time."

"That's why Nicky must die slowly."

Bryce muttered an oath. "I'm not looking forward to this."

"Neither am I. I've been thinking about it, and his ingesting poison is all I've come up with. I'm good at murdering villains, but murdering someone I love is a different matter altogether."

"Och, you don't love Nicky. You love me."

"I can't separate the two of you very well. That's the scariest part."

"Don't turn coward on me now."

"I won't." I frowned. "What about freezing? They say it doesn't hurt to freeze to death."

He shook his head. "A friend of mine almost froze to death when he was stranded in a car in a snowstorm in Austria. He lost both feet and both hands to frostbite. If my body took on the symptoms of frostbite, you might be able to reverse the death, but could you reverse the damage to my body? I don't want to risk it. I'd rather die than lose my limbs."

"Okay, freezing is out. There's always a bullet. But if a bullet tore into a vital organ of Nicky's body, maybe it would cause serious damage to your body—or maybe somehow, at some unexpected moment, you'd actually get shot, just the way you did with the spear gun. No.

No trauma stuff. We'll have to stick with an illness, then I can control the symptoms.''

"I can find a doctor who might give us some medical advice. Maybe it wouldn't hurt to have a doctor present."

"Yes! We should. But what doctor won't think we're...insane?"

"I can find one."

"You really want to go through with it, then?"

"Love, I can get over an illness. There's no use pretending this spell isn't getting stronger. Our lives aren't going to work apart or together unless something stops it. I don't care how bad the cure is, it's worth a try."

"Before this is over, you're going to hate me."

"I won't hate you." Bryce rose. "I'll do some phoning to get a doctor here."

"What? Tonight?"

"I want to get this over with. Can you plan Nicky's murder in two or three hours?"

"Oh...I...Bryce...I'm so scared!"

"So am I, but I have faith in you."

This declaration bothered me even more. "My faith is not in myself, but in Grizel's love for you. I just can't bring myself to believe she meant to hurt you or that she'd let you die."

"Maybe you're right," he said from his desk, searching through a notebook for a telephone number.

Shaking, I gathered the teacups onto the tray and carried them into the kitchen, where I put on the kettle to heat water for another pot. The sherry Bryce had poured me was almost untouched, but I felt so cold that I wanted something hot to warm my insides. It was a tiny kitchen, rarely used, from the look of it, too neat for two transient bachelors. There were few dishes on the shelves and even fewer pots and pans. The white-tiled cabinet tops were polished to a shine, more evidence that housekeeping service came with the lease of this luxury apartment. The refrigerator was empty except for a package of sweet rolls, butter, jam, mineral water and milk.

Colin King had left a box of tea bags on the counter. I made a pot of tea, rinsed out the cups, and took the tray back into the living room. By that time, Bryce was off the phone.

"Diana," he said, "you're as white as a sheet."

"Did you find a doctor?"

"Aye. I had one in mind." He rose and took the tray from me. "Look, I know it's frightening. Tonight we'll treat this as an experiment. We'll see how long your written words take to start affecting me, and we'll see how good I am at staving off your power. An experiment, Diana, okay? And there will be a doctor here."

"It's a well-accepted fact of science that doctors can't save people from spells," I said, plopping onto the couch.

He began to pour the tea. "I know. But it's a way of gauging when to pull back, perhaps."

"I didn't know how brave you were."

"I'm not brave, I'm desperate."

Even the steaming cup he handed me didn't seem to warm my ice-cold hands. "I suppose then," I said, almost choking on my words, "that what I'm going to have to do is poison you."

Chapter Eight

AT ELEVEN-THIRTY that night we were gathered in the flat—Bryce and Colin and a physician named Patricia Conoroy, a flamboyant woman in her forties who wore a bright red skirt and a silk blouse with a red and pink floral design. My initial skepticism turned to confidence after talking with her for an hour and a half, for she was a medical expert with enough knowledge of witchcraft to take our dilemma seriously. There were hints that it might not be the first case involving sorcery that Dr. Conoroy had been consulted on, but specifics were never mentioned.

Bryce, in jeans and a white T-shirt, settled onto the sofa. He pushed back his dark hair and said, "I'm tired of talking. Let's just get on with this."

I looked from Colin to Dr. Conoroy. Panic rose in me like nausea and I fought it down as I took up my pencil. I'd chosen a pencil with a large, soft eraser. The eraser was very important. Bryce gave me a smile and a wink for encouragement, but he didn't try to hide the fact that he was worried.

With eyes closed, I brought images of Nicky into my head. In about two minutes, the scene I had been contemplating and discussing with them began to unfold. As a group we had decided to use an undisclosed poison. An eerie silence filled the room while I wrote. Ten minutes of utter silence, until Bryce's deep voice broke it.

"My head is spinning," he said.

I gritted my teeth and kept writing. Bryce lay with his arm over his eyes until he started to cough. In a few minutes he struggled to his feet, went into the bathroom and was sick. None of the others said a word.

"Unbelievable!" he howled afterward, flopping back onto the sofa. "I'm powerless to resist this."

He tried his best to fight me, but before long he was shivering with fever. Doubling over, holding his stomach, he cursed like a marine. His body became soaked with perspiration. The doctor stayed close, monitoring carefully. Colin, fascinated by the scenario, decided to read over my shoulder. It irritated me, but I soon forgot Colin was even in the room.

Watching Bryce suffer was dreadful. I thought I couldn't stand it. But I forced myself to remember what was at stake in this experiment, and as soon as I dared, I introduced to Nicky's conscious mind the concept of dying. It hurt to do that—far more than I'd ever imagined it could, and the hurt was proof of how real Nicky had always been to me. The poison spread through his body, causing fever and weakness. I tried to minimize the pain, yet Bryce seemed to be suffering a great deal. He writhed, holding his stomach.

Dr. Conoroy talked to him constantly, trying to distract him, telling him he was all right, that the symptoms were not real, that he had the power to resist the illness, that he was in no danger. But her efforts were in vain, and after a time he didn't seem to hear her voice at all.

She kept looking at me more and more frequently, showing concern mixed with disbelief, until finally her warning came. "His pulse is slowing dangerously. Blood pressure is dropping."

The room was cold, yet perspiration rolled into my
eyes, blurring the page in front of me. We had made the
agreement that I would not take it upon myself to reverse the symptoms; that choice would be the doctor's.
But the fear was overwhelming me. Bryce was growing
more ill by the second as Nicky approached the thresh-
old of death, and I was terrified we could lose them
both. I wanted desperately to erase the concept of death
from Nicky's mind and give him back his strength.
Bryce was having difficulty breathing. But still nothing
came from the doctor except mutterings about the state
of his blood pressure and weakening pulse.

Shaking like a leaf in the wind, I pressed on, as I'd
promised Bryce I would.

The dark spirit hovered. Nicholas knew it and tried
to get out from under it, but he was too weak.
Breaths came only with the greatest effort. The
spirit, dark-cloaked and menacing, reached out to
him—reached out to touch him. *One touch,* the
spirit breathed in a silver, hissing voice.

"Stop now!" the doctor shrieked. "Stop quickly,
Diana! Life is rapidly slipping from him, and I'm powerless to do anything about it!"

Terror provided me with the superhuman strength of
determination. Frantically I erased the last words I had
written, giving Nicky the power to fight the advancing
spirit of death, to pull out from under that malignant
shadow. Instead of letting him die, I gave him sleep.

The sleepiness was a drug moving through his
body, washing pain away in its wake. Nicky slept
sweet, dreamless, healing sleep, softly, in the

sleep he struggled back to life, rallying quickly, miraculously.

Bryce responded less quickly. Dr. Conoroy was assisting his breathing with an oxygen mask, but he had lapsed into unconsciousness. I kept on writing until Nicky had overcome all possible danger, and still I wrote, until I heard the doctor say, "Vital signs are near normal again."

The words on the page blurred through a mist of tears. Bryce lay on his back, lips parted, his eyelashes forming delicate shadows on his cheeks, his fingers loosely curled. He was all right.

But I wanted to scream! I ripped out the pages, crumpled them in my fists and hurled the diabolical paper balls across the room. My own handwriting—incantations in black magic. Voodoo! The signature of a witch! It was all I could do to keep from pounding the walls.

Dr. Conoroy slumped onto the floor, using language I would never have expected to hear from a female physician with graying hair. "I didn't realize the power we were dealing with here! Where the devil is it coming from?"

"From the moon," I mumbled, my head in my hands.

Colin leaned over Bryce, shaking his shoulder, but the unconscious man was not responding. The doctor, still on the floor beside him, held her hand on his neck, monitoring his pulse. "I thought his heart was going to stop!" she said. "It would have if you'd kept on. Diana, from what I've observed here, nothing can be done medically to help you. Even putting him into a hospital emergency room with emergency equipment wouldn't help. Physical interference can't penetrate this power.''

"I can't believe this!" Colin wailed.

The woman in red looked up at him. "There is more than one reality, Colin. I've seen sorcery before. I've seen sorcery kill. I'm afraid Diana and Bryce are stuck with this one."

My neck was so stiff that I could barely move my head. *No!* a voice inside me was screaming. *There has to be an answer—there has to be an answer... somewhere!*

Aftershock was taking its toll on me. This had been too close! What if I hadn't been able to bring Bryce back from the grip of death? What if there was a point of no return? What if it had been Bryce who'd died instead of Nicky?

Slowly Bryce came back. The doctor stayed for another hour, until he was sitting up and able to talk. But he was too exhausted to say very much. With Colin holding him up, he stumbled into his bedroom and fell into a very fitful sleep.

Colin left to drive Dr. Conoroy home. In the soft light of a small bedside lamp I sat watching Bryce sleep, trying to deal with my anger. Hating Grizel MacCreath wouldn't help. I wanted to battle with her, though. There *had* to be a way to win.

Bryce's chest moved with quiet, steady breaths now. With his face partly in shadow, he looked beautiful, sleeping as peacefully as a little boy. I conjured up an image of Grizel, the witch who loved him, bent over the child as he slept, touching his cheek, his forehead. How many times had she tucked the little boy between his blankets on cold moorland nights, and kissed him while he slid into innocent sleep? I pictured moonlight on his eyelids.

Was it really motivated by love—this sorcerer's spell—as Bryce believed? No woman could resist his eyes, his smile or the beauty of him. No woman, not even that one. Especially not that woman.

Help us, then! I begged the ghost of the witch who loved him. *You got us into this. Help us to get out!*

I must have sat there for over an hour, and in all that time Bryce barely stirred. When exhaustion began to overtake me, I took off my clothes and crawled into bed beside him. Almost automatically his arm came around me. "Diana..." he whispered. "I want to hold you..."

But it was I who was holding him when he fell asleep again. I was so spent that it was only minutes before I was asleep myself. I didn't hear Colin return, but I couldn't have had less concern over what Colin might think about my sharing Bryce's bed. My last thoughts before I escaped into sleep expressed dread of the morning, for in its light we would have to face our failure tonight.

THE ESCAPE wasn't to last until morning. In less than an hour, Bryce was tossing around in the bed.

In the dark I asked, "Are you all right?"

"Is the moon full tonight?"

"I don't know."

"It must be. I can't sleep."

"You've been through hell tonight, Bryce. It could be that."

"No, it's the moon."

I drew closer to him, needing his strength. "I wonder if the phase of the moon has any effect on the power of the spell."

"Never thought about it."

"Neither have I, but maybe we should have thought about it. The power had unbelievable force tonight."

He yawned. The short sleep had apparently revived him; his voice was groggy but strong. "Grizel and her talk of the moon's power over me. We should have thought of it, Diana. The night of a full moon was the worst possible time to try to kill Nicky."

"Try to remember," I said. "The night of the eclipse, did you become ill before or afterward?"

"After. When the moon was pulling out of the shadow. During the actual eclipse I was fine. I could look at it with the shadow covering it. But when the moon was showing again enough to hurt my eyes and I looked directly at it, I felt pain all through my body. Grizel told me to turn away from the moon, and she closed the curtains quickly.

In his bedroom in the London flat, there were metal shutters over the single window. Thin streaks of moonlight showed through the slats, otherwise the room was black. I squeezed his hand. "Darling, it's possible the power is greater or lesser, depending on the moon phase. The pull could vary, as with the tides."

He sat up. "I'm thirsty. Do you want anything?"

"No. But let me get you whatever you want. You could barely walk a while ago."

"I can walk now."

He went to the kitchen and came back carrying a glass of water. With the door open, the living-room lamps cast a soft arc of light into the room, just enough to see by. Bryce stripped to his briefs and sat on the edge of the bed with the glass in his hand.

"Diana, I've been thinking about it—about how Grizel told me to turn away from the moon on the night of the eclipse. Turning my back on the moon or closing curtains at night has always lessened the discomfort, but it doesn't work effectively anymore. These blinds cut out almost every bit of moonlight, and yet look what happened tonight. The spell is getting stronger.''

''I know. It scares me to death that you were in more pain than Nicky. I didn't anticipate that. My idea isn't going to work, is it?''

''We're too connected, your arrogant Nicholas and I.''

When I laid my hand on Bryce's knee, his skin still felt too hot. Or perhaps I was cold. I felt weak and sick with disappointment. ''I don't know how to separate you and Nicky. I thought I could do it, but I don't know how. Damn, I thought we had a chance. I really did.''

''It was worth a try. But the way his symptoms hit me, Diana, I'm not sure I could survive another one of Nicky's brushes with death.''

''You couldn't fight it.''

''Heaven knows, I tried.'' He finished the water and set the glass on the floor. ''This...experiment has taught me there's no use trying to fight this damned spell. Being apart won't help. Nothing will help. Like it or not, we're going to have to live with it.''

''Then I won't leave you. It will do no good to leave you.''

He smiled bitterly. ''You couldn't leave me now if you tried. And I couldn't leave you. So here we are.''

Here we are *where*? I wanted to scream. In some kind of hideous limbo! Wildly in love with each other, and not by choice. Trapped forever...without choice...

But I loved him. More deeply than I thought I could ever love any man, I loved him. More desperately than

I'd ever wanted anything in my life, I wanted to be with him. I no longer felt whole when I was away from him.

I knew that it was the same for Bryce. He lifted my hand to his cheek and held it there, while his warmth pulsed through me. What else was there to say? We were together.

He pulled me closer and kissed me. My body responded to his kiss with wild and uncontrolled desire for him, stronger than ever before.

We heard Colin moving around in the other room. Bryce rose, quietly closed the bedroom door and felt his way back to me. He got into bed beside me. "Diana, I've thought of you every night. I've turned out my light and felt alone, knowing the most important thing in my life was missing. In Greece. Holland. London. Wherever I was, it was the wrong place because you weren't there."

"It was the same for me. I never want to have to leave you again."

"I don't know what's going to happen to us, but you're here beside me and I want you here. That's all I know."

I cradled his head against my breast. *No man but me,* he had said once. Oh, how well he knew me!

I ran my hands across the wide expanse of his bare back, savoring the feel of him. With my hand against his chest I could feel his heart beating steadily and strong. I let his heartbeats penetrate my hand with their rhythm and enter into my body as if our hearts were one, pumping my blood, pumping his.

Our hearts seemed to set the world back on its axis. When we were touching each other, everything was different. Stars shone brighter. The darkness was softer.

Fears began to thaw and melt. And peace took the place of turmoil.

"I can't see you very well in the dark," I whispered. "I can only feel you."

"Do I feel good?"

"You feel alive and strong. And wonderful."

"And you," he said, lightly caressing my breast. "You feel like silk . . ."

His gentle hands moved over my body in the dark, lingering with intimate warmth. I began to tremble with the ache of wanting him. More than wanting him, I ached to know him, to know every line and mark and groan and throb. I wanted to be a part of the mystery of him. And with his touch, he welcomed me back into his life.

He touched my face, found my lips with his fingertips. Fingertips like candy—I savored the taste of them, memorizing his fingers one by one with my tongue, over and over again, until at last Bryce's lips were there instead, kissing me deeply. So deeply that the bed began to spin and us with it.

Fever on my lips. Fire against my palms. I could feel the tightening of his body while he held me, the tensing of his thighs. And the deep, erratic rasp of his breathing.

"Diana . . ." he whispered.

"Bryce, are you . . . ?"

"Am I what?"

"Are you up to this? Not even two hours ago you were unconscious."

"I'm conscious now." He took my hand in his and guided it down the length of his body. "Proof enough?"

"You're unbelievable. You're . . . Superman."

"I'm in love."

"So am I."

"You're in love only with me . . . forever."

Only you, the voice inside me vowed. Drenched in the enchantment, I was awash with the strongest feelings of love I'd ever known. I closed my eyes and called upon the silence to try to calm me, knowing Bryce alone could do it, but only after the storm had passed.

He kicked away the encumbrance of the guilt. No longer feeling the cold, we soon lay naked against the night, against each other.

"I need you. Make love to me, Diana."

I floated on the sound of his words. To be needed by this man—this powerful, mysterious man—stirred my dreams to life. Tonight, still slightly weakened by what he'd been through, he needed me. He was asking me.

"Make me forget," he whispered.

I knew his body—incarnation of a thousand fantasies—in the dark. And it came to me like a divination that we had not been apart a single day since our spirits had met, when the dark of the earth's shadow had blocked away the moon. We'd met then, although we hadn't known it, and we'd been together ever since. Our bonded spirits knew it—our bodies too. And those bodies, bonded by love all those weeks ago, needed to be one again.

With hands and lips I explored his body, remembering. Kissing his scars, his chest, his stomach, his thighs. All of him. Tasting the strength and the passion of him.

Letting myself love him. Imbibing the pure joy of loving him.

A moan came from deep in his throat and with it the sound of my name—his name for me. "Diana . . ."

"Diana . . . let me . . . reach you . . . too . . ."

Seeking me, he shifted around in the bed, guided in the dark by his own hands. Enchanted hands, impassioned lips, expressing his love for me, reaching back to me with the same intimacy with which I was possessing him.

Giving, receiving, without knowing which was the giving and which the receiving. Kissing him, I felt his kisses all through me until I thought I couldn't stand any more. A great moan from his throat told me he couldn't either. I moved over him.

Only you... my heart was chanting in the new rhythm of love. *Only you.... only you*... Deep inside me, stirrings beyond emotion pitched and dived...and soared.

Bryce was with me, his senses merging with mine, becoming mine...taking...giving....

Bryce was with me, his reflexes merging with mine, his need crystallizing...climbing with mine... climbing...soaring...

Soaring....

Bryce was with me, accepting everything that was mine to give. And he gave me all of him.

SOMETHING KEPT ME AWAKE long after Bryce had drifted into sleep beside me. Light streaming from the full moon seeped through the narrow slats of the metal blinds. Moon dust pushed through the shuttered window as if it had a life and strength of its own, as if it had been seeking Bryce and now had found him. Ghostly light illuminated his handsome face.

I remembered what the sisters had said about Grizel's second sight, and began to shudder. She had always known that the moon would bring Bryce grief. Had she forgotten it the night of the eclipse? No, of course not. Could she have been trying to reverse it with a love spell? Had she underestimated the force?

From somewhere far away I heard my own name. His voice. "Diana? What's the matter? Can't you sleep?"

Whether real or imagined, I was certain I could see the moon dust floating away, back into the night.

He reached for me. "What is it, my love? I thought I heard you crying."

"The moon," I answered.

"The moon can't touch you here."

"But it can touch you! It can find you anywhere! No wonder you aren't able to look at it!"

His voice was surprisingly patient. "I don't think it will help for you to lose sleep over it tonight. I wish I could change things. I can't make sense of this cursed spell. But you don't have to be frightened as long as I'm here, as long as you're with me. I'm helpless in a lot of ways over this, but my ability to protect you isn't affected." He touched my cheek tenderly. "I'll protect you with my life, Diana."

Tears filled my eyes in the dark. His life...his strength were controlled by me. And yet I desperately needed the strength he promised me—that incredible strength I saw in Bryce when Nicky wasn't around.

I COULDN'T get away with trying to hold my thoughts at bay, and I knew it. Nicholas Paul was a part of my life, and it was impossible not to think of my work, my books, and the hero I had lived with night and day for years. Nicky crept along the back roads of my mind. He raised his head and took a breath of life at unexpected moments.

I tried at first to keep those moments from Bryce, but he often knew. He found out in terrible ways. I still shudder to think of that night at the Gold Crown restaurant, when Bryce and I were having dinner after he'd taken me to an opening of a small theater production.

From the moment I walked in, I was distracted by the fact that the restaurant was so like one in an early scene I'd written for Nicky. Surely this was coincidence, I thought, trying to blank it out of my mind. But that scene had been a powerful one—a violent one that was imprinted like a memory from my own life. Nicky had been extremely apprehensive, because he was under surveillance by a foreign government. Undercover villains were following him with orders to make his death look like an accident, and he knew it. Sitting there in the Gold Crown, I remembered. It didn't help that I desperately missed creating adventures for Nicky. My books had become like my life's blood; without them I'd been drained of purpose.

Bryce felt the tension. He ordered lamb and afterward complained that he didn't like lamb. He asked for a Greek wine the waiter had never heard of. I was perspiring, because in the scene, when Nicky eventually spotted the hired killer at another table, he rose to leave and stabbed the assassin with one of the thin oriental blades he always carried, as he walked by the man's table. So subtle was Nicky's move that no one else in the restaurant knew the thug in the tuxedo was dead in his chair.

It became increasingly difficult for Bryce to sit still, and every now and then his eyes would scan the softly lighted room. His fists tightened. The muscles in his neck looked stiff. He drank too much and ate too little. The more I tried not to think of what was happening, the worse it seemed to get. I was desperately working at canceling my memories, frightened because I didn't know whether they could be canceled or not. I had to tell Bryce, but I hated to. The situation was becoming more intolerable by the day—so intolerable that I concealed from Bryce the fact that he was acting out my thoughts. I no longer had to write anything. My thoughts alone could manipulate his mind and his body. This night, I knew he realized it.

I was going to suggest we leave before something happened but Bryce was ahead of me. He threw his napkin onto the table and said, "Diana, something is going on. Some kind of tension is killing me. Let's go. Let's get out of here."

With only a nod I rose. Glancing around the room at the men seated at the tables between us and the door, I couldn't make myself take the lead. "Go ahead," I said.

He glared at me, his eyes saying that a man does not walk ahead of his lady. "Please," I urged. "I'll follow you."

"Diana..." We stood there awkwardly. I knew he wouldn't do as I asked, no matter what I said, so I had no choice but to clench my jaw and walk out ahead of him, praying he was all right. Inside the foyer, he settled the bill hurriedly in a hushed huddle with the maître d'. I was shaking.

Neither of us mentioned the ruined evening until we were back in the living room of his flat, drinking coffee.

"How often does it happen?" he asked in a bitter, injured voice. "Does it happen every day, Diana?"

It was hard to look at him. "It happens...more at night."

"When we're together."

"Yes. and especially when we're out somewhere. I try, Bryce. I try desperately to clear my mind..."

"So you don't have to write the scenes anymore. You think of Nicky and something hits me." He leaned his head back against the cushions of the sofa and closed his eyes. "It isn't humanly possible to clear one's mind. We both know that."

"Yes," I answered miserably. "Bryce, I've been wanting to mention this for several days now and I haven't known how. I think it's better if we don't go out . . . at night."

"Stay out of the moonlight, you mean. It's worse than I thought, isn't it?"

"The spell is getting awfully strong. I desperately try not to think of Nicky. But I get letters from my publisher constantly. And of course, the pressure of *not* thinking just makes me . . ."

"I know. I know. Like tonight. What did Nicky do in a restaurant, walking out, that had you so worried?"

"He stabbed a man who was dining at another table."

Bryce swore. "No wonder you say we should shun public places."

"I think . . . we have to. I was terrified something would happen tonight."

He got up and began to pace. "You have to leave me! My life is practically ruined, but it's not necessary for yours to be. We mustn't both stop living."

"I won't leave you. I couldn't, even if I tried. You admitted yourself I couldn't. The force holding me to you is so strong now, I *can't* leave. Not ever."

I slept that night with my arm across Bryce's chest, feeling the beat of his heart and wondering if—in spite of his love for me—somewhere deep inside he hated me.

When he flew to Athens early the next morning for a three-day business trip, there was no relief, no lessening of my fear because he was away from me. I had to get out of the flat, it was becoming a prison. I shopped. I tried to write a scene with my new hero as I sat in a tearoom, eating chocolate pastries so rich that they were sure to make me sick. Something was wrong. Everything was wrong. I felt as if the world were closing in on us.

At seven o'clock the next morning, I was in the kitchen making tea when I heard the front door open. Colin had left for Hong Kong two days ago, so I knew it was Bryce. Home two days early. My hand began to tremble as I took down two cups from the shelf.

His body shadowed the doorway. I looked up. His clothes were immaculate as always, but there were dark circles under his eyes. With only a grunt as greeting, he walked to the sink and swallowed several aspirin.

"What is it?" I asked, going cold with dread. "What's happened?"

Chapter Nine

"YOU DON'T WANT to know," he answered.

"Why did you leave Athens early? You must tell me, Bryce."

He drained the water glass. "My life is shot to hell. I can't work anymore."

He was right; I didn't want to know what I had done to him. Shakily I set up the tea tray and followed him to the living room. He was standing at the window looking down on the early-morning London traffic.

"I missed my appointment in Athens. Forgot it completely. A client has acquired a small sculpture from the Byzantine period, from Rhodes. The bloody thing is worth a fortune, because carved figures were considered idolatrous by the Christians in that period, and very few exist. An acquisition like that...and I was four hours late."

"Where were you?"

"Wandering around under the pine trees on the Hill of the Muses, thinking about making love to you."

I could do nothing but stare at his back and curse my knees for buckling.

"Nicky has been on the Hill of the Muses, hasn't he?"

"It was...several books ago."

"But when you thought of me in Athens, you remembered."

"I suppose I must have. Oh Bryce, I'm so sorry...."

He turned. "It isn't your fault. I don't blame you. I blame Grizel."

He strode to the couch and poured himself a cup of tea. "I'm in serious trouble, Diana. We've got to do something."

I was near tears. "We tried. It nearly killed you."

"I thought about that. I was in such bad shape that I thought about going down to one of my favorite resorts on the beach for a few hours, and then I realized I didn't know which of us wanted the beach—it was probably Nicky. I don't know who the hell I am anymore. Instead, I feigned illness and bought a ticket home. Perhaps that was Nicky's idea, too."

He dumped four sugar cubes into his tea. I'd never seen him take more than one.

"On the flight home I was thinking about the beach—thinking about how good the sun would have felt, and I remembered something, Diana. In your book *Bulawayo Sunrise*, Nicky suffered from a bad case of sunburn."

"Oh dear. Don't tell me you got sunburned, too?"

"Yes, but I wasn't in the sun. I wasn't in Bulawayo then, either. I was in London under gray skies, and so up to the ears in work that I hardly went outside for a week. When I did get out, I went to a concert at night, under the stars. The next day I had such a bad burn that I had to see a doctor. He said it was sunburn, but I hadn't been in the sun. I got it from the moon."

I switched into full alert. "You got sunburn from the moon?"

He nodded. "I didn't tell the doctor that, or I'd have been written up in medical journals."

A surge of illumination hit me like a bolt. "The sun and moon—balance of opposites! Like a photo negative, in which the black is really white and the white is really black! Moon and sun, good and evil, night and day. You've talked about that, remember? Nicky is only the negative of you! What affects him in the sun comes to you in moonlight!"

He gulped at the tea. "Yes, and it makes sense. We know the phases of the moon influence the spell. I was burned when the moon was full. I distinctly remember that, because we watched the moon rise during the concert. No doubt the burn would have been milder under a quarter moon." He unbuttoned his suit coat and pulled off his necktie. "I've been thinking about this for hours . . ."

"I have the same thought, Bryce! The sun can kill people, but the moon can't!"

"The moon can't kill other people, but I think it could kill me."

"Right! Suppose moonlight was blocked from you. Suppose Nicky were stricken with sunstroke and you were shut off from the sun *and* the moon? You didn't get his sunburn until the moon touched you. Maybe other afflictions caused by the sun couldn't get you, either."

"Who the hell knows? I do know something about sunstroke, though. It's agonizing, and it kills—but if it came without the sun . . ."

"It's too risky!"

"Perhaps not. We did prove with the poison experiment that you have the power to save me. I'm going to telephone Grizel's sisters to see what they have to say about this theory of opposites. I haven't talked to them since the day we left Dunfermline. They might have learned something more."

An hour later, when he felt it was late enough to phone, I sat across from Bryce, fidgeting nervously, while he put in the call to Scotland.

Morag answered. Bryce greeted her by name, so that I would know which woman he was talking to. Glancing at me from time to time, he launched into a detailed explanation of why he had called. He began by describing our failed experiment in accomplishing Nicky's murder. He told her about being burned in moonlight after Nicky had been blistered by the sun. Meticulously, cautiously, he led her toward the inevitable question: was there anything in our theory of the balance of opposites?

And the more important question: did he, Bryce, have a chance of surviving, should Nicky die from exposure to the sun?

His questions brought a long response. Listening intently, he sat ankle over knee, his brow deeply furrowed. I was on the edge of my chair.

"I'd very much appreciate that," Bryce said finally. "Aye, we'll both be here. Reverse the charges." He gave her the number and looked at me as he hung up. "They're going to think hard about this and they'll phone me back."

"What was her reaction, though? Initially?"

"Receptive. Very interested. I got the feeling I struck some kind of chord. They're going to consult their books and some other sources. My feeling is that they're going to consult a psychic, not a sorcerer. The answers to this lie in interpreting the old, so-called magic. Morag said we have the advantage of living in a new age of understanding, and there may be a way to pit that understanding against the old magic."

"They sincerely want to help us, don't they?"

"For Grizel's sake, as much as for ours."

I sighed deeply, wishing words existed this morning that could quell the foreboding, the fear in me. "Whatever they discover from a psychic, their answer to your question scares me to death, and we haven't even heard it yet. I don't like the idea of putting you through so much hell, and I don't like having your life in my hands. I'm as much a witch as Grizel was. It's her power that's coming through me."

Bryce reached over and touched my knee. "I'll submit to anything short of death to end this bloody nightmare. A nightmare to cure a nightmare. Some choice."

"Morag sounded . . . actually hopeful?"

"Hopeful might be too strong a word, but she listened with intense interest. The balance of opposites of sun and moon obviously was a new concept to her. They hadn't had that information before."

"I'm a wreck! This suspense! I wonder how long it will take them to call back."

"Elspeth was heading for the attic even before Morag got off the phone."

"The attic? More digging through old secrets." I studied Bryce as he sat across from me, showing no signs of the terrible ordeal of last night. "You seemed so at ease around Grizel's sisters. Having been raised by a sorcerer, of course, it all wouldn't seem as strange to you as it does to me. Do you think you were influenced by Grizel in other ways?"

"I've never thought about it."

"Think about it."

"I don't know. Unless it was the cats. She liked cats, but taught me never to touch them or trust them. I went against her wishes on that once, and befriended one of the strays that came around the estate. A few days later was playing at the riverbank, and fell in where the water was very swift. I'd have drowned, if there hadn't been a sheepdog nearby that got the attention of its master. At the exact spot where I was pulled ashore, they found the cat dead. No one knew why. Grizel said it was taken by the kelpie, the bad river spirit who wanted me, but was persuaded by Grizel to take the cat instead."

I blinked, feeling a chill. "And you believed it?"

"Not only me. Many people feared the kelpie. Still do. It's a water goblin that hunts rivers and pools for victims. Grizel said she'd saved me this time, but she doubted her power to do it again, if I ever picked up another cat."

"Good heavens, Bryce! Do you think she drowned the cat, thinking it would save you?"

"She implied as much, but never actually admitted it. I was upset about the cat, but I was also terrified. It was a convincing lesson about the evil of cats."

"How old were you when all this happened?"

"Four, but the memory is vivid. I believed I was going to drown. And afterward...I believed the cat caused it. I was young enough to develop one hell of a phobia, if that's what you're thinking."

"It's exactly what I'm thinking. You still have the phobia, and it's so strong that I picked it up and gave it to Nicky."

He winced. "There's one thing I have to ask you, Diana. Please don't think about cats. Anything else—wolves, gorillas, tigers, venomous snakes. But not cats. I can't take it."

"It would seem," I said, "that Grizel wasn't as modern in her thinking as her two sisters are."

"Aye, perhaps so. Messing about with a love spell is more evidence of that."

"Bryce, I'm getting more nervous by the second, waiting for that phone to ring. Our whole future could depend on what we find out this morning."

A gray London sky sent light through the east windows. It looked as if it was going to rain.

"It always rains when I'm in London," I said.

"And it always rains when you're not in London."

The radio played softly. The morning was so dark that we needed the lamps. Bryce had opened the window, and the smell of the damp air reached us. This strangely quiet, dark gray morning held in it the feeling of a coming storm. Clouds were gathering in.

He took my hand into his. "Your hands are like ice."

"Yours aren't as warm as they should be."

"Don't be afraid on my account." Gently he brushed my hair back from my neck and kissed me. It was a reassuring kiss. I clung to him, wanting his strength and his warmth.

He kissed me again, lingering this time, until we both jumped at the jangling of the telephone.

"Could it be them already?" A chill hit me the moment his body moved away. I held my breath when he picked up the receiver.

"Yes, operator," he said, and glanced at me.

I hung on every word he spoke, watching his face. It was impossible to guess what he was hearing, but I knew it was important.

"I was in the sun for about four hours and not affected at all . . . It was full moon . . . Yes, I'm absolutely certain it was full moon . . ."

He shifted about as he listened. "Aye, sunstroke. If we used sunstroke to kill Nicholas Paul, would a delayed reaction in moonlight be fatal to me? I don't know.... Are you certain about that? . . ."

I couldn't sit still and listen. I began circling the sofa like a bird in dizzy flight.

"If we have to," he continued. "Aye, the risks. We know there are risks to my life, Miss MacCreath, and we're willing to take them. Well, yes, Diana is a wee bit hesitant to . . . Jaye . . . Diana is the name I call her now. I can convince her." He paused, while I stared. "No, it's real. It's her middle name. Why?"

He glanced at me strangely. Elspeth MacCreath talked for a long time without pause. Finally Bryce said, "Aye, I have it. Is that everything? You're sure? It's a promise. Thank you both."

Bryce heaved a jerky sigh as he dropped the receiver back into its socket. He sat back and closed his eyes. I sat down beside him again.

His voice came huskily. "Elspeth thinks it's possible."

"Oh, thank heaven!"

"But it won't be easy. She got out Grizel's notes again and the old books, then made a telephone call to a medium and discussed the balance of opposites. The verdict is that it's possible—as long as the moon doesn't touch me. Morag made sure I understood that she couldn't guarantee success, but she did tell me exactly how we should go about it. The idea is to weaken interference from the moon any way we can." He rose suddenly. "I'm going to get more tea. Do you want some?"

"There is still hot water on the stove. I can get it."

"I'll get it. I need to move."

"What did Elspeth say about my name?" I called to him.

"Goddess of the moon. She says no person's name is an accident. Power play with the moon was preordained for you."

"Power play? What does that mean?"

"The will of the moon is your will, but it has to be invoked in a certain way, turned to help us. This is a big plus in our favor."

He brought back the full teapot and set it down on the table in front of the sofa. "The balance of opposites is the key. Therefore we must use it to our fullest advantage. Because the spell began here in the northern hemisphere, it has to end in the southern—in the opposite hemisphere. Grizel's moon was the moon of England. Elspeth suggests we try southern Africa."

"Africa? We've done Africa! The spell was so powerful in Africa that you were attacked by the snake!"

"It was probably in bright moonlight. In fact, I remember shadows on the path caused by moonlight that night, because the camp was so dark. All the conditions will be different this time. Our instructions are to wait until the new moon." He hesitated, scratching the back of his neck.

"And? What?"

"Elspeth's hocus-pocus. It sounds silly to me, but we'll have to assume there's a good reason for all of it. She said I must cover my eyes for three nights before Nicky's death, moonrise to sunrise, and the night of the new moon, when he is to die, I must put on the blindfold at high noon and keep it on the entire day—and, of course, all that night, until the spell breaks. We are to keep the room free of any moonlight, and you are to write by candlelight. Specifically, with two blue candles and one white candle."

"What? I thought Morag said these...props were outdated."

"I think they're just symbolic recognition of the ancient power, for stronger manipulation of the subconscious, and it's easy enough to do. We begin three hours before midnight, and under no circumstances can we continue after sunrise, or there will be a delayed reaction from the moon the following night."

I felt myself go pale. "You mean, if we'd tried the sunstroke idea the first time instead of poison, and I'd let Nicky die, thinking you were all right, there would have been a delayed reaction once the full moon came out, and the moonlight would have killed you?"

"That's right."

I shrank back in horror. "Oh, Bryce! There are just too many unknowns here! There's too much danger! We don't know what we're doing! I could kill you!"

"We know what we're doing now—I think."

"What if Elspeth MacCreath is wrong!"

"She could be. It's a chance we'll have to take."

"A chance with your life!"

"Yes. But there are certain precautions. Elspeth was very specific as to what we should or should not do this time. She says we must research sunstroke and the treatment for it, and then, as an added precaution, I can undergo the treatment at the same time Nicky is suffering the symptoms. So we'll need medical help, if we can get it. We haven't got any choice, Diana. I no longer have any kind of a life."

"Okay," I agreed with a shaky sigh. "Okay. I guess we go to Africa."

He smiled. "Elspeth considers your name an encouraging sign and says she wishes she'd known about it sooner. I'm going to take it as a good omen. The new moon is less than two weeks away. How soon can you leave?"

"I can leave today. But what about you—your job?"

"I put myself on indefinite leave yesterday. I had to."

I stared at Bryce, trying to comprehend what was happening. "It's awfully strange. I was planning to take Nicky back to Africa in the book I'm writing—or was writing, until I met you. The story begins in Madrid, where he's hired to solve a murder in a castle. Turns out the victim, like the victim of an identical murder over half a century earlier, was killed with poison. But the substance is so rare that no scientist can locate its origin. My plot took Nicky to the farthest reaches of the Kalahari Desert in search of a rare plant. By this time, of course, the villains have killed two or three more people with the poison, and an antidote is desperately needed."

Bryce slapped his fist into his palm. "The Kalahari? That's made to order!"

"It's almost too perfect."

"Strange forces *are* at play here. I want to be free of them, whatever they are."

"Something unforeseen could happen in Africa. The Kalahari is so terribly isolated."

"Let me guess about Nicky. The villains follow him to the desert. Correct?"

"Right. And they wreck his Land Rover and cause Nicky to get stranded out there."

"Stranded," Bryce repeated incredulously. "Stranded in one of the wickedest deserts on earth. Where, of course, he can't avoid sunstroke."

"This is eerie! I don't like it!"

"Perhaps it's a sign that we're on the right track."

"One thing's for sure. It can't be coincidence—which is more proof that we have no idea what sorcery we're really up against."

"Perhaps it's a manifestation of your power, Diana. You thought it up before the fact, rather than after."

"I still don't like it! There's something wrong, something missing, something else we should know about and don't!"

Bryce crossed the room to get the phone book from the desk. "Tell me. How did you plan to rescue Nicky when he was stranded?"

"Some Bushmen would find him."

He was leafing through the pages, then abandoned the task and looked up. "Elspeth mentioned your having to create an appropriate setting, and she said we should get as close to the site as possible, but also that we shouldn't be under open sky. I don't know about the advisability of heading off for the far reaches of the Kalahari. There are areas out there where no white man has ever been. And there certainly wouldn't be shelter."

"We'd have to have a sturdy, tight tent. In my story the mysterious deadly plant had to be in a very remote area of the desert, but you're right, we can't get too far from civilization. We'll compromise."

"We'll fly in. And out again. No plane can land safely on that shifting sand, but a helicopter can. I'll make the arrangements from Johannesburg. We'll need these two weeks to organize." Bryce looked solidly at me. "Are we crazy, Diana? Are we actually planning to take off for the opposite side of the world, because a seventy-year-old witch says the African moon will have less power over us than a British moon? Are you listening to this conversation?"

"I stopped listening to our conversation when we got serious for the second time about plotting murder."

He exhaled noisily. "Let's just keep reminding ourselves that one day—and it'll be one day soon—all this will be over. A couple of weeks from now, either the spell will be broken or I'll be dead."

"Bryce!"

"It's the way it has to be. The power is too strong to live with. Look at this Africa thing—the weird way it's come about. I have to be freed from Grizel's spell, or die trying."

"Why would Grizel's spell be so dangerous—if it's a love spell?"

"As her sisters said, something went hell wrong."

"Many things went hell wrong. Nicky was born, for starters."

Bryce scowled and picked up the phone book again. "Nicky, with more damn lives than a cat. Nicky the bold. I trust you to get rid of him next time, Diana."

"You're phoning for plane reservations, aren't you? For when?"

"Tomorrow. If you're ready."

"I can pack in thirty minutes. We can buy or lease equipment after we get there. I'll make a list, starting with a book on sunstroke, its symptoms and its curses. We don't want to forget insecticide and matches and flashlights..."

"At least you've been in the bush before," he said. "I'd hate to think of most women I know taking on the Kalahari Desert."

"What kind of a chauvinistic remark is that?"

"Hell," he said. "Most men I know couldn't take it. Treat it as a compliment, and let's be grateful it's winter down there. If it was summer, we'd have to wait months.''

While Bryce dialed, I noticed rain spatters on the window. Before long, I thought, we'd be longing for the smells and sounds of England—rain on wet streets, rain on the rooftops, rain on the soft green hills of the English countryside.

''Don't forget to put candles on the list,'' Bryce said in a brittle, suddenly alien voice. ''Blue candles. For you to write by.''

BRYCE WAS FEELING more relief than apprehension. It seemed as if any hope to him was better than none, however dim the ray. As for me, I felt the sensations of little bubbles of terror starting in my stomach, the way water churns before it reaches a full boil.

All these instructions. All this information. I didn't trust Grizel's sisters completely, because by their own admission, they didn't fully understand what had gone wrong with Grizel's spell. It bothered me that the spell was getting so much stronger. I needed to know *why*. The explanations didn't sit comfortably with me. What was it we should know that we didn't? Something was missing, I was sure. Something had been overlooked.

That feeling assailed me constantly during the long flight. When we reached the southern hemisphere, it became even stronger, as if the clear, vast southern skies were trying to tell us, trying to warn us. We were flying blindly into the greatest danger yet, and Bryce would not listen to my fears. He'd made up his mind that he would rather die than lose complete control of his life to me. I knew I had no moral right to try to block his decision with my power. I loved him too much to force him to live in Nicky's shadow.

Chapter Ten

THE HYENAS didn't start to scream until the third night, long after the wind had died with the sinking of the sun. No sunset adorned this wasteland; the bright red ball dropped over the edge of the horizon and the day was gone. Nightfall sent down cold from the sky in a canopy of frost, mean and penetrating. We sat by the fire in heavy parkas and listened to night sounds: cries of birds, screeching insects, and tonight—from somewhere out there—the unspeakably hideous laughter of hyenas—according to African witchcraft, living symbols of evil.

"No human could ever describe the laughter of hyenas," I said.

"No human could listen to it for long without going insane."

I thought it was probably true. When I moved nearer him, he shifted his legs. "Bryce, be careful! If you get your feet any closer to the fire, you're going to burn the toes off your boots!"

He tugged with discomfort at the bandages we had used for a blindfold and drew back his feet. "Can you see the moon?"

"It's just a sliver. The stars are incredibly bright against the pitch-black night. It's beautiful. But I wish those hyenas would stop their ghoulish laughing. The sound is giving me chills. Will they come near us?"

"They probably won't come into our camp if no food scraps are left around and we keep the fire bright. It's not hyenas I worry about. It's lions."

"Trevor swore there were no lions around here in the dry season, and we haven't seen signs of any."

"Just the same, I feel helpless with this damned blindfold. If you were in danger, I wouldn't know it until too late, and then it would take me half a minute to get this bloody thing off."

"We just have to get through tonight," I said. "Trevor and Pieter will be back in the morning."

"I hope they don't forget anything."

"What could Trevor forget, except his helicopter or his one passenger? And Pieter knows what we need out here better than we do. Have some faith, darling. You've got to have faith in them as much as in me."

"I do have. I'm just nervous."

We'd been lucky to find Pieter Vaan through a Transvaal university. He was a medical student who worked as an ambulance driver and paramedic, experienced in emergency treatment. Raised on a farm north of the Orange River, he had grown up with the superstitions of Africa; he'd seen the powers of sorcerers' spells firsthand, and believed in them completely.

Trevor Lund, the pilot of our chartered helicopter, knew the Kalahari as well as any white man in Africa. He knew the seasons and moods of the vast desert and spoke the language of its mysterious people: the elusive Bushmen. We had let Trevor choose our campsite and we believed him about the lions hunting farther north of where we'd landed.

Trevor brought Pieter out with us, but neither of them stayed. It's hard to describe how it felt, standing beside Bryce in the middle of nowhere, watching the helicopter lift off, taking the two of them back to civilization. The hot wind blew into our faces. Blades were whirring, churning up the sand around us—hot, stinging sand—as the helicopter rose and turned its nose east. Then overpowering silence. We stood in the sound of the wind, facing three days alone before the two men returned on the dreaded day of the new moon.

Bryce proved to be a man's man in the bush, adaptable to the discomforts and disposition of nature at its meanest. He had secured the tent to the trunks of scrubs, because the sand was too loose to hold stakes. He had gathered in a good pile of firewood from the sparse supply, chopped larger branches, and taught me the best way to build a camp fire. He had worked hard, perspiring, his bare back gleaming in the sun, and complaining not about the work, but about my being there. "This is one of the most hostile places on the planet earth," he had said half a dozen times. "It's unfit for humans. I hate the idea of dragging you out here."

"I don't recall being dragged," I had answered, gathering in my armload of branches for the fire. "I'm no stranger to adventure, nor to the bush, so stop worrying about it. Let's just worry about getting out of here alive."

That remark could always make him pause to wipe his brow and smile.

This third night, the night of the hyenas, the temperature had dropped drastically. I dreaded leaving the fire's warmth to crawl into an ice-cold sleeping bag, even if Bryce was going to be in there with me.

"Could you give the tent a thorough check tonight, Diana? Last chance to make sure it's absolutely tight."

"I've already checked. It's as black as velvet in there. No moonlight can seep in, not a drop. There isn't going to be much light from that splinter of a moon, anyway."

The fire blazed brightly against the night. Its flames leaped high, turning our faces a soft, glowing orange. Bryce looked incredibly handsome in the firelight, even with the thick band of black around his eyes.

"You're quiet tonight," he said. "Are you worried about tomorrow?"

"Of course. Aren't you?"

"Let's not think about tomorrow." He huddled in the parka. "Damn, it's cold."

"Let's think about the hot, sultry nights of Madrid. That hot, reckless, wonderful city, where I found you."

"Where I found *you*."

"Were you looking for me?" I asked.

"I'd looked for you all over the world. I just wasn't quite aware of it, but now that I think back, yes, I was searching for you. I had searched for a long time. Does it warm you, thinking of the hot, sultry nights with me?"

The hyena cackled again—a sound like a zombie screaming from the netherworld, and a second hyena answered from a distance, filling the whole night with the sound of demons. I shivered. "It helps. But to tell you the truth, I'm really dreading that cold tent."

"I'm ready to go in, if you are. What time is it?"

"I don't know. Does it matter?"

"Not in the least." He rose from the camp stool. "Is the fire all right?"

"I just threw on the biggest log we have." Taking his arm, I led him toward the tent. The first night he had stumbled about with the blindfold, but he was getting used to it now and had learned the distance between the fire, our tent, and the table on the opposite side that held boxes of our supplies, all tightly sealed in tins, so as not to attract the night-prowling scavengers.

"Necessary bush walk," he said. "Point me in the right direction."

Using a flashlight, I led him a short distance away, and went in the opposite direction myself, thinking what a failure I'd have been as a pioneer. Some things about camping in the African bush were wonderfully exciting, but necessary bush walks at night, when the snakes were out, along with other, growly creatures, was not one of them. How Bryce stood it with a blindfold, I don't know. But then he had certain advantages over me on bush walks—men were better equipped for surviving in the wilderness.

The desert, so deathly silent by day, was noisier than usual on this night with the sounds of animals and birds we couldn't see on the prowl and in flight—hunters all. I hurried back toward Bryce, shining my flashlight across the scrub and the sandy ground. I took his arm and led him to the tent.

We slid out of our coats and crawled into the thick sleeping bag, which was actually two bags zipped together to make one.

Bryce hugged me. "We could turn the gas heater on."

"It's too dangerous to have it on while we're asleep."

"We wouldn't have to sleep."

I smiled. It had been wonderfully intimate out here with Bryce—just the desert and us and the bright heat of the Kalahari afternoons. We had made love in sunshine. But during the icy nights we had slept fully dressed in a tent so dark that I might as well have been blindfolded, too.

"On this of all nights, you need to rest," I said.

"On this of all nights, I need you."

His hands, still very cold, pushed up my sweater and shirt, and warmed themselves against my bare skin. Practiced fingers unhooked my bra and found my breasts. His large hands, so strong and gentle at the same time, caressed me, a familiar caress. Could I ever live without it? I wondered. The thought flashed through my mind that by tomorrow night, if our plan worked, the spell that bound his love to me would be broken. And then? Would our love be ended?

I couldn't think about that, especially not now, with Bryce lying beside me, touching me...wanting me...

Unable to resist the sensations his touch aroused, I unbuttoned his shirt and ran my open hands through the hair on his chest.

He reached for my face, feeling the lines of my features, and found my lips. I kissed his fingertips one by one, and then his lips were there instead, and he was kissing me hungrily. I lost myself completely in his kiss. Moaning, writhing, I tugged at his thick hair, wanting him more desperately than I'd ever wanted him before as the kiss lingered, leading us both past the sparkling, tingling point of no return.

Still kissing me, Bryce found the buttons of my jeans, undid them easily by feel and slid them down. His kisses traveled over my neck and my breasts, while he wriggled deeper into the double sleeping bag.

"How can you breathe down there?" I asked. "You're going to smother."

"A happy way to die," he mumbled.

Erotic kisses, intimate caresses—Bryce's language of love—made me forget I'd ever been cold. My fingers moved through his hair and touched the back of the blindfold. He knew my body so intimately by now that when he was blindfolded, the language of his love was even more arousing than when we could see.

"I never wanted a woman like I wanted you...." His voice came muffled from inside the heavy down bag. "Never... wanted... so much..."

With the churning passion filling me, I reached out of our cocoon to the table beside the thick foam mattress on which we were lying. The cold hitting my bare arm came as a shock.

"What are you doing?"

"Looking for something."

"For what?"

"You know what."

"Did you find it?"

"Yes. I have the flashlight."

Bryce poked his head out to breathe the cold, fresh air.

"You're not smothered yet," I said.

"No, but I can get a little claustrophobic, completely covered like that."

"Not me!" I slid down inside, pulling my head in, and teased, "I still have the flashlight."

"I thought you might." Bryce shifted his body and said huskily, "I'd be back down there in the sleeping bag with you if I could see..."

"You don't have to. I can see."

"Yes." He unbuttoned his jeans and wriggled out of them. "You can see to make love to me..."

At my touch, his soft moans filled the silent tent. I forgot there was little air in the downy bag, forgot about tomorrow's fears. Only Bryce existed for me, Bryce and these moments of togetherness, and my love for him.

He startled me when he jumped. "The flashlight's cold, Diana."

"I didn't mean to drop it on you."

"You're warm, though...your touch is so warm...and so sweet...it's different with my eyes bound. I feel so..."

He paused.

"So what? So...captured? Good. You are captured, and I'm laying claim to what's mine."

Out of a long, breathy silence, he mumbled, "The beam...is warm...and your lips are...so...warm..."

By the rasping of his voice and the writhing of his body I knew what he didn't have to tell me. This time all responsibility for precaution fell on the one who could see. When I shifted my body over his, I was filled to brimming with the joyous sensations of him—the pure joy of loving and being loved by him.

EXACTLY ON SCHEDULE in the early afternoon of the fourth day, Trevor Lund's helicopter set down once again at our campsite. Trevor and Pieter Vaan had brought sleeping cots, more food and, of course, the medical supplies.

Bryce was in a foul mood because, according to Elspeth MacCreath's detailed instructions, he'd had to put on the blindfold at noon, which meant he could do nothing but sit around, while the other two men took over responsibility for the camp. Sick to death of the blindfold, which was even more uncomfortable in the heat of the day, Bryce was less than successful in his efforts to keep from complaining.

He grew more nervous with every passing hour, and so did I. In search of a little time away from him, to try to control my own mounting fear, I took an umbrella

Pieter had brought me for protection from the sun, and went for a walk out into the scrubby desert with my notes on sunstroke. As though rehearsing for a bizarre play, I read over the notes for the hundredth time. The desert on a winter afternoon was as silent as death, except for the never-ending howl of the wind. I couldn't hear a bird or an insect. The sun beat down relentlessly.

The Kalahari is sparsely inhabited by bands of yellow-skinned Bushmen who were once hunted like animals by neighboring Bantu tribes. Their numbers are small, so we had thus far seen no signs of them, nor of their crude little shelters made of sticks. They knew we were here, though, because of the helicopter. No doubt they had even been watching us. Trevor had told us they knew every individual shrub and every tiny flower with which they shared their homeland.

My heart went out to Bryce. He was facing an awful ordeal tonight, but he wasn't receptive to sympathy. When I got back to camp, the three men were sitting at the table drinking beer and eating peanuts, and Trevor was making preparations for an evening meal of lamb steaks, boiled potatoes and curried corn with tomatoes. The vegetables evidently were going to simmer over the low flames for the next hour. I was skeptical, but glad they were taking care of their own needs. Food could not have been less important to me.

When I joined them, the two African-born men were talking about black witchcraft. Trevor, who knew the ways of the bush, didn't like it when he heard that the hyenas had howled last night. He considered it a bad omen, and so did Pieter, but they tried to conceal their concern from Bryce, who could not see the glance that they exchanged. I saw it, though, and that scary feel-

ing came over me once again. Something was wrong—
something was missing—some vital thing we didn't
know that we ought to know. I didn't want to admit it
to Bryce or to myself, but that feeling was growing
stronger by the minute.

As dusk descended, the wind died as it always did,
and the cold came creeping across the desert floor.
Bryce asked, "Is the moon visible yet?"

"Yeah, it's dangling up there like a little gold chain,"
Pieter answered.

"Koew," Trevor said, leaning back on his elbow and
looking at the sky. "That's the Bushmen's name for the
moon. They don't like to fall asleep with their faces in
moonlight."

"Why is that?" Bryce asked.

"Something about the moon being displeased if they
look at her, so she causes pain in their faces."

I sat forward. "The Bushmen worship the moon?"

"They seem to, from what I've observed, although
I've never got far with asking them questions about
their beliefs. Their answers are unreliable, because they
believe an outsider has no right to know. They give
more attention to the moon than they do to the sun.
They dance on nights of full moons, sometimes all night
long, celebrating the fact that the moon has come to life
again. To these people, there is spirit in all things—dust,
springs, clouds, stars..."

"The ancient Celts believed the same thing."

"Did they? Sometimes out here in the bush, I believe it myself. I've been out here lying by the fire, just
me and one lonely baobab tree over my head, and I've
talked to the tree and felt the living presence of it and
known it has a soul, and its soul somehow touched

mine. Yes, I believe it myself, Diana, damned if I don't."

As he said this, Trevor's soul certainly touched *mine*. I looked at him, sprawled comfortably by the fire—a big man wearing heavy, laced boots and jeans and a fleece-lined khaki jacket, his light hair reflecting gold in the firelight. Trevor lived almost as close to the wild as the little aborigines that were out there, not far away, unseen. I was glad he was with us.

And I felt a certain comfort in knowing that the people of the desert night were longtime friends of the waning and waxing moon and understood its mood and its power. Bryce and I were not as alone out here as we had supposed.

"The Bushmen are here, aren't they?" I said to Trevor.

"Certainly. We're intruders on their territory. I talked to a couple of them when we came out, before Piet and I flew back, and obtained permission to stay. Only a formality, perhaps, but quite necessary nonetheless."

"You talked to them?" Pieter asked. "I didn't see you. Or them."

"I didn't want to make it obvious. They're elusive people. We found each other in the bush easily, or rather, I allowed them to find me."

"You're as good as your reputation," Pieter said and smiled, while he dished up the food onto metal plates.

When Trevor held out a plate of food, Bryce smelled the curry, winced slightly and politely declined. "I can't eat, and the sounds of the night are so damned loud I'm getting jumpy. I don't feel right. I think I'll go inside and lie down."

Without a word I got up to lead him into the tent because the camp table had been moved during the day.

He said nothing until he was inside, sitting on the edge of one of the cots Pieter and Trevor had brought.

He leaned into his hands. "Are you all right, Diana?"

"Yes. Are you?" I sat down beside him and put an arm around his shoulders. "What do you mean, you don't feel right?"

"Fear, I suppose. I'm not looking forward to this."

"I'm not, either. You'll be all right. I won't let you die."

He groaned as if he were already in pain. "The tent is tight? You checked?"

"They did. Several times."

"Are you sure? My eyes are bothering me. I feel as if the moon is seeping right through this blindfold."

"That's impossible. It's completely dark out." I brushed my lips against his cheek. "You want to be alone for a while, don't you?"

He nodded. "I just want to...think."

"And not have to talk. I understand. Try to rest if you can." I hugged him. The hug was going to have to last until tomorrow.

The heater was set up in the tent, and so were the candles. During our three days in the desert I had been writing, so Nicky was deep in the Kalahari, too, being pursued by trouble. I picked up my writing pad and clipboard from the camp stool at the foot of Bryce's cot and took it outside with me.

Perched on another stool, I tried to write by firelight, but it was necessary to use a flashlight to see my own words on the page, because the night was so dark.

I wrote with numb, reluctant fingers. The sun was rising on the last day of Nicky's life—sunrise in a lost and brutal land. He woke to find that someone had tracked him, kidnapped his guide, emptied the gas tank of the Land Rover and stolen his supply of food and water. It was clear to him why he hadn't been murdered: there would be search parties if he didn't come back. And they would find his sun-scorched body. Why should his elusive enemies murder him, when the desert needed only hours to take his life. Death by natural causes, no murder investigation. His guide would be found some distance away, also destroyed by the desert. A perfect crime.

I had brought Nicky to his last hours, and it felt terrible. For a long time I stared into the fire, barely aware of the two men who sat opposite me talking very softly, respecting my need to concentrate.

Pieter looked at his watch. "It's eight forty-five, Diana."

"I guess we'd better get started, then."

Bryce was not lying down; he was sitting on the edge of the cot, waiting for us. While Trevor tended to the fire, Pieter followed me inside to finish organizing his medical supplies, which included syringes and oxygen. Earlier he had brought in some large jugs of water.

I lighted the three candles and gave Bryce's hand a squeeze before I sat down cross-legged on the foam mattress with my clipboard and a pencil. Shadows of the candle flames danced eerily against the sides of the tent. Outside a night bird cried shrilly.

A rush of cold air came in. Trevor stood in the entrance, the heavy tarpaulin flapping behind him. Bryce covered his eyes with his fists and let out a howl of pain.

Pieter grabbed his shoulders. "What's the matter?"

Trevor rushed forward. "Bryce?"

"My eyes!" he wailed. "The moonlight is killing my eyes!"

"There isn't any moonlight!" Pieter said. He looked back. The door flap was slightly open. A sliver of light from the night stars shone through.

Trevor closed the flap. Bryce covered his eyes with his arm and groaned. "My eyes...are killing me! What the devil did you just write, Diana?"

The candle flame trembled on my paper.

"The land was undulating as the sea. Sand dunes rolled between dry riverbeds—white quartz rivers, swollen dry. Skeletons of dead streams, rusted red. Hot winds whipped the crackling air. Small animals had gone underground, and insects hid in the shadows. But there was no place for Nicky to hide. Not even a shadow, not even his own."

"It's too intense," Bryce moaned. "I can't take it."

Trevor bounded around the tent like a man possessed. "I don't believe this! All that power? This puny slip of a moon?"

"We had hoped the power of a new moon would be diminished enough," I said. "Even the new moon wields too much power when it's balanced with sunlight that intense."

Trevor plopped onto the floor, huddled in his black parka. "It's incredible! How could this sliver of a moon through a crack in the tent flap...Cripes! A total lunar eclipse isn't much darker than the sky tonight!"

Pieter and I turned simultaneously and stared at Trevor.

I was the one who found my voice first. "An eclipse!"

"Eclipse!" Pieter echoed.

I grabbed Bryce's hand. "That's the answer! The only time Nicky can die without the moonlight interfering! When there isn't any moon at all!"

"Mmm," he mumbled. "And when is the next total eclipse? Ten years from now?"

Trevor grinned. "Two weeks from now."

Bryce weaved, holding his aching head. "What? Are you sure?"

"Of course, I'm sure. I check the sky charts every day. The next full moon will eclipse."

"A total eclipse?" I asked. "A full, total eclipse?"

"Total. Which means there will be a few minutes when the surface of the moon is invisible."

Bryce said, "That's it! That's what's caused the spell to get stronger—because we're headed into an eclipse. Cycles. Grizel always talked about cycles!"

I reeled with fear of the unknown. "Maybe with the moon in eclipse, I won't have any power, either!"

"You got your power during an eclipse."

"We're assuming...assuming...but what if something should go wrong? What if...?"

"If something should go wrong," he cut in, "I might die. That's the accepted risk. But as far as I'm concerned, there is less risk with the moon eclipsed totally than there is tonight."

I looked at Pieter. "What do you think?"

He scratched his blond head. "I think it's the only hope you've got. When you were reading, I was checking Bryce's vital signs, and it didn't look good. If you want a medical opinion, I wouldn't take a chance tonight. Bryce is having problems already, and you've barely got started." Pieter's mouth twisted thoughtfully. "It's odd that an eclipse would be coming on so soon..."

"Maybe, maybe not. Strange forces have always been in play with this spell, and it keeps getting stranger—and stronger. I'm sure Bryce is right about the spell getting stronger because of the approaching eclipse. I don't think any of it is coincidental! The timing—even Trevor knowing the date of the eclipse."

"That's not strange," Trevor insisted. "Any bush pilot can tell you about the sky. It's part of a guide's business. Some people come out here mainly to watch the sky. No place in the world is better for stargazing. I wish I'd thought of the coming eclipse sooner. I just didn't realize what you were up against."

Bryce rubbed his neck, fatigued. "Diana, you've said all along you felt there was something more we needed to know. Maybe we've just found out what it is—the approaching eclipse."

I took a deep breath. "Oh, maybe that *is* it! Bryce, the wilderness nights make the moon seem so...so strangely alive! It will be the full moon that eclipses...a full moon, out here! Could we do this somewhere else? Would we have to be in the Kalahari at full moon? It's so...scary."

"We're safer out here," Bryce answered. "We're safer experimenting with witches spells out here in the middle of nowhere. In civilization, if I should die of sunstroke in the middle of the night, how the hell would you explain it?"

"*What?*"

"Think about it. If Nicky dies when the moon is invisible, you might lose your power to bring me back. It's a gamble we have to face. I don't mean to be unecessarily morbid, but you could have a corpse on your hands, and that would take a lot of explaining with a story no one would believe.

"We've got one chance, and this time you're going to have to go through with it. You might not have the freedom to choose, anyway. If I should die, the three of you have to come up with a believable story. You sure as hell couldn't tell the truth."

Silence fell between us. Bryce was right, but no one wanted to say so. My heart was already pounding with fear. Here we were again—working with forces far too powerful for us—without truly understanding what we were doing.

Sensing my fear, Bryce reached out and gently touched my face. "I'm asking you for my life back, my sweet. You're the only chance I've got."

Chapter Eleven

NEW MOON to full moon. We had two weeks, less if we were to use the last few days for preparation. After the cold of the Kalahari we longed for warmth, and Bryce still had beaches on his mind. Privacy was essential, because with the nearing eclipse, we had no idea how bad things were going to get as the moon waxed brighter every night. Pieter suggested we go down to a secluded resort he knew about on the south coast. He flew us back to civilization, where we hired a car and headed for the southernmost shore of Africa.

The small hotel was situated on a rocky ledge overlooking a sweep of golden beach and the dark blue water of the Indian Ocean. We arrived late in the day.

Bryce, in jeans and sweatshirt, drinking wine ordered from room service, was sprawled across the bed with some folders he had picked up in the lobby.

"Good Lord, Diana, we're at the beach without swimsuits."

I stood at the window looking out at a pink sunset over the sea. "We can probably get by with shorts or underwear. The beach down there is utterly deserted."

"It's off-season. The water's cold. Pieter said it isn't a good swimming area, even in summer, because the currents are dangerous."

"We can play around the beach and soak up sun."

Bryce was rattling paper behind me. "There's an ostrich farm not far from here and an elephant herd near

Knysna...and here, how about this, Diana? It says here that these big caves at Oudtshoorn were the inspiration for *King Solomon's Mines*."

I turned around and smiled. "Sometimes you're nothing like Nicky. He hates touristy things."

"He thinks he's too sophisticated for the common world. He's a conceited ass."

I picked up the glass of wine Bryce had poured for me. "Yes, I suppose he really is. I love it when you're different from Nicky."

"That's because you're searching for me...for who I am. I'm not him, Diana. I don't care what anyone says."

"I want to find you." I sat down on the bed beside him.

He reached out to touch my hair. "Promise me you'll kill him, no matter what happens."

Fear shot through me. "We've been through this. I'm not going to promise to let you die."

"If you love me, you'll promise to kill Nicky."

His silver-blue eyes were intense. I nodded weakly, then gulped the wine. Outside the wide window, the pink sky was fading to gray as darkness rolled down from the high, black mountains and the plains and deserts to the north, where the rest of the world was. The weight of the earth seemed to be on top of us, while we clung to the watery edge of a continent in the same way we were clinging to our sanity.

Bryce sat up. "Let's take a look at the beach while we still have some light."

He took my hand on the steep, rocky path that led down to the sea. At the bottom, we kicked off our shoes and ran across sand that still held the warmth of the sun. The long sweep of beach was wide and wild. Birds were playing on the sea foam between the million little polka dots of crabs' burrows.

Bryce sucked in a giant breath of sea air. "I'm stale from staggering around so many hours with that damn blindfold. I need to run off some energy." He released my hand and headed out on the wet sand along the washing tide, running hard. I watched the ghosts of the twilight swallow him.

Darkness spiraled down. High in the sky the small, crescent moon appeared.

"Bryce...where are you?" I muttered against the low roar of the ocean. The moon was dangerous for Bryce, especially here under an open sky.

To bring him back to me I thought of Nicky.

When he came loping into sight along the line of tide bubbles, he was limping.

"The tide's rising," Bryce said.

"We'd better go in."

He scowled. "Are you cold?"

"Now that you mention it, yes."

"Och, I thought we came here to swim!"

I watched, horrified, as he waded out to meet the rising waves. He plunged in and began to swim toward the open sea. Nicky had done that the day he was pursued by the nautical killers who speared him. Damn! Remembering Bryce's spear wound and Pieter's warnings about the currents, I thought of Nicky and tried to force Bryce back, but Nicky hadn't come back in that scene; a boat had rescued him, and because it had all been so vivid and still was, I couldn't seem to reverse it. I couldn't get him to turn around and swim back to shore.

Desperation cleared my mind. Bryce had been convinced that the sliver of moon had had so much power because Nicky was in blinding sunlight. Balanced opposites! Would it work? I concentrated on the black of the night sea, the descending night, and Nicky returning in darkness. It seemed forever before Bryce finally came panting and dripping onto the beach.

"I'm freezing!" he wailed.

I grabbed at him as if he were a lifeline. "Hurry up! Let's find our shoes!"

OUT OF THE HOT SHOWER, he sat naked in bed, the blanket pulled to his chest. "My leg is killing me. That old wound. Why didn't you stop me, Diana?"

"I tried. Oh, Bryce, let's not talk about it. I'm trying so hard to just...to not think about...him..." I had changed into a warm sweatsuit. "You're still shivering. What do you want to eat? I'll call room service."

"I've lost my appetite," he answered. "If you could just find me a handful of aspirin...and a leash."

I cringed, and found the aspirin in his bag. He swallowed them with a mouthful of water and leaned back against the pillows in a sulk. The curtains, rubberbacked to keep out light, were tightly closed, and I was so conscious of trying to control my every flying or hiding thought that my head had begun to ache.

His skin still felt cold when I held his hand. "Bryce, have you noticed anything different since we've been in Africa? You seem...somewhat changed. Not always, but sometimes. Sometimes the spell seems so much stronger here, and other times it seems weaker."

"It's the sky. The southern skies are very different from those in the north, and we were told planets are involved in the spell, if you recall. I can feel a difference."

"You have less control?"

"Sometimes I have more. When the moon's not out."

I straightened. "It's true! In the daytime you're . . . you're Bryce! Aren't you?"

He opened his eyes and stared at me. "Aren't you?" I repeated. "Think back!"

His brow wrinkled with concentration. "Perhaps. I don't know much of anything anymore, except that I'm lucky I didn't drown myself tonight. I hope I last until the eclipse. No more twilight walks. Just chain me to the bedpost after dark."

"It's that bad?"

"It's a constant pull now, Diana. I might have to resort to the blindfold when the moon nears full."

I caressed his bare shoulders lovingly. How could I tell him that I'd had a very difficult time controlling the situation tonight? That here in the southern hemisphere I was no longer sure of the perimeters of my power?

"Tomorrow," I said, "I'm going to telephone the sisters. I have to ask them if I'll lose my power completely when the moon eclipses. If I do, you could die."

"I'd rather not know."

"Don't be ridiculous! We have to know!"

He sighed and closed his eyes again. His energy was sapped. I curled up beside him as he drifted into sleep.

"NONE OF THE TIMING is coincidence," Morag told me the next day. "There is no such thing as coincidence. The eclipse might well be the secret of breaking the spell, but we cannot be absolutely certain of it."

The phone line crackled. "Mrs. Campbell, I don't understand my power. I can't tell if it's good or evil!"

"It is neither," the witch answered. "It is merely power. Like electricity. It can be either good or evil, depending on how it's used."

"I'm terrified. What if my power leaves with the moon, and the spell's evil is too strong, and I can't save Bryce?"

"My dear, you must remember it isn't a matter of good versus evil, but of how much power you have. We are sure that in eclipse the moon won't be able to control Bryce. Whether or not *you* can is uncertain. But without having to go against the moon's force, I believe you can. It is, after all, a love spell. Grizel formed it of love. You just concentrate on the love. Freedom is the essence of love, and you are trying to give that to Bryce."

In the seconds that followed, images formed like darts of light and shadow moving around my heart. A witch was speaking to me about love—and I believed everything she told me.

I was beginning to understand what she was saying about power, but I was so ill-equipped to handle the power I had that I ached with the fear that I might not be able to use it to save the man I loved. Inside, deep inside me, I sensed there was some secret to reining in this power and then releasing it to him. But I had no access to the secret! If Morag knew that secret, she had been unable to convey it to me.

IN THE LATE-MORNING SUNSHINE we sat on the terrace, eating shrimp salads and drinking wine coolers. Chewing, Bryce asked, "Who is the new character you've been writing about these past weeks?"

"His name is Dirk Chadburn."

"Oh, Lord."

I grinned. "He's very different from Nicky. Dark beard and glasses and a background in acting, so he's an excellent impersonator. It's hard getting used to him, I'll admit."

"Poor stupid Nicky."

"I love Nicky. None of this is his fault."

To my surprise, Bryce smiled. He rarely smiled at the mention of Nicholas Paul, but now he did. "You know what his problem is? I mean, other than his conceit and his lack of humor, which have already been mentioned?"

"I'm dying to hear it."

"He knows nothing about love."

I set down my fork. "What?"

"What is love without loyalty? Old Nicky is loyal only to himself... well, to his principles, as you call them. Who the hell puts love of principle above love for a woman?"

"A hero," I answered.

"I could not love thee (Dear) so much,
lov'd I not honour more."

"Honor's, all right," Bryce conceded. "But I'll tell you this. If your arrogant Nicky would stop allowing himself to be seduced by a different beautiful woman in every adventure, and give himself body and soul to one woman who loves him, I'd have a lot more respect for him."

I dissolved into laughter. "So would I."

Birds were singing in the trees around us. The winter lawn was velvet green, and flowers were blooming along the terrace walls. "Isn't your life-style a lot like his?" I asked.

Bryce shrugged. "I suppose it was. Grizel complained that it was. But not any longer. Now I know what real love is." He folded his hand over mine. "I love you, Diana. And loving you is worth everything."

"For me, too. As long as we're together." My voice choked with emotion.

He reached across the table to caress my cheek with his fingertips. His hand moved lightly, feather-softly, across my cheek and over my lips. I shivered in the ecstasy of his touch.

The sun shone in his dark hair and into his eyes. He had always sought the sunshine, hadn't he? He wasn't even blinking in the sun. These were not Nicky's eyes, meeting mine in sunshine. And this tender, sensuous touch that made my heart go wild...this was not Nicky's touch!

"Darling," he said, "we have this time to play, from sunup to sundown for another week. Let's take advantage of it. Let's stop moping around, scared and dreading what's ahead. There are speedboats for hire on the lagoon and ostriches to ride. Have you ever ridden an ostrich?"

"Ridden? Of course not. Have you?"

"No, but it appears to be a local sport. I'll bet it's tricky staying on. I'm game, if you are."

"Sure! We'll have an ostrich race. Last one to fall off wins." I finished my wine cooler with one long gulp. "Let's go!"

In our room, changing into our jeans, Bryce kissed me.

"We aren't in a hurry for the bird race, are we? All I can concentrate on is how much I want you."

I was wrapped in the power of his embrace, the nearest place I'd ever come to heaven. "What...bird race...is that?"

His kiss—strong and hard and wanting me—was not Nicky's kiss. His body—strong and hard and wanting me—was solid, touchable and real.

WE DID NOT race ostriches that day. In fact, we barely left our room for twenty-four hours. The next morning, though, we drove up to Oudtshoorn to an ostrich farm, and felt like idiots trying to keep from sliding off the feathered backs of the awkward, giant birds. Bryce won the "race" because he had better balance then I and stayed on to the finish.

Later, zooming around in the speedboat on the inland lagoon, his good sense of balance failed him. Bryce stood up, slipped on a wine bottle that was rolling in the bottom of the boat, and fell overboard. We had to go back to the room, so that he could dry off in the nude behind the high walls of our private lanai. He made love to me with the heat of the sun on our skin and the water sparkling in his hair like diamonds.

Bright mornings we walked the beach at low tide, gathering shells. Bryce discovered a hidden tide pool in the sandstone reefs. Shirtless, wearing khaki shorts, he climbed over the rocks like a child who was part of the world of the sea. When I caught up with him he was balanced on one knee, one hand in the still, clear water, humming a strange, haunting melody. I stood, immobilized, listening to his voice blend with the calls of the seabirds.

He looked up. "My voice carries through water this shallow. It attracts the little fish."

I spoke in a near whisper, not wanting to break the spell of his song. "I've never heard of such a thing!"

"Come and look."

The pool was alive with tiny sea life, little fishes that were not frightened by Bryce's hand in the water. They seemed as mesmerized by his voice as I was.

"This is one of the most incredible things I've ever seen!" I said softly.

He lifted a shell from the water and sat back to show me. "A pink murex. Pretty, isn't it? They're carnivorous, you know."

"I didn't know."

"Certain varieties of them eat nothing but oysters. They've got this little tongue that drills through the oyster's shell. Voilà, sucked oyster."

"I had no idea you were so at home at the sea."

He carefully set the shell back into the pool. "I spent a year in Australia in my younger days, messing about the beaches and the reefs."

Oh, yes, Australia, I remembered. It must have been where he met his Australian wife. I dug a handful of shells from my shorts pocket. "Can you identify these?"

He poked through them. "This is a tellin. These are arcs. Mussels, of course. This is some kind of triton."

"I won't remember."

He smiled, reached into one of the deep outside pockets of his camping shorts and pulled out his Swiss knife. With a pick blade, he carefully drilled little holes in the soft shells, humming while he worked. He strung several shells on a string he produced from his pocket, and tied it around my wrist.

"You won't remember the names," he acknowledged, closing his knife. "But you'll remember today, because of them. And I'll remember their pastel colors against your skin."

My gaze moved from the bracelet of shells to his sky-blue eyes. "I once spun a childhood fantasy around a sailor—after I saw a film called *Winds of Paradise*. You've made me remember him."

"Let me guess. You were a South Seas princess. Did he take you home with him, or did he stay on your tropical island forever?"

"Oh, neither, I'm afraid. Like in the movie, he sailed away with his ship, promising to return. But I guess he never did."

"What kind of fantasy is that?" Bryce took my hand and urged me to my feet. "Come on, I want to show you something."

I followed him across the rocks, climbing slowly and carefully. When we reached the soft white sand, he took my hand again and trotted across to the widest stretch of beach, where he stopped, shading his eyes and gazing at the ocean. No one else was on the beach that morning. Gulls circled overhead. The slowly rising tide was singing. Bryce pointed to the blue horizon. "There! Do you see it?"

I saw only gently heaving waves, the dark blue line where earth met sky, and sun gleaming on the water. I shaded my eyes and squinted. "Do I see what?"

"Out there. Look carefully and you'll see it, Diana. It's a ship—my ship—sailing away without me. See it? And here I am, still here. With you." His arm circled my waist.

"Yes! I see the ship! Of course I see it!"

Bryce picked up a small clump of drying seaweed. "Gardenias for your hair," he said as he began to hum the ocean song again, and whirled me around in a little dance.

Nicky would never have sung a song to little fishes. Nor made a gardenia of seaweed. Nor would he have found my lover's ship out on the heaving waves. Nicky would never have understood about that ship...

But with the sinking of each day, the magic ended. Rapidly the moon was waxing full. At night, Bryce became so sullen and short-tempered I hardly knew him. He complained both about food he didn't like and the unceasing sound of the ocean outside. If I had even a passing thought of Nicky, Bryce would react in some bizarre way and blow up in anger. The pressure grew more unbearable with each passing night.

In daylight he would sometimes squeeze my hand or kiss me for no reason. In daylight he would sometimes pick a flower and place it in my hair. Once he built a sparkling castle in the sand. But as the moon waxed to full, even in daylight his head began to ache, and then when he squeezed my hand in silence, I knew the reason.

One bright night the pain in his eyes began. From then on, he slept on the floor of the bathroom with the door tightly closed.

WE BEGAN TO FEEL the mystic effects of the coming eclipse the moment the helicopter set us down in the heart of the lost world of the Kalahari. Something different was in the air. The ever-present wind was tame, subdued. The nights sat back in eerie silence, warmer than before, for spring was approaching the arid land; soon it would be the season of the locusts.

Our mission was secret. It amounted to a pact, actually, an agreement that whatever happened in the

Kalahari on the night of the eclipse, only the four of us would ever know. If, God forbid, Bryce lost his life, Trevor and Pieter would protect me by lying about what happened. Bryce was the one who insisted upon this agreement, and the other two men quickly agreed on its necessity.

So Bryce and I were less alone than we were the first time, and better prepared. Trevor, who had done his homework, explained to us that the twentieth century would see no less than one hundred forty-seven partial eclipses, but the total eclipses were much rarer. When we studied his charts by the fire, we discovered that Grizel MacCreath had cast her spell during a partial eclipse. The earth's shadow had covered seven-eighths of the moon that night, but hadn't hidden it completely. Tonight's eclipse would be total.

The fateful night was full of mystery from the time its twilight slipped away. The earth was uncommonly still. Stars of the southern constellations shone so brightly that they seemed to sing in the sky. And people we didn't know and couldn't see—moon worshippers— crouched somewhere in the shadows.

A moon of moons rose out of the eastern hills—a luminous globe of gold, changing to silver as it climbed. Slowly it turned the black-coated night ghost-white and set it trembling. So bright was the full moon that fragile shadows of the bushes, dancing in a faint wind, gave the illusion that the desert floor was alive and moving.

Two things caught me in a vise of fear. One was the brightness of the September moon, which meant the power of the spell would be at its strongest before the eclipse began. The other was Bryce's insistence that I promise to go through with killing Nicky this time. He was afraid Pieter and I would back off again in fear. Under his grueling pressure we both complied. But it was a terrible thing to promise, because none of us knew what was really going to happen once the moon was hidden. We understood Bryce, though, and why he made us promise.

Bryce couldn't stand to be out in the moonlight, even blindfolded. He went into the tent while the rest of us watched the sky. Shortly after nine o'clock a small dark area appeared at the edge of the moon. "It's beginning!" Trevor said.

The three of us sat by the camp fire and watched the shadow creep over the face of the moon. "Do the Bushmen know about tonight's eclipse?" I asked Trevor.

"I told them," he answered. "I don't know what they think about lunar eclipses. I've never talked to them about an eclipse, except today, to tell them to expect this one."

"If they worship the moon, they must be superstitious about it. I wonder if their witch doctors know anything about moon spells."

"They don't have witch doctors in the same sense the Bantu tribes do, Diana. Bushmen doctors practice healing with plants and herbs, but they don't get into the kinds of magic and the evil other African witch doctors practice."

"They do their own divining with bones," Piet interjected. "Every Bushman I ever saw carries bones and tosses them before he makes any decision. Won't go into a hunt if the bones indicate ill luck."

"I don't think they adhere to their superstitions as strictly as one might expect," the bush pilot said. "At least not in the tribes I know best."

Pieter lighted a cigarette. "*Ja?* You never saw them step on their shadows, I'd wager." He turned to me. "It's my understanding that they look on their shadows as their other selves. If they step on someone's shadow, it's like stepping on the person's other self, his soul, if you will."

"His other self?" I echoed. "Two selves, like Nicky and Bryce?"

Trevor thought about this, squinting into the fire. "They believe it's a person's other self that dreams. And the other self that an enemy can sometimes get control of."

"You mean an enemy can destroy a person by getting control of his soul…his…his shadow? That sounds like a spell to me."

"Maybe. Since they don't regard death as a natural phenomenon, its cause is interference by bad spirits."

This sounded disturbingly familiar. It was the same belief the ancient druids held, and I pondered for a moment. Evidently similar interpretations of the mysteries of living and dying were made by people who lived close to nature. Nature—the signature of its creator. Nature—the realm where life is not breath, but spirit, where life and spirit are one. I looked out at the moonlit African veld and felt the spirits of life around me. The desert itself was a living thing, its heartbeat the wind, rustling in the night. The moon above me, creeping slowly behind the shadow of earth, was a living thing that walked the night eternally. I thought I could faintly hear the chants of the yellow-skinned women and the sound of gourd rattles on the dancers' feet from Bushmen's camp fires in the distance. But I couldn't be sure. It was too mystical a night to be sure of anything, except my fear of the living moon.

I looked up at Trevor. "You told us Bushmen believe the moon dies and comes back to life. Does that apply to people, too?"

"No. Actually, according to Bushman folklore, the moon sent a message that said, *As I dying am restored to life, so you dying will be restored to life.* This was the will of the moon, but the messenger, who I think was a hare, got the message wrong, so ever since then men have died only once."

My heart began to beat louder. I repeated, "*As I dying am restored to life, so you dying will be restored to life. This* was the moon's message?"

"According to Bushmen folklore, yes."

"The waning and the waxing of the moon symbolize rebirth! Nicky *can* live in Bryce!"

Pieter held a twig over the fire until the end was flaming. He pulled it out and relighted his cigarette. "What are you talking about, Diana?"

"It's this place," I said. "This...this lost world. These people know things we don't, I feel it. Nicky is the shadow of Bryce, and I have to somehow return that shadow to him, not to kill Nicky, but to give Nicky's spirit back to Bryce." I looked up at the shrinking moon. "But *how*? If only I knew how!"

"Think the moon's message," our bush pilot advised. "It's the only thing I know to say that might help. *Dying, you'll be restored to life.* Think those words as hard as you can. If that Scottish witch courted the moon, you can, too." He shifted his feet, raising a small cloud of dust that sparkled in the firelight.

Trevor moved restlessly, his eyes on the sky. "The moon is more than half-hidden, Diana."

Fear crept over me like a cold wave. "I'm going inside," I said.

I took my writing pad and clipboard into the tent. Wearing a heavy gray exercise suit, Bryce was lying on the cot with his head on a hard pillow. I stood over him for a few seconds.

His voice was raspy. "Who is it?"

"It's me. We're well into the eclipse. The moon is about two-thirds covered."

"Then it's time to get started."

I touched his forehead. "Are you okay?"

"I won't be for long."

"Bryce, what are you thinking about, lying here."

"About you and me. I'm wondering how this is going to affect us."

"You're wondering if we really love each other."

"Something like that."

"I know I love you," I said.

"You can't be sure."

"I know my own heart. I'll always love you, Bryce."

He felt for my hand. "I hope so. I'm not as good at knowing my own heart, but I can't conceive of not...loving you."

"We'll be okay," I said, trying to convince myself as much as him.

"Let's get this over with, shall we?"

"I'm lighting the candles now. Pieter has everything set up. He'll be in in a few minutes, and Trevor is going to stay outside to keep us informed of the progress of the eclipse."

In the dim light of the candles and the kerosene lamp, I sat down and gazed at Bryce, connecting with him, loving him. My love for Bryce supplied me with a reserve of strength. Finally I picked up my notebook and began to write about Nicky for what *had* to be the very last time.

Chapter Twelve

THE SUN WAS BRIGHT in Nicky's eyes and hot as fire on his shoulders. He shaded his eyes and wouldn't look toward the sun, knowing this ancient god of fire and light had the power to kill him. In the intense heat, the blood vessels dilating near the surface caused his skin to become flushed.

Pieter was keeping a careful eye on Bryce as the first symptoms of sunstroke began to show—the flushed skin, the body temperature beginning to fluctuate. In an actual sunstroke emergency, he would have immersed his patient in cold water when his fever rose, but in the icy desert night, Pieter had decided against this drastic treatment, for fear of giving Bryce pneumonia. We counted heavily on the success of balancing nature's opposites.

While I wrote, I could feel the heat sear Nicky's lungs when he breathed. My head throbbed. I loved Nicky. His agony was mine.

And Bryce's. His temperature was rising. "Fight it," Pieter kept saying while he monitored Bryce's temperature and pulse. "Fight it and keep on fighting. It makes a difference if you fight."

"My eyes..." Bryce muttered, tugging at the blindfold.

"It's the fever. Here, hold this cloth on your forehead while I turn down the heater."

The heat of our three tense bodies was enough to take the chill from the tent. Pieter turned down the stove and removed the first layer of Bryce's clothing.

Nicky had walked several miles, hoping he might stumble on a Bushman settlement he had seen some miles back when he drove out here, but by now he knew it was useless to go any farther. He no longer had any sense of direction and the desert was vast. His chances were less every hour and he knew it, but he no longer knew how to measure an hour against a minute or a day.

Bryce's heavy gasps filled the tent. I knew his delirium could result in coma if his body temperature kept rising, and the blood flowing through his brain grew too much hotter.

Some minutes later Bryce had stopped perspiring; it was a very dangerous sign that meant he was dehydrated from the profuse sweating, in spite of the liquids Pieter had poured into him for as long as he could swallow. While Nicky was suffering from thirst, Bryce was being saturated with water. Now he could no longer swallow.

Pieter started an intravenous infusion and placed an oxygen mask over Bryce's face. "His pulse is racing, Diana, and his color is bad. He's burning oxygen faster than his body can replace it, even with the mask." He glanced at me, his eyes full of concern.

My hand was perspiring so heavily that the words smeared on the page. Bryce was hovering on the edge of death. A half hour had gone by. "Trevor!" I called through the tent. "How much time do we have?"

He was directly outside with his eyes on the sky. "The moon is barely showing. I'd estimate we have one more minute!"

I drew a painful breath. In sixty seconds or less the moon would be totally hidden by the shadow of earth, and once in complete shadow, we would have less than three minutes before it began to move out again. Within those three minutes, Nicky would have to die!

Trevor had told us the next total eclipse of the moon was eighteen years away. In view of the promise we had made to Bryce, this had to be it. It had to be now.

Bryce had been in agony for half an hour, while Nicky had been stumbling deliriously over the burning desert sand, knowing the end of his life was near. The last adventure, the last ending. Nicky knew. Aching, I sobbed for him.

From outside the tent Trevor began to yell. "There they are! The beads! Brilliant lights are flashing out in a crescent shape! Lords of heaven, look at this! It's the instant of totality, Diana! The moon is covered!"

The instant of totality. A hideous instant. My mind went haywire! Suddenly Bryce and Nicky merged! I could see their bodies merge into one—one reflecting the other, like the illumination of light refracted by earth's atmosphere against the moon. It was exactly what Trevor was describing in the sky—the red refraction of sun around the swallowed moon! As in my vision, the bodies of Bryce and Nicky reflected as light, one against the other—and I couldn't tell which was which!

In panic, I screamed inside myself, *No! No! Don't merge! Don't become one . . . not now!*

Not now! I had to keep them apart. I had to *get* them apart. I couldn't kill Nicky if he was one with Bryce! Desperate, I tried everything to separate them, but I seemed to have no power now! The force of my power had been cut off by the membrane of our planet's shadow.

Tears stung my cheeks. The candle-lit page swam before my eyes. I concentrated so hard on Nicky that I lost hold of the reality of the tent. I was here in the sun-blanched desert with Nicky...he seemed to be Nicky...I concentrated so hard that I shook. He was *my* character, I said over and over. I was the master of Nicholas Paul. My character! He was not real. He was only a shadow. He was in my control.

Time was running out.

Nicky...Nicky...

His eyes were blinded by reflections of the sky's fire on sand. His lips were parched from thirst. His body no longer responded to his weak commands; his body was of no more use to him. This time he had lost.

Part of me was dying with him, for his consciousness was mine. But his consciousness was also Bryce's.

His consciousness. Consciousness of life! *That* was the refraction of light that connected Nicky and Bryce! Suddenly the voices of the witches rushed back to me. *Power of human thought,* they had said. *Thought—consciousness—power—they were all the same thing!*

Dying, you will be restored to life. Life meant consciousness! My mind swam. The answer was coming...coming...consciousness...conscious thought...the secret of power lay in the energy of the mind. My mind against the forces...no...no, my mind *connecting* with the energy of all nature's forces. Not fighting them, but connecting with them. *Using* them!

The word *live* hammered inside my head. Nicky was dying, but that didn't mean he had to give up. I concentrated so hard that it hurt. *Nicky, fight!*

Wanting desperately to survive, despite knowing he couldn't, Nicky began to fight for his life, to reach for it, to scream for it, to demand it. I wrote hard and fast. Nicky fought with his whole being, with his body and his mind, to stay alive.

This was Nicky's gift to Bryce: his strong will to live.

He fell. The desert sand was blistering hot against his face, and the sun's breath was relentless. Even when Nicky closed his eyes, the fire still burned inside his eyelids. No longer able to move, Nicky thought of his life. Of living!

He thought of the son he'd never had. Of his dreams as yet unlived, of love still unfulfilled. He thought of one special woman who loved him—I was that woman, because I was all the women who loved him. He thought of the summer hills of home and of how he longed to be in cool green hills again. He thought of favors owed and adventures not yet spun. He planned, in those waning seconds of his life, what he would teach his son about living and loving and being a man...the son he wanted and could have had...would have had...had there been time...

Death moved in a shadow. The shadow of a large, black bird drifted across Nicky's closed eyes. He didn't understand why a black bird would be diving down out of the blinding sun, but the shadow of the spreading wings was a welcome darkness. He remembered a hawk circling the skies of home...how free it was...how filled with life spirit, yet free from the bonds of earth...

MY PENCIL dropped from my hand. My heart was bursting with pain. I was terrified to look at Bryce. Pieter and Trevor had been so silent during the minutes of the total eclipse that it seemed as if all life on earth had stopped. Nothing moved. Nothing breathed.

I couldn't hear Bryce's gasping any longer.

Outside the tent Trevor began to shout. "The beads of flashing light are there again! The moon has started out from behind the shadow! Diana! Diana?"

"I hear you," I called back to him. "It's over..."

Reality rushed back like a flood. Tossing the notebook aside, I jumped up from the bench. "Bryce?"

I knelt beside his still form, shaking him hysterically.

"He's breathing," Pieter said, trying to stop me. "He's alive, Diana! Is Nicky...?"

"Nicky is dead."

I fell onto Bryce's body, blinded by tears. "Oh...Pieter...Bryce is breathing!"

Pieter's voice was choked with emotion. "His heartbeat was damned weak for a few seconds, but it's getting stronger."

I felt for the throb of pulse in his neck. "Pieter, I was terrified! When the eclipse totaled, Bryce and Nicky merged. I was afraid their destinies were merged, too!"

"Their destinies opposed each other—like the sun and the moon."

"But how could they, if Bryce and Nicky were one?"

He shrugged. "Maybe they were always one."

Of course they were! Bryce and Nicky had merged at the end of Nicky's life because they had to. Because they *were* one! In the moment of total eclipse they were no longer separate; they were both Bryce.

"It's true!" I said to Pieter, who was still sponging his patient's face. "Nicky was only my fantasy then—at the totality—and the fantasy was dying without the power of the moon to make it live!"

My fantasy was gone. Bryce was real; he was alive.

The spell was broken.

Trevor had been standing in silence in the doorway. "How is he?" he asked.

"His pulse was so thready I thought he was in shock," Pieter said. "But he pulled out of it. He was mumbling about a bird . . . a hawk." He handed me another tissue.

I touched Bryce's hot cheek. "I'll take off the blindfold."

"You're shaking, Diana. Let me do it."

Wobbling, I got to my feet. Bryce lay still, his breathing almost normal. He appeared to be asleep. Suddenly I had to get out of there—outside. I backed out of the tent and into the darkness. The night's silence assaulted me; the chill hit my face. I looked up at the miracle—the waning eclipse—the bright, living moon moving eastward out of the shadow of its parent planet.

Slowly the moon was reclaiming its shape and its brightness. It spread itself over the mystic Kalahari like a silver flood, filling every sinister shadow, every dent and paw print on the sliding dunes. Even tiny flowers hidden on the rippled shores of dead rivers were found by the September moon. It ruled the silent land as it had ruled us, with a cold power, without compromise.

I don't know how long I stood there in communion with the night. I was so drained of energy that I could barely think. Only one thing was real in my world: Bryce was free of the danger of me now.

Suddenly Trevor was beside me.

"Bryce is bloody sick," he said softly. "Piet says we'd better fly him back to hospital as soon as we can get packed up."

I whirled around. I had been in a daze, so relieved that Bryce was alive, without thinking past that. Now reality, balance and feeling were returning. *Was* Bryce all right?

I hurried back to him. Pieter, packing medical supplies, looked up at me. "No signs of consciousness, Diana. I don't like it. I won't feel easy until he's awake and alert."

I touched Bryce's forehead. "He still has fever."

"It was up to forty degrees. We've taken a hell of a risk tonight."

Forty degrees Celsius—one hundred five Fahrenheit! No wonder Pieter was worried.

"We anticipated having to move Bryce out in a hurry," Pieter said. "So we're prepared. We'll get him into the helicopter, and you can keep an eye on him there while we pull up camp."

By the time the helicopter lifted us off the floor of the desert, the moon was completely full again. We headed toward civilization, leaving the lost world behind us, leaving Nicky there forever.

THE SUN SHONE on a bright September morning—African spring. We had been two days out of the Kalahari, and still Bryce slept. The doctors couldn't explain it; they could find nothing physically wrong with him. I had spent every waking hour of those two days at his side, trying to hold back my terror that something had gone terribly wrong and, like Nicky, he was never going to wake.

In my hotel near the hospital, I had a dream the second night about gardenias. Bryce had bought me a real gardenia at a little flower shop in London, but more dear to me was the make-believe gardenia made of seaweed that he had presented to me on the beach as we watched his ship sail away without him.

I left Bryce's side for a short time the following afternoon to get something to eat and take a short walk in the fresh air of the hospital grounds. Passing a florist shop off the hospital lobby and remembering my dream, I was compelled to go inside and purchase a gardenia. I think I needed the beauty of it then, and the sweet fragrance instead of the antiseptic smell of the hospital, to help me recapture the lovely moments with Bryce.

I held the delicate flower in its little round container as I stood over Bryce. He was pale, unshaven, lying without a pillow on the high bed, and wearing a blue short-sleeved hospital jacket that looked too stiff to be comfortable. Watching him, I realized how much I loved him. That hadn't changed; it never would.

I touched him and said his name for the hundredth time. This time he stirred.

"Bryce?" I leaned close to him. "Bryce, can you hear me?"

"I smell gardenias," he said in a sleepy whisper.

Relief flooded me. He was awake. I said his name.

Slowly he opened his eyes and stared up at me, clearly disoriented. "Jaye?"

"It's over," I whispered.

His eyes closed again. "Thank God."

"Bryce, are you all right?" I asked, taking his hand.

He didn't answer. His hand went weak in mine and he turned his head away. He slept again.

A sickening feeling of rejection came over me, not only because he had turned away from me, but because he had called me Jaye. I wasn't Diana anymore.

The spell was broken. I walked out of the hospital and into the afternoon sun. Jacaranda trees were blooming everywhere along the streets; their blossoms fell over lawns and sidewalks, adorning the spring day with a gown of purple. I walked for a long time, trying to gather the courage to face Bryce again, to face what his feelings were, now that he was free.

When I returned two hours later, the head of his bed was rolled up and a young nurse's aide was urging him to drink a glass of juice. The gardenia was still on the bed table.

When he saw me, he pushed aside the juice. "Jaye. They tell me I've been here two days. I don't remember any of it."

The nurse glanced at me and took away the tray. I moved closer to his bed, wanting to bend down and kiss him, but instead I set my handbag on a chair and asked, "What's the last thing you do remember?"

"The heat. The pain. Strange thoughts..."

"What thoughts?"

He shook his head weakly. "Thoughts about life, wanting to live, wanting a future, wanting...a son. Wings of a bird."

I waited until the nurse was out of the room before I answered. "The bird came when Nicky died."

He looked at me strangely. "Those thoughts—that desperate will to live—were they thoughts you gave to Nicky?"

"Yes. It was my way of giving you more strength."

"It worked. I was fighting like hell. You made Nicky fight for my life. How did you know to do it? How did you...figure it out?"

I thought about this and answered slowly. "By trying to wake up, I think, by listening...to the witches about the power of thought...to the Bushmen about the spirit living separately from the body...to my own heart about the power of love...and to the moon about the restoration of life through death.''

Bryce closed his eyes weakly and said, ''I knew I was dying when I saw the bird, but it wasn't what I'd assumed it would be. There was no sense of finality about it. It was like...it was a feeling of doors opening, not closing, and it was a familiar feeling. I mean, I knew it was death, but it wasn't death.'' His eyes opened. ''There's no such thing as death, Jaye. I didn't know that before, but I know it now.''

He said it with such conviction that a great emotion surged in me. ''You...came hideously close.''

''I know. I knew it then. I felt Nicky fighting to push me back, and I started fighting, too, but not because I was afraid, only because I'm not finished with my lifetime yet. I have things to do, things to live for. I was too ill to fight and I felt Nicky doing it for me.''

''Nicky was part of you. He still is, somehow. It was as if he...merged into you.''

''He had your strength, though. Thank God for that.''

I touched Bryce's arm. ''You rallied very slowly. The doctors were getting concerned. How do you feel now?''

''Still sleepy. I feel as though I've fought a battle with a dragon.''

''You have. But you won.''

He leaned back and closed his eyes. ''Jaye, you've been through a bloody lot because of me.''

''And you've been through a lot because of me.''

''I'll never forget it. I'll never forget you. I'm sorry you lost Nicky.''

"So am I," I said, while my heart screamed, *I've lost you too, haven't I?*

"I want out of this hospital. I've got a life to get back to, and so do you. By tomorrow, I think I can make the trip."

"So soon?"

"There's nothing wrong with me. And I can rest on the plane."

"Do you want me to make the plane reservations?"

"Aye, if you wouldn't mind. What are you going to do now, Jaye?"

I studied him carefully before I answered. "I have a book to write."

"You're going home, then."

I nodded. He wasn't going to say anything to try to stop me, I knew, and the pain of knowing this was very bad. "Do you feel different?" I asked.

He rubbed the stubble of beard on his chin. "I feel lighter. Like a weight is off my shoulders."

"And off your heart?"

"What do you mean?"

"You know what I mean. I'm talking about how you feel about me."

He reached for my hand, frowning. "What happened between us was caused by powers outside ourselves. What we felt for each other wasn't real."

"Are you so sure about that?"

His voice became husky. "Aren't you?"

"No."

"I don't understand," he said.

I met his gaze. "My feelings are the same as before."

He lapsed into an uncomfortable silence. I waited for some response. Finally, after what seemed an eternity, he said, "We've been cut loose from a . . . a bondage.

You know, I think I've been influenced by Grizel's sorcery since I was just a wee lad, because I feel this... incredible freedom. It's been a very long time since I was free. I can't tell you what that means to me...not to be controlled by some...witch.''

"I can understand what it would mean not to be controlled," I said.

He smiled, but it wasn't a real smile. "You're free too, Jaye. Your feelings couldn't be the same as before because you were under a spell before.''

"Don't interpret my feelings for me.''

Pain filled his eyes. "It's just residue. We've been very close, and suddenly the bond is broken. And there is this...residue. It will pass. Right now I can't think beyond the sensations of freedom. You were incredible out there, and I owe my life to you. I owe my freedom to you, which is the same as my life.''

And to what do I owe my pain? I thought. *To you?*

There was no use discussing it. Bryce was still somewhat groggy, not quite himself. Perhaps he would never again be the Bryce I had known. Each moment that passed moved my worst fears further into the path of new reality. The spell was over, and so was his love for me.

THE FOLLOWING EVENING we boarded a flight to London. Bryce was still a little shaky, and he slept much of the way, his seat tilted back, his head to one side, facing me. We were returning to a familiar world in which nothing was familiar anymore. Nothing fit anymore.

My life had turned on its axis. The man I loved slept beside me, his shoulder touching mine, yet he was far away. The interior of the plane was dark, and stars in a black velvet sky shone through the small windows. I listened to his quiet breathing and remembered other nights he'd slept beside me, when he'd loved me.

At the first light of morning, flight attendants came around with warm washcloths and cold juice. Bryce stretched groggily and looked over at me, as if he were trying to remember where he was. He muttered a raspy, "Good morning."

"Good morning."

"Did you sleep?"

"I can't sleep on planes," I answered.

"Neither can I as a rule."

"Many things in your life will probably be different now."

He gulped down a glass of orange juice. "It's hard to define the ways I feel different."

"You told me. You feel free."

"Aye, but this morning I feel sort of...empty. I imagine it'll take some time to know who I am again. Are you all right, Jaye?"

"Sure," I lied.

"I'm going to look forward to reading the book. Do you think I ought to read it?"

"It'll bring back some of the pain to read of Nicky's death."

"Nothing could stop me reading it. Do you think I could just walk past it in the bookshop?"

"No...I'd hate it if you did that. It would be as though it had never happened." I excused myself, went into the nearest rest room and splashed cold water on my face.

Splashed cold water on my life. I felt so ungrounded, as if I belonged nowhere. It was because of loving Bryce, of course, knowing that he was lost to me.

The sooner I got away from him, the sooner I could try to put the pieces of my life back together.

EUROPE WASN'T the answer for me now. Home was. My adobe hacienda in the desert with its round-windowed study on the roof that looked out at pink sunsets. Daydreams ran rampant up there at sunset. In Arizona I waited for the phone to ring or a letter to come, but there was no word from Bryce. He was just...gone. His memory was a shadow darkening my life, the way the shadow had darkened the moon on the night I lost him.

There were moments when I felt I was groping in the dark of that shadow for my sanity. I plodded through days and long nights, pounding out the damned book, wanting to be rid of it and all it stood for.

And trying to give my all to the new man in my life—Dirk Chadburn, Nicky's permanent stand-in. Trying to pump breath into Dirk's lungs and blood into his veins. Trying to snap life into his eyes and resonance into his deep, English voice.

Slowly Dirk struggled to life over the hurdles of Nicky's memory. I came to like him, but I didn't love him. The real man I did love was no longer caught in a spell of love, but I was less lucky. At night I could hardly bear to look at the moon.

THE FRANTIC CALL from my editor came exactly one week after I sent the completed manuscript express mail to New York. I answered the phone at five in the morning, and felt a terrible foreboding as soon as I heard Alan's voice.

"Jaye, get on the first plane. We've got to talk. Dirk Chadburn isn't going to work."

A sixth sense told me what he meant, but I didn't want to believe it. "I know I introduced Dirk a bit late in the book, but I thought his and Nicky's relationship laid the base for—"

"I'm talking about Nicky's death! The whole office was sobbing for half a day. People are outraged. Marketing people are having a fit and they've been buried in surveys for the last sixty-four hours. They're saying your readers won't stand for this. You can't kill Nicky!"

My heart sank. "But Alan, when I suggested it, you gave me the go-ahead..."

"All I said was that I was open to the idea. Nothing was firm, if you recall. I didn't anticipate the reaction this would bring."

"Alan. Nicky is dead."

The strain in his voice took on the sound of a whine. "Look. I know you're used to doing things the way you want to do them. We've always trusted your instincts. But this time it's different. Nicky has a following of his own—people who wouldn't even recognize your name. Nicholas Paul is important to millions of people, and they don't want to lose him."

"Damn," I muttered.

"Surely you considered that," Alan Buchanan said.

I couldn't answer him truthfully. Of course I'd thought of it. I had tried not to. "Nicky...is dead and I can't bring him back," I repeated weakly.

"Nicky isn't dead until *España Farewell* hits the presses. We have to change this, and fast, in order to meet the deadlines for our advance publicity, which is going to be enormous for this book. I'll work with you on it. Can you be on the next plane?"

"Alan, please be reasonable."

"I'm asking the same of you. You have no choice in this, damn it."

I closed my eyes, feeling ill. "All right. I'll be there as soon as I can. We'll talk."

"We'll write, love! We'll write like crazy! I've just been handed another research survey report. It's confirmed. Your readers won't let you get away with this."

I could taste the sourness of defeat as I hung up the phone. What the devil was I going to do now?

Chapter Thirteen

MY FIRST IMPULSE was to slide back down in bed, pull the blanket over my head and pretend Alan Buchanan's call hadn't happened. But the panic in his voice spurred me on. I went to the kitchen in my pale pink pajamas to make myself a pot of coffee strong enough to get me through the next few hours. I'd memorized the airline schedules, so I knew that the next flight to New York would leave at twelve-thirty, six hours away. I had a little time.

As my coffee maker growled in the sunny blue and yellow kitchen, I phoned my travel agent and booked the flight. Sitting at the table, I picked absently at a bouquet of daisies that were beginning to wilt in their vase, while a dozen scenarios raced through my head. What would happen if Nicky were resurrected from the dead? The spell was already broken, wasn't it? Surely it wouldn't return! Or would it, if Nicky had never been dead?

What would it mean to Bryce if Nicky had never been dead, if he were still alive? Did one dare play around with forces as powerful as these? Did I dare use that kind of trickery? Bryce's life had been endangered numerous times because of me. I was terrified that I would put his life in real jeopardy if I brought Nicky back. Not to mention what it would do to him to be under my control again.

And yet . . . the spell was broken, wasn't it?

My head was spinning. My editors were not going to give me a choice on this. My publisher wouldn't allow me to do something that would be a market disaster. It would cost me dearly to refuse, but what else could I do, if it threatened Bryce's life?

That damned spell of Grizel MacCreath's! Was it broken forever, or wasn't it? Did the witches know? Perhaps they would! I looked at the clock and counted forward seven hours. It would be afternoon in Scotland.

Elspeth answered the phone, surprised, but pleased, to hear my voice. Bryce had called Elspeth and Morag from London after we got back from Africa, to tell them our plan had worked, and I suppose she hadn't expected to hear from me again.

"Diana! Where are you?"

"Still in Arizona."

"I would like to think this is merely a friendly call. But I fear otherwise. Is something wrong?"

"I have another problem, Miss MacCreath. I need to know if the moon spell is broken for good."

"Aye. Quite so. Are you all right?"

"I'm fine, yes."

"Bryce telephoned not long ago from Edinburgh, just to say hello. He says he's fine."

"He's fine?"

"He says he is. I'm not absolutely sure."

"Why not?"

"A feeling. The lad's a wee bit restless, seemed to me. Perhaps a wee bit lost. But what is the problem you have, that you'd be asking about the spell?"

"My publisher doesn't want me to do away with Nicholas Paul. I'm being pressured to bring him back. What would happen if Nicky came back to life?"

The old woman was silent for a moment, then her voice came through clearly over the cable that stretched under the Atlantic Ocean. "Once a spell is broken, it cannot return."

"But is it truly broken? And not just . . . suspended? I mean suspended for as long as Nicky is dead?"

"I do not believe so. When you killed Nicholas, you believed with all your heart that he was dead, did you not?"

"Of course."

"Belief is the blood of sorcery, the source of power, Diana. Nicholas did die, because there was no doubt in your mind at the time. Aye, the spell is surely broken for good."

Elspeth sounded so confident. "There's no danger in resurrecting Nicky, then?"

"Not unless there are forces at work that I am not aware of. I would say there is most likely no more danger."

That isn't good enough, I thought. *Because you're not absolutely sure!* But it was the best she could give me, and at least it was encouraging. "I don't want to have to do this," I said. "I'm really scared, but I think I'm going to have to."

"Keep us informed, will you now?"

"Of course I will. Miss MacCreath, I haven't talked to Bryce in over five months. He is all right, isn't he?"

"That I cannot say. He is pleased to be free of the powers of sorcery. He told us he had gone back to the place of his childhood and walked the moors alone, feeling the lightness of freedom for the first time in his memory. There's a sadness in his voice, though. He has some adjusting to do."

"Yes, I suppose so." She could surely hear the sadness in my own voice, however hard I tried to disguise it.

"And you?" she asked. "Are you all right?"

"Yes."

"I think the spell is not broken for you, Diana. You still care very much for him."

I winced. "Yes, but the truth is I never really knew him—the real him. I fell in love with the fantasy of him, and the real man is . . . a stranger."

"Time heals," the witch said, sounding more like a grandmother than a witch. I needed to believe in her wisdom.

WORKING on a rented word processor in a New York hotel room, I brought Nicky back to consciousness from the coma he had fallen into in the relentless African sun. Because I had destroyed the pages of his rescue by Bushmen tribesmen, I had to go through it all again. So did Nicky.

The shadow of death that he'd seen as the wings of a bird now became the wings of the majestic African fish eagle. Nicky hadn't known when he lost consciousness that he had reached the outer perimeter of a shallow inland delta. The Bushmen hunters discovered his trail half a day behind him. These wary trackers, who could follow the spoor of a wounded animal for days, determining its condition exactly, knew they were on the trail of a dying man, and their swift feet lost no time. They immersed his burning body in water pooled from one of their secret springs, until he began to cool enough to transport him to the mossy delta. It was several days before he opened his eyes in the shelter of a thatched hut.

An enormous pain stabbed through my body the moment Nicky opened his eyes. I didn't know the cause of it, but looking back, I believe it was a constriction of pure fear. For several grueling weeks I wrote in Nicky the rest of the way through the book, teaming him up with Dirk Chadburn to solve the murder and get into a showdown with the villains. It took a lot of rewriting. Subconsciously I was fighting it all the way, because of my terror that the power of the spell would somehow be resurrected.

THE NEW AND FINAL VERSION of *España Farewell* was completed only three weeks behind schedule. Alan Buchanan put up with my frustrated outbursts during those final weeks. My nerves were frazzled. A thousand memories of Bryce had resurfaced with Nicky. How could I ever hope to get over Bryce, with Nicky back in my life to constantly remind me?

I had nightmares of Bryce in some awful accident because of what I wrote, and I'd wake perspiring, convinced the dream wasn't a dream, but a bleed-through of the spell's power. From Nicky—back to Bryce. The worst part of it all was that I never could be sure my dreams were only dreams.

I lived in dread of the day Bryce would discover that Nicky wasn't dead. I owed it to him to tell him before he got the shock of reading about it. I owed it to myself, too, because I didn't want Bryce to think I was trying to deceive or trick him. As soon as the first copies were off the press, I mailed a book to his London address with a brief letter, explaining. Then I held my breath.

But nothing happened. Three and a half weeks passed, more than enough time for him to have re-

eived the books. His silence was a clear message that
all he wanted to do was forget he ever knew me. He was
probably angry about my betrayal in bringing Nicky
back from the dead; I could hardly blame him if he was
furious about it. It had now been seven months since I'd
left London, and in all that time, not even a card. Seven
empty months. Seven full moons.

España Farewell hit the book stands and was enthu-
siastically received, partly thanks to good advance
publicity. So the entire adventure, so far as I was concerned, was over. I wanted desperately to return to a
normal life again, whatever that was, but how could I,
when my first thought every morning and my last
thought every night was of Bryce Macklin? At times I
seriously believed that I remained under the power of
that awesome love spell. Time didn't heal the pain of
losing him. Nothing did.

MAYBE I SHOULD HAVE known better than to go to Europe again. Europe was Bryce's playground. But of
course it was Nicky's, too, and I, carrying on with my
life, had to carry on with Nicky's. Another Nicholas
Paul novel to write. Europe was a big place, after all.

Thinking back to Madrid nearly a year ago, remembering the shock of my first sight of Bryce, one would
have thought that experience would have cushioned me
against the shock of the unexpected. But Madrid hadn't
prepared me well enough for what was still to come. I
didn't know it, though, as I set about outlining the
forthcoming adventure of Nicholas Paul.

Nicky, thoroughly recovered from his desert ordeal,
was about to take on his most dangerous assignment
yet. And to set off the danger, I chose a setting of tran-

quility and beauty: Lucerne, Switzerland, and its Vierwaldstätter See—known as Lake Lucerne, in English.

I flew to Zurich and took a bus down to Lucerne. It had been several years since I'd been there, but I remembered at once why this particular city was known for its tranquility. A feeling of peace came over me with my first sight of its spires, bridges and ancient, wood-shuttered buildings.

My hotel was very old and quaint, with a view of the lake from my room and from its open-air restaurant on the floor below. Standing at my window, looking out at the most spectacular scenery in the world—the magnificent Alps rising over a crystal-blue lake—I couldn't help but remember that Mark Twain had loved this view and found peace and inspiration here. With luck, so would I.

I strolled the shore of the Lake of Lucerne, along the city's edge. Gulls were soaring and crying overhead. Swans were gliding regally among little cliques of ducks and black and white coots. Surrounding the lake, towering mountains stood silent and calm with their shimmering frozen peaks and their dark-forested slopes. There were flowers everywhere. It was spring again.

By now I believed Elspeth MacCreath had been right about the moon spell being permanently broken, because I had heard nothing from Bryce. If bringing Nicky to life again had brought the spell back with him, surely Bryce would have known at once and contacted me. So we were both safe. At least I thought so.

Opportunities for Nicky's adventures were abundant in the environs of Lucerne. Nicky first encountered the villain, Claus Wolf, on a red carriage of the cog train that chugged up to the top of the Rigi, a mountain singing with the yodels of herdsmen. In another scene, Nicky tailed Claus onto a lake touring ship, where he discovered that the man was traveling with a large cat on a leash. One look at the cat, and Nicky recoiled in revulsion, while his stunned adversary looked on. Nicky would not go near the cat, and Claus managed to slip away easily in the ship's restaurant, dissolving into a crowd of six hundred passengers. I wrote the scenes sitting on the deck of a steamship on a day-long excursion out of the harbor of Lucerne.

Claus, a cat lover, had the advantage from the moment he discovered Nicky's phobia. So he surrounded himself with cats to keep Nicky at a distance, and the ploy was working.

One afternoon after I had tea at a sidewalk café in the once-walled Old Town, I made my way in warm sunshine along the River Reuss to the Museumsplatz, to see again the great stone Lion of Lucerne. Statues had always interested me, but the sleeping lion with his head resting on one massive paw, his brow frowning with dreams of a just-fought battle, was to me the most moving sculpture in stone in the world. Hewn from a cliff, the monument was framed by green branches and overlooked a tiny lake. The first day I came, I had decided that *The Lion of Lucerne* was the perfect title for Nicky's latest story. Symbolic. Nicky was himself a lion of strength. How long I spent at the monument, I couldn't even guess, because whenever I gazed at it, I became inspired, and I could sit nearby and write for what seemed hours.

On this particular Thursday afternoon there were few people, which was surprising, because the Swiss are always out in fine weather. Perhaps they were gathered along the garden parkways at the lakeshore. Absorbed in Nicky's story, I sat on a bench and wrote, oblivious to those around me who were walking and sitting in the park area. An uneasy feeling began to come over me as I worked—a hard-to-describe feeling of not being alone, mingled with a sense of foreboding. I blamed it on the sky, which was beginning to darken with high, gathering clouds.

Nicky had taken lodging not in the city, but at one of the plush resorts on the slopes above the lake, where he mingled with the elite of Europe. In my writer's fantasy I was with him there in a garden of cypress and fig trees, where he was engaged in dialogue with one of the most beautiful and mysterious women every to appear in one of his stories. Nicky was in danger; the woman was a part of the conspiracy, and she had set a trap.

Scarlet rhododendrons, silver firs. A lush garden where a wire could be strung invisibly among the greenery. Very sharp wire, strung at the height no man wants to be hit with anything. When Nicky walked into the wire he would be hurt and incapacitated for some time, and the woman, who pretended to be luring him into her boudoir, would be able to continue her game of seduction without having to prove her promised expertise. Nicky would remain in her confidence, but he would be no threat to her in her bed until he recovered.

I winced at the scenario, so typical of the kinds of situations in which Nicky was constantly getting entangled. It took a devious mind to do my job. Lucky for Bryce, though, that I hadn't thought of this one while the moon spell was in full force. It would have been one of the more disagreeable things I'd done to him.

The seductress had wandered to the opposite side of a cluster of cedar trees, then pretended she'd twisted her ankle and cried for help. Nicky was moving pretty fast when he hit the wire.

Just at that moment, for some reason I thought of gardenias. Half-conscious, Nicky would smell gardenias when he fell. I closed my eyes and smelled the heavy sweetness, myself—that poignant sweetness of memories, so real that it would be unbearable to have to let it go. I placed a gardenia in the flowing blond hair of Nicky's conquest, so that when she bent over him, feigning horror, the fragrance of the flower invaded his senses. Perhaps, I thought, he had even given the gardenia to her earlier.

A shadow came over me. Not a cloud, but a hovering shadow, darkening the page on which I had been writing. For an instant I thought the shadow felt cold, until I realized it was a sudden, unexplained fear that sent the rush of cold through me. I looked up.

Bryce!

He stood framed by the backdrop of the enormous stone lion, legs apart, squinting at me. My heart dropped to my feet. My mouth fell open. I sat paralyzed, staring at him. He was holding a gardenia!

He must have known he'd frightened me, yet he didn't apologize. He just looked at me for what seemed an eternity, then held out the flower and said, "You're wearing blue, Diana. I always picture you in blue."

My heart was pounding so hard that I could hear it over the velvet sound of his voice. The flower, held in a round, open plastic container, looked so delicate, so perfect. Its heavy fragrance made me reel as I took it from him with shaking hands.

"You're...here...?" I whispered.

"Aye, and about time."

I couldn't believe this. It was starting all over again! Hesitantly, because I didn't really want to know the answer, I asked, "Why are you here?"

"I'm here because you are."

"Oh Bryce! Please, I don't understand!"

"Why are you staring at me like that, Diana, as if you're afraid of me?"

The blood had drained from my face. I must have looked like a ghost. "You're calling me Diana again."

"Haven't I always?"

"No!"

He looked puzzled. "I like it, and it suits you." He sat down on the bench beside me. "I missed you like hell. I had to see you."

"You didn't even write."

"I apologize for that. I had a lot of things to try to work out."

Part of me wanted to throw my arms around him in an embrace that would last forever. To have him beside me was like coming alive again after a long sleep. He looked wonderful, he sounded so wonderful that it was all I could do to keep from reaching out to him—to touch him. How I longed to touch him! But another part of me was consumed by fear, and needed desperately to face those fears. There were questions that had to be answered—awful questions. I dreaded the answers. "How did you find me?"

"Simple detective work. I tried to get in touch with you and finally remembered the name of your editor, so I phoned Alan Buchanan, and he told me where you were."

I gritted my teeth. "He told you I was sitting here by the Lion of Lucerne."

Bryce smiled. "He told me the name of your hotel. When you weren't there, I decided to take a walk along the riverbank. I thought about how you love fountains and statues, so I looked for you at the Weinmarkt fountain in the square, and when you weren't there, I thought I'd try the lion." He looked up. "I love this bloody lion. Such an unusual commemoration of the death of Swiss soldiers."

I looked at him with skepticism. "Bryce, I might have been anywhere in the entire city. You came right to me."

"I struck lucky. It was a fine day for a walk, anyhow, until these clouds moved in."

Yes, lucky, I thought. Bryce could find me anywhere, under the power of the spell. He had found me many times, without being able to explain it. The perfume of the gardenia was making me ill.

"The lion is a cat," I said softly.

He glanced at me sideways.

"Stone cats don't bother you."

"Or Nicky, either, I'll bet." He leaned back against the back of the bench, stretching one arm behind me. "So Nicky is back."

"I explained why I had to do that. Elspeth believed it was perfectly safe."

"You should have told me."

"Are you angry about it?"

"I could never be angry with you. I'm afraid you're mad at me, though, and justly so, for not staying in touch with you. I wasn't sure I wanted to at first, because I was feeling so different...I mean, the freedom. Did you know you can feel freedom as a physical thing? I kept thinking about open sky and open sea...and open roads. Like a lad on his own for the first time. I needed some time to adjust to all that. For a while I didn't think I'd come back, but I was kidding myself. I missed you constantly. It took some time before I finally admitted to myself just how bloody much I missed you."

I closed my eyes, trying to still the thundering of my heart. More than Bryce could ever imagine, I had longed for those words. But they were coming too late. Now that I had resurrected the black magic again, it was too late. I was witch Diana, and Bryce didn't even seem to realize it. "This...change of heart was recent, then?" I asked, eyes still closed.

Bryce seemed a little stiff. He was watching me so carefully. I could feel his eyes on me. Somehow he wasn't as natural as before. He hadn't scooped me up in his arms or even kissed me. Instead, he seemed obsessed with what my reaction was to his being here—walking back into my life so suddenly. He seemed almost unsure of himself, and I wondered what that meant. Actually I knew so little about this man.

"It wasn't a change of heart," he answered. "I just finally admitted what I really felt. You told me at the hospital that your feelings for me hadn't changed, wouldn't change. Yet after Africa I believed that everything that ever happened between us was caused by Grizel's spell. I believed that once away from me, you'd forget me." He shifted self-consciously on the narrow bench. "To be honest, I was afraid your love for me was gone. I haven't helped by being such a bastard about writing or calling. It was just such a damned weird thing to try to work out...my own confusion...and yours."

"My feelings have never changed," I assured him.

"Mine haven't, either. I know that now." He reached for my hand and squeezed. "I want your forgiveness. I want you back. We were meant to be together. That's what I came to Switzerland to tell you."

Emotion was almost choking me. I looked at him and couldn't answer. He touched my cheeks affectionately and looked into my eyes. "I love you, Diana."

The emotion turned to moisture in my eyes. What if this was real? What if he really loved me! If only... if only... But common sense said otherwise. He had materialized so suddenly, handing me the very gardenia I was writing about. And calling me Diana again.

"You... love me?"

"More than I believed I could ever love a woman." Gently he brushed the drop of moisture from the corner of my eye. "What's happened, love? What's the matter?"

I swallowed. "What's happened is that... Nicky is alive."

"What does Nicky have to do with anything?"

"Bryce, what if the spell isn't really broken?"

"What are you talking about?"

"I'm worried that—"

"You think I'm here because Nicky is here?" he interrupted. "That's absurd! After all we went through to break that damned spell? You think just because I say I love you, the stupid spell is back?"

"It's... the timing."

He scowled. "I should have written you last winter. Last winter was hell. I shouldn't have just... surprised you like this. Diana, you're wrong."

"It's a very real possibility, based on the... facts." I looked not at him, but at the gardenia and touched its delicate, cream-white petals.

He was looking at the flower, too. "Can't you trust me to know my own feelings? Never mind, scrub that. All the time you've known me, I haven't known my feelings. Perhaps all my life I haven't. But now I do."

I continued staring at the flower on my lap.

"Look," Bryce said. "I've taken a week's holiday to be with you down here. Will you stay with me? We have to talk."

"You know I will. I'd go with you anywhere, Bryce."

The sound of my own words horrified me. What did I mean, I'd go with him anywhere? Even if he didn't really love me, would I go with him then? Was I as unable to choose as he was? Or was I just so madly in love with this man that nothing else mattered? I didn't know the answers. I simply didn't know!

He leaned over and kissed me lightly on the mouth. Even so light a touch sent my spirits dancing.

"Shall we go, then?" he asked.

Tucking my notebooks under one arm, I rose. "Back to my hotel?"

"Let's go to mine. I've taken a room at a Burgenstöck hotel."

I froze. Burgenstöck. On a cliff jutting up from the lake, this summer resort was a favorite of celebrities from all over the world. Nicky's kind of place. It was the location of Nicky's hotel.

Bryce was watching me closely. "Why do you look so surprised that I'd have a hotel?"

"I'm not surprised," I said honestly. "Because Nicky's hotel is in Burgenstöck."

"Damn." His arm went around my shoulder protectively. "Would you rather go somewhere else?"

"Of course not. It's a beautiful place. The scenery is indescribable. I've never stayed at Burgenstöck."

"Nicky and I have similar tastes. Only the best for us. But never mind him. Forget Nicky, Diana. Concentrate on me. On us. From our hotel we'll have a view of the lake and the peaks. There are terrific mountain paths and we can hike in the high Alpine meadows and look for the edelweiss. We can take the outdoor lift to the top—to Hammetschwand. The view is magnificent from up there."

I shuddered. "The lift is fast and terrifying. I think I'd be scared to death. You too, after your last experience in Switzerland, when the cable car fell with you, and you were hurt so badly."

"Och, that accident is part of the past. Everything is different now. But we can take the funicular around, if you'd prefer, or a steamer, or, hell, get our own boat. You'll take a holiday with me, won't you, Diana? To make up for all the months we've been apart? You can spare the time for us, can't you? Away from your writing schedule and your deadlines?"

He made it sound like something from a dream. Time for the two of us to be together again, in the most beautiful setting in the world! It seemed too good to be true. I smiled. "Do I have time for us? How can you ask such a thing?" I inquired.

I felt his strong arm tighten around me. He leaned down to kiss my temple, and his kiss was magical. It set off silver sparks and caused my body to tingle.

"Experience me," Bryce whispered into my ear. "Experience my love. To hell with everything else."

Helpless with love for him, I looked up. His pale blue eyes were different from the last time I'd seen them at London Airport. His eyes had been unreadable then, confused. He had been elated over his freedom, yet his eyes hadn't shown his joy. Now they shone with happiness, and I knew his joy was in me.

His eyes met mine. "Let's go and sign you out of your hotel and get your luggage."

I glanced up at the lion, symbol of strength, a lion at rest with one great paw on his battle shield and supporting his head, his mane curling back over his shoulders. He seemed to be at peace, yet his forehead was curled in a strange frown.

Bryce and I walked hand in hand along the river through the oldest part of the city, past the old water tower, which Bryce told me had once been a torture chamber, and over a covered wooden footbridge. I barely looked at the paintings on the gables of the bridge; my mind was on Bryce. Why had he really come to Lucerne? Why?

And why did I feel so vulnerable, as if there was nothing in the world that could ever take me voluntarily from his side? Love? It felt like love!

My hotel was at the edge of the lake. Bryce carried my bags down to the piers, where we boarded a boat to take us along the south shore to Kehrsiten-Burgenstöck. From the lakeside village, we took the cog train to the hotel. The rail was so steep, I don't think I took a breath during the six-minute ride. I was too busy muttering prayers of thanks that I had not yet put Nicky on this funicular, nor given the villainous Claus Wolf any ideas about tampering with the safety brakes. The danger of my written words had returned, I knew it.

Bryce, marveling at the view of the white peaks of the Bernese Oberland, was in excellent spirits. "This scenery certainly looks better than the Kalahari Desert!" he exclaimed.

"It couldn't be more opposite, could it?"

"Is that why you chose Switzerland?"

"I want to forget the Kalahari," I answered. "I wanted beauty and peace."

"Beauty surrounds us. I probably won't give you much peace."

My knees weakened with anticipation, and I felt the familiar fluttering in my stomach. Bryce squeezed my hand. He easily read my thoughts; they were the same as his. I held tightly to his hand, wanting him—desperately wanting him again.

The brooding secrets of the netherworld—secrets of witchcraft—shivered out of mind when Bryce was touching me, wanting me. The instinct of fear lost its hold; I could think only of him. Only of him.

We stepped from the railway coach into cool mountain air. From the south blew a warm, strange wind. Warm and sweet—the foehn, the dreaded wind. While Bryce was getting the bags, and I stood looking down at the breathtaking view of the lake, the breeze felt like cobwebs against my face. I trembled. This haunted wind—what sort of omen was it?

Chapter Fourteen

OUR SECOND-STORY ROOM had a magnificent view of the Lake of Lucerne and the mountains beyond. A picture window and a private balcony seemed to bring the Swiss panorama to our doorstep. It was a large, exquisite room with antique furniture and fresh flowers on every table.

"Honeymoon beds—double beds to us—cost extra in this country," Bryce said, after he'd tipped the bellman. "I made certain we had the proper accommodation."

"You were so sure I'd come?"

"Yes, because I believe you still love me, Diana." He opened his arms to me, and I found myself under the spell of his incredible eyes.

"Yes, I still love you," I said softly. "It was you who changed after the Kalahari. I never changed."

"I hurt you. Damn, I hurt you and I didn't even realize it at the time."

"You didn't mean to hurt me, Bryce. You were trying to deal with something very heavy, very difficult, and a lot of newfound feelings. I understood that. I didn't like it, but I understood. I thought the spell was broken."

"It was. And I had to rediscover all my senses and emotions. I was like an explorer, walking through an uncharted jungle, hacking my way through a tangled mess of feelings to find out which were real and which weren't. You can see why I had to know, can't you? It took a long time. Months. I'm sorry it took so long. I want to make that time up to you, now."

I touched his cheek, looking up at him sadly.

"Why do you look so worried, Diana? Everything's all right now. It is, isn't it? I'm here. And you're here. We're together again. Damn, how I've missed you! It's been six months!"

"Seven."

"You could have found someone else in seven months!" he wailed. "What a fool I've been!"

"I couldn't have found someone else when I was obsessed with you. How long ago did you decide you still loved me?"

He took off his jacket, unbuttoned the top of his shirt and kicked off his shoes. "It's been rather gradual, but for the last several weeks the doubts have disappeared and I've known for certain."

About as long as Nicky has been resurrected, I thought, aching.

He continued. "I was going to write and I was going to telephone, but then I knew that wasn't good enough. I had to see you, tell you in person. But I was too tied up with work to travel across the Atlantic. And when I got the time and tried to locate you, I found out you weren't even in the States."

He kissed me, and the kiss deepened, until once again I began to lose all hold on reality. "I'll never leave you again," he whispered, between kisses. "Never, ever again."

I was still holding the gardenia, and it was getting crushed by the press of his body against mine, so that its sweet fragrance became part of our embrace.

"Undress me," he said, gently taking the flower from my hand and letting it fall to the floor.

Slowly I unbuttoned his shirt and slipped it from his shoulders. He interrupted me with kisses on my own shoulders while I unfastened his belt buckle and moved his slacks down over his hips. When he stood naked in the soft light, Bryce took a step back from me so I could look at him. "This is me, Diana. My body, not Nicky's. These scars are mine, not Nicky's. This is my heart pulsing with love for you. Feel it. It's real. It's me. There's no more black magic."

He placed my hand on his chest, so that I could feel his heart beating. "Tell me I'm real to you."

I understood. Bryce was offering himself to me, not as the puppet, but as the man. Should I accept for his sake his conviction that there was no more witchcraft—even though I was far from convinced of it myself?

The sight of his body heated my blood and made it impossible for me to think clearly about anything but loving him. "I scarcely know the real you," I said softly.

"I want you to know me. Don't be afraid to know me. It will take a little time, but you'll like me. I'm more solid than Nicky, and I find life a hell of a lot more fun than he does. He was always too bloody serious, if you want my opinion."

He cupped my face gently in his hands and kissed me, and his warm body pressed against mine. I held him tightly, clinging to everything I'd ever wanted, ever needed, ever really cared about. Spell or no spell, I loved Bryce more than I had ever loved anyone, and I knew I always would.

"Don't be afraid to know me," he whispered. "Don't be afraid."

Desperately I wished to believe that this was the first time, that we were in love and we were free. Bryce seemed to believe it. But then he didn't know about the gardenias...

Gardenias be damned. His chest was hard against the palms of my hands. He received my caresses—savoring the soft circling of my hands over his naked body as though it *were* the first time my hands had ever touched him.

Or my lips.

He wanted my love this way, this time, determined that I accept him as a man and not a fantasy. This time he wanted to be the receiver of my total acceptance of him.

My hands explored his body, slowly at first, then nimbly and boldly. While he stood, tall and strong, in the pale light of late afternoon, my own legs weakened with passion and would barely hold me. Caressing his hips, I slipped to my knees. I touched his scars with my lips. The warmth of him and the strength of him belonged to me. This was what he was silently telling me. This was what I was telling him, in a language more eloquent than words.

Bryce accepted my love. Welcomed my love. He hadn't known, even I hadn't known how much I had to give.

Murmuring something about how long he'd been without me, Bryce groaned. The fires of his need flamed out of his control. His thighs trembled violently in a rush of passion. There were ripples and moans of passion. I accepted, too...

A long silence did not seem silence. His thighs still quivered. I looked up at him and whispered, "You're still standing."

"Barely. . . just barely. . ." He reached down to me. "Come here."

He kissed me and undressed me simultaneously as we fell upon the bed; he muttered something about hoping I was as good at receiving as I was at giving. There were fireworks in my head, igniting my whole body. The passion we unleashed in each other was the issue of a hundred thirsting nights and dust-dry days apart. And now, the end—and the beginning—of wanting.

Something was subtly different about the way Bryce made love to me that first time in Switzerland. His passion came like a wild wind over an echoing sea, rushing upon me like waves, drenching me. He had never before loved me so wildly, so tenderly and so completely.

BRYCE STIRRED. "Did I doze off?"

"Only for five minutes," I answered, combing my fingers idly through his dark hair.

His blue eyes looked up at me. "You're beautiful."

"Everything in the world is beautiful." I looked around at the room. "This hotel. The view. Have you ever stayed here before?"

"No. But it was recommended."

"I love it." Pulling the crumpled sheet from the bed, I wrapped myself in it, got up and opened the French doors that led to the balcony. That strange south wind hit me again. The sun was setting behind the snow-swept mountains, casting a pink glow over the darkening water and the white peaks. Villages dotting the opposite shore of the lake were in shadow; only a few lights shone from their windows in the silver-pink twilight.

From the balcony railing, looking down, I gasped and drew back in shock. My heart lurched and then nearly stopped. Below was the very garden I had been describing in the scene I'd been writing when Bryce suddenly materialized! It was a garden lush with foliage—fig trees and silver firs, scarlet rhododendrons and cedar, and lined with cypress. A few hours ago Nicky had been hurt in this garden by the hidden wire! I made a weak attempt to rationalize that there must be many such gardens in the grounds of the luxury hotels, but my hand was grasping the railing so hard that my fists were white.

Bryce moved up behind me, wearing only slacks, his belt unbuckled. "That wind," he said. "It's the föehn."

"It's so unseasonably warm." I tried to keep my voice steady and my eyes away from that cursed garden.

"Warm enough to melt the winter snows on the peaks, but it's not a welcome wind. People say the föehn causes bad dispositions and is often followed by a terrible storm."

"It doesn't look as if it will storm."

He raised his eyes to the sky. "Not tonight, anyway. Want to get dressed for dinner? We could have a cocktail down there in the garden."

"The...garden?" I felt the blood drain from my face. "Oh...must we get dressed? Couldn't we just... stay...here?"

"Certainly, if you'd rather. We'll have dinner in the room, and I'll order a bottle of fine Valais wine sent up."

I was trembling. Bryce was being drawn to that damned garden! No matter what, I had to keep him out of there, or take the chance of something horrible happening to him! Along with Bryce, along with the joy, the awful nightmare had returned.

The gardenia...the hotel...and now the garden...
Was it also a coincidence that the moon was nearing full
tonight?

He went back inside to order room service. My
thoughts were racing. I had to change what I had written about Nicky being hurt by the hidden wire in the
garden, but it would be extremely awkward to try to do
it now, especially with Bryce insisting the spell was
gone. How could he be so naive about it? Wasn't it obvious what was happening?

Wasn't it?

Bryce had turned on soft music in the room. I went
back in and closed the French doors behind me to keep
out the ghostly wind and the night's chill.

His mood was festive. "I took the liberty of ordering dinner for us with my wine order, so we won't be
interrupted twice. I decided on a meal that would taste
as good cold as hot, so we can eat when we're ready."
He glanced back at the menu he was holding. "Gruy-
ère quiche, pickled salmon and stuffed tomatoes. Do
you approve?"

"It sounds great."

He smiled. "I'm pleased you suggested staying in. We
have a lot to catch up on, and we can make some plans
for the next few days. And I can make love to you
again. We have to make up for lost time."

I dropped the sheet I'd been wearing, and pulled my
pink silk robe from my bag. "Maybe we should just stay
right here in the room for the next few days." *And stay
the hell out of the garden,* I added to myself.

"Mmm. I'm for that idea. But you want to play outside, too, don't you? Let's take the cog train to the top
of the Rigi. And see the lakeshore sights by steam-
boat."

I felt slightly ill. The Rigi train and the steamer were, of course, the places where I had just put Nicky. Bryce looked so happy and content, sprawled in the chair, that I couldn't bring myself to tell him so. Not now.

But soon I was going to have to tell him what was really happening—that his love for me was only illusion. Again. And the freedom that he cherished so deeply—that was illusion, too.

What were we going to do? Go through all the hell of trying to kill Nicky again? In eighteen years' time, when there was another total eclipse? What the devil was I going to do with the book I was writing now? For Bryce's sake, I vowed to keep up a pretense of sanity while I tried to figure out just how I was going to convince him of something he was determined not to believe. It was all I could do to keep from crying. But Bryce was so caught up in our love for each other that he didn't even notice anything was wrong.

We settled in like hermits, unpacking, smoothing the rumpled sheets on the bed, soaping each other in the shower, and toasting our reunion with the excellent Swiss wine. And in the night sky, surrounded by shivering stars, a bright, three-quarter moon was shining.

We were curled in each other's arms, sipping wine and listening to the music when the phone rang.

"Och! It's probably my office. I should have given them the name of the wrong hotel." Bryce had to cross the room to pick up the phone.

"It had better be important," he said to the caller.

After a long pause, he replied to the person on the line. "I know I did the first appraisal, but they'll have to get someone else on this if they want it right now, because I'm on holiday. No, hell no, I won't."

The bubbles in my wineglass were like miniature crystal balls, and in each one lay a wish. While he was talking, I made wishes on the bubbles, every wish the same, and then I watched the little bubbles burst.

Bryce had launched into a business discussion. Restless, and preferring not to eavesdrop, I got up, grabbed a heavy sweater and went back out onto the balcony to look at the view and the night.

The moon was showing above some wispy clouds. Rain clouds that had threatened earlier had been blown off; the sky was almost clear. In spite of its warmth, I didn't like the feel of the wind on my face. The garden below was partially illuminated with soft floodlights; its shadows danced wistfully. The moon cast a silvery glow over the lake, the snowy peaks and the dark-forested slopes.

Greenery and flowers surrounded me. The garden's trees reached as high as the railing. Potted shrubs and planters of fresh flowers were all over the balcony. Standing at the rail, I spotted an incredibly beautiful rose on a viny branch that had grown through the wrought iron bars and out onto the other side. A drop of moisture on the rose caught the light of the moon and shone like a tiny diamond. Its beauty enchanted me. To touch it would be to touch a little piece of eternal beauty... just to touch it... I leaned over the railing, balancing on the toes of one foot, trying to reach the flower.

Suddenly, from the shadowed foliage directly in front of me, the diabolic shine of yellow eyes! Iridescent, unblinking eyes, staring out from the depths of night. Startled, I shrieked and lost my balance. An eternally long second passed, during which I found I couldn't retrieve my footing. Terror rushed through me; the garden was a floor below!

"Diana!" A strong arm caught me, pulled me in. Bryce held my trembling body tightly against his own.

"Diana, my God!"

I went limp. "You came just...in time."

"What happened?"

"I was reaching over for a flower, and I saw these glowing yellow eyes right...right in front of me! It must be a cat, but it startled me, so that I lost my balance."

"What eyes?"

I pointed to the shadows. The eyes were still there, ancient eyes, split by shadows of their narrow, dark pupils. Light from the moon was reflected from them. Cat's eyes—symbols of fear from centuries past. Symbols personifying witchcraft. I shivered.

"It's only a cat, Diana."

"I know. It just...frightened me for a second."

"You almost tumbled over the railing!"

"Not almost, I did tumble over. You just saved my life."

"Are you all right?"

"I'm fine. I'm sorry. That was stupid of me. There's a beautiful rose...." Suddenly I didn't want to explain in detail how foolish I'd been—feeling this silly urge to touch a rose in moonlight, and then getting frightened half to death by a cat.

With one arm around my shoulder, Bryce moved to the railing. "Just a wee tyke, she is. She must have climbed up from the garden."

My eyes were growing used to the dark, and the cat had moved farther into the light. "It's black...it's pure black," I muttered.

"Aye," Bryce answered. "Sign of good luck."

"*Good* luck? Black cats are symbols of evil!"

"Not in Europe, love. Here it's the white cat who's unlucky. Black ones are lucky."

"Are you serious?"

"Absolutely."

I watched in stunned silence as Bryce reached out an arm to the branch and coaxed the cat toward him.

"Come on, baby," he cooed. "Look, Diana, she's hardly more than a kitten."

"She's a cat! How come you're not recoiling in fear like you did the last time you saw a cat?"

"That was then." Bryce stretched forward until he could reach the little creature. When he touched it, it came to him willingly. He scratched its neck with two fingers. "Ahh...poor wee thing...what'd you do, climb up and couldn't get down again?"

"I don't believe this!"

"What?"

"Your...your phobia!"

He looked over at me. "It's gone. All of that is gone. I told you."

"But . . . but the gardenia—"

"The gardenia?"

"At the lion this afternoon. I was sitting there all absorbed in writing a scene that took place in a garden—*this* garden—and there was the scent of gardenias when Nicky... There was a gardenia in the scene, I looked up and there you stood—with a gardenia! Just like...like it always happened before."

"My sweet, I'd been standing near you for several minutes before you saw me. You looked so beautiful, and it had been so long. I just stood there watching you write. You smelled the gardenia long before you saw me."

"I did?"

"You did."

"Of course I did! The perfume. That's what made me think of gardenias!"

With the kitten settled contentedly against Bryce's chest, he said, "Were you so frightened of the spell, Diana? You couldn't bring yourself to believe me that it's gone?"

"There were other...other things. You wanted to do the same things Nicky did—the ride to the summit of the Rigi, a lake excursion...."

"*All* tourists do those things. You know that."

"I do know that," I admitted. "And that garden below us. It's rather typical of this area, isn't it?"

He looked down. "This garden? I suppose so. It reminds me of the garden in your little hotel on the lakefront. I was there when I was looking for you this afternoon."

"You were in the garden of my hotel?"

"Just walking through, to get to the back street. Would you believe there are wild chestnuts growing there?"

"You walked through the garden?"

"What's the matter, Diana?"

"Nothing is wrong. I was thinking about the... the...garden."

He took my hand gently, patiently. "Why are you thinking about the garden?"

"Just the...scene..."

"I see. More problems for Nicky."

"Yes."

"Forget him. Forget about everything except us. Do you hear the melody of the wind in the high meadows?'' He turned toward the night. ''Do you hear the music, Diana?''

I gazed at the man I loved. He took my breath away as he stood tall and handsome with the moonlight silvering his softly blowing hair. Moonlight bathed his face, lightened his eyes, fell over him like soft mist. He held the black cat against his bare chest while his pale blue eyes focused on the face of the moon without flinching!

I gasped.

He knelt to release the kitten. ''What's the matter?''

''The moon! Bryce...the moon...'' That wistful, splendid portrait of him, half-naked, holding the cat and looking at the moon was etched on my memory forever. Forever...

He turned back to the sky. ''It's magical, isn't it? I've lived my whole life without ever really seeing the moon—until now.''

''It doesn't hurt you anymore!''

''Nothing can hurt me anymore.'' He brushed my hair from my face.

I was aware of the sensation of the breeze blowing the silk of my robe against my legs. I was aware of the music in the trees—the music of night, of grass in high meadows and night-blooming flowers opening—music I had never heard before.

Bryce gently kissed my cheek—and my mouth less gently. He gathered me into the shelter of his arms. ''Do you need more time to get to know me?''

''I've known you since long before I ever met you. In some ways I know you better than I've ever known anyone. I just didn't understand that you were real.''

''I'm real.'' His arms around me were sure and strong.

"Yes."

His smile was soft. "Today in Lucerne I passed by a fine jewelry shop with a display of wedding rings. Where shall we be married? London? New York?"

My mind was moving like a flower in the wind, yet at the same time, a peace like none I'd ever known came over me. "Switzerland," I answered.

"I was hoping you'd say that." His eyes were shining as he gazed hard into mine. "It's going to work for us, Diana."

NICHOLAS PAUL was the perfect man. The man who would soon place a wedding ring on my finger, whom I love so deeply, would not be perfect when I got to know him. But he was perfect for me. Forces we would never understand had brought us together and then pulled us apart. But a greater power—the power of love—had brought Bryce back to me.

From *New York Times* Bestselling author
Penny Jordan, a compelling novel of ruthless passion
that will mesmerize readers everywhere!

Penny Jordan

Silver

Real power, true power came from
Rothwell. And Charles vowed to have it,
the earldom and all that went with it.

Silver vowed to destroy Charles, just as surely and
uncaringly as he had destroyed her father; just as he had
intended to destroy her. She needed him to want her...
to desire her... until he'd do anything to have her.

But first she needed a tutor: a man who wanted no one.
He would help her bait the trap.

**Played out on a glittering international stage,
Silver's story leads her from the luxurious comfort of
British aristocracy into the depths of adventure,
passion and danger.**

AVAILABLE IN OCTOBER!

 HARLEQUIN

A BIG SISTER
can take her places

She likes that. Her Mom does too.

BIG BROTHERS/BIG SISTERS AND HARLEQUIN

Harlequin is proud to announce its official sponsorship of Big Brothers/Big Sisters of America. Look for this poster in your local Big Brothers/Big Sisters agency or call them to get one in your favorite bookstore. Love is all about sharing.

BB/BS-1A

Six exciting series for you every month... from Harlequin

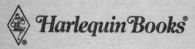

From America's favorite author
coming in September

JANET DAILEY

For Bitter Or Worse

Out of print since 1979!

Reaching Cord seemed impossible. Bitter, still confined to a wheelchair a year after the crash, he lashed out at everyone. Especially his wife.

"It would have been better if I hadn't been pulled from the plane wreck," he told her, and nothing Stacey did seemed to help.

Then Paula Hanson, a confident physiotherapist, arrived. She taunted Cord into helping himself, restoring his interest in living. Could she also make him and Stacey rediscover their early love?

Don't miss this collector's edition—last in a special three-book collection from Janet Dailey.